What Others Are Saying About
Pat Simmons and In Defense of Love

Author Pat Simmons has done it again. She has written another powerful story that draws you in from the beginning and keeps your attention until the end. Pat has a way of telling a story that makes you feel as if you are a part of each character and also prompts you to take an inventory of your own life.
—*Ellowyn Bell*

This book is the sweetest romance crafted to perfection and saturated with God's love.
—Tanishia Pearson-Jones *Characters Book Club*

It's the story of our lives—the ups, downs, and emotions of relationships. An exciting read!
—*Andrea Alexander Binion*

@2015 Whitaker House Publishers
@2018 Generations Quest Press/Pat Simmons

Interior design: Kimolisa/Fiverr.com
Cover design: Ultrakhan22/Fiverr.com

In Defense Of Love

By

Pat Simmons

Dedication

To an amazing sister-in-Christ at Bethesda Temple Church who shared an astonishing testimony about the Lord's presence. Rest until the trumpet sounds, Sister Patterson.

Acknowledgments

This story would not have been possible without assistance from the following people:

Jessica Hougen, curator, U.S. Marshals Museum in Ft. Smith, Arizona.

Cory Thomas, U.S. Marshals Service, Ft. Smith, Arizona.

Jessica Sinkfield, Assistant State Attorney at Miami-Dade State Attorney s Office. (She also happens to be my cousin.)

Major JaRai A. Williams, attorney, United States Air Force Judge Advocate General's Corps.

Family, friends, readers, book clubs, my street team, and Jersey captain Mia Harris.

My dark and lovely friends and family: Diamond Flanagan, Joylynn Ross, Rene Daniel Flagler, and Krystal Mims.

Sister Cynthia Patterson (1950-2012).

Special thanks to Chandra Sparks Splond for giving me clarity for *In Defense of Love.*

The late Bishop James Johnson and former first lady of Bethesda Temple Church, Lady Juana Johnson.

Descendants of Cole, Wade, Simmons, Sinkfield, Carter, Wilkerson/ Wilkinson, Brown, Palmer, and others I have yet to meet.

Most definitely my husband, Kerry Simmons, who enjoys our road trips, and my son and daughter.

For I know the thoughts that I think toward you, saith the LORD, thoughts of peace, and not of evil, to give you an expected end.— Jeremiah 29:11

Chapter One

Garrett Nash's Boston homecoming was bittersweet. The majority of his family and most of his friends were glad to see him—but not all. There were some who seemed to take pleasure in his discomfort in the aftermath of breaking up with his fiancée. At least their whispers couldn't be heard in Philly, where he had relocated months ago.

If only he hadn't needed to return home so soon. But it was his grandparents' fiftieth wedding anniversary, and nothing would keep him away, especially since he was spearheading the program. Only one problem had arisen as the event neared: The original band had canceled, forcing Garrett to scramble to find a replacement.

John Whitman, an old college buddy and the band director at his new home church in Philly, had offered the ensemble's services. Talk about a godsend. Garrett hadn't thought twice about accepting the offer.

The instrumentalists would arrive an hour or so before the ceremony. Garrett's only request was that someone performs one of his grandparents' favorite songs, Walter Hawkins's "Thank You." John had assured him that a fellow saxophonist could play the selection flawlessly.

He hoped so. The slightest off-key note would be a blaring error to his maternal grandfather, Moses Miller, who had taught music theory both in high school and also at a historically black college before retiring. Plus, Grandpa Moses had toured with a band in his heyday. Most in the Miller dynasty didn't bother reading music, since they could play almost anything by ear.

Sighing, Garrett glanced out the window of his childhood bedroom in Roxbury. The radiance of the sunrise was surreal. It seemed like yesterday that his fate had been sealed without a heads-up.

Grandpa Moses had been livid when he'd gotten the news that Garrett's fiancée, at the time, was expecting a baby. The rumors, accusations, backbiting, and shame from longtime friends in the church had caused the Miller clan to call for two days of consecration with fasting and prayer. After all, they were a godly family, living a God-fearing life, and scandal was not something that was connected with the Miller name.

Then, on the infamous night of the gathering, a family member had spoken in tongues, and Garrett and his grandfather had both received the interpretation.

"What did God tell you?" His grandfather's eyes had been weary, reflecting the same heaviness Garrett had felt in his heart.

Garrett had frowned, feeling confused and disturbed. The word from God hadn't made sense to him. The Lord had told him to walk away from the job and family he loved and the woman he had vowed to love—everything that was in Beantown. "I'm supposed move." That hadn't sounded right to his ears when he'd said it. And now, a couple of months later, he was still baffled.

Deborah, his older sister by two years, had been outraged. "Your fiancée got herself pregnant," she'd insisted. There had been no love lost between his only sibling and Brittani.

The fault didn't lie with his ex alone. Regardless of his sister's outburst, Brittani hadn't gotten pregnant by herself.

"Granddaughter, my spirit bears witness to Garrett's. God's ways aren't like ours. His decision is final," their grandfather had stated in a voice that left no room for bargaining.

Their grandmother Queen—a classy, garrulous grand diva who had been aptly named—had seemed to age in seconds. Sniffing, she'd held her peace as she linked her arthritic fingers with her husband's.

"This pregnancy is not only an embarrassment to our family but a humiliation before God," Moses had said. "There's no excuse for any sin, and sexual immorality..." He'd shaken his head.

But he'd been preaching to the choir. The Millers were three—going on four—generations strong of committed Christians. Garrett had been born, reared, and educated in Boston public schools; had completed his undergraduate studies at Boston University; and, at age thirty-one, had transferred from the Department of Homeland Security to the Justice Department as a U.S. Marshal less than a year ago. Life was good. Everything had been going smoothly, until, through no fault of his own, a night of passion—one that never should've happened—had altered his life forever. Garrett scowled whenever he thought about it.

"Haven't I spent years telling you and your cousin Landon, my only grandsons, that you're supposed to walk uprightly before God, not touching a woman unless she's your wife? I'm so disappointed. Brittani was bewitching from the start, but God can forgive instantly, as each of us is a work in progress. Look at your move as a blessing in disguise."

Deborah had snorted. "A blessing, Grandpa? I see it as Brittani dolled up in a church disguise."

Their mother had frowned. She was long-suffering toward her children until they stepped out of place.

Garrett cleared his mind of the memories. That night had been traumatic. At times, he hadn't known where he was going—a new city, a new job, a new place of worship. There had been so many questions, but, one by one, the Lord had opened doors and led him to where he lived currently—in Philly, attending a great medium-sized church where he was the new kid on the block and where no rumors circulated about him and his ex-fiancée.

And now he was home, where the pain had escalated. But it was just for a few days. After giving his grandparents the anniversary party of their life, he would be back on the road to Philly, ready to resume his fresh start.

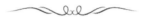

"Great," Shari Carmen groaned when her smartphone chimed. Climbing out of her vehicle, she fumbled with her purse and briefcase, then tapped her Bluetooth. "Hello?"

"I need you," the caller greeted her in a raspy, desperate-sounding male voice.

Shari curled her lips into a mischievous smile. "Does your wife know?" she whispered in the huskiest voice she could muster. She strolled up the pathway to her childhood home, which she shared with her widowed mother. Although Shari could afford pricier real estate in Center City, closer to her downtown office, she preferred her mother's company—any company, other than a cat's—to living alone.

"Who do you think put me up to this?" John Whitman demanded in his regular voice.

Laughter spilled out of Shari's mouth. The church band leader and his wife were known pranksters. She groaned as she inserted the key in her front door. "You and Rita have no shame. Whatever it is, my first and final answer is no."

She had to watch out for that duo. The only thing that topped their antics was their notorious matchmaking schemes directed at the members of the band and choir at Jesus Is the Way Church.

The pair seemed to have the gift, not necessarily from God, for predicting a couple's compatibility. They had even beaten out a church busybody who was infamous for her get-your-hope-chest-ready-because-you're-about-to-be-married prophecies. And the church folks were keeping score. So far this year, the Whitmans were leading, five happy couples to Mother Ernestine Stillwell's one. The senior citizen had cited her last three fiascos as false starts.

"Wait, Sharmaine. Hear me out."

Sharmaine? Whatever he was calling about, it had to be a doozy. She was surprised John didn't tack on "Esquire" to her given name.

"It's a favor for a frat brother, a new church member, a fellow band member—"

"Hmm. Am I supposed to have warm fuzzies by now? I'm not feelin' it, whatever it is." She hiked up the steps to her spacious bedroom on the second floor, kicked off her four-inch heels, flopped on the bed, and wiggled her toes. Exhausted from back-to-back court appearances, she was hardly in the mood for granting favors. A deep-conditioning shampoo and a warm bath were the only items on her agenda for the evening.

John sighed. "I'll cut to the chase. Brother Garrett Nash is in a bind."

Now *that* name made Shari pause. His dark complexion, handsome features, and muscular build would make any lady smile—even one with cataracts. The handsome package reminded her of actor Lance Gross. God really did know how to create masterpieces. But dozens of female bees at church were already swarming around him. Shari shook her head. No surprise there.

She recalled the formal introduction of the three new band

members—all male—at the last practice she'd attended. Garrett had been the standout of the bunch. Unfortunately, due to her other church ministry obligations, Shari hadn't rehearsed with the band for almost a month. Still, Garrett was unforgettable.

Curious now, Shari took the bait. "So what does that have to do with me?"

"Garrett asked if some band members wouldn't mind traveling to Boston to play for his grandparents' fiftieth wedding anniversary party. Apparently, the musical talent he had booked had to cancel at the last minute. He's covering the transportation costs, so there's no expense on our part. Please."

Shari wasn't opposed to the travel aspect. The six-hour road trip—five hours, if John drove—would be a piece a cake. She'd traveled with other groups from her church to gospel choir competitions, the pastor's preaching engagements, and other events; as long as she was back in time to play at Sunday services, it wasn't a problem. Her lips were forming an "o" for "Okay" when he dropped the bombshell.

"I need you to play 'Thank You' for the ceremony," John said quickly, then rushed on. "Terrell was going to play his sax, but he's down with the flu. Rod could manage it on his guitar, but, as you know, the horn rules on that song."

John had just wasted ten precious minutes of his cell phone plan. No wonder his wife had put him up to badgering her. The answer was still no, and Shari felt no shame in telling him so. "Sorry, can't do it."

That solo belonged to one man: her father, Saul Carmen. He was the one who had taught her to play that timeless Walter Hawkins tune, and Shari had thought it would be appropriate to play it one last time at her daddy's funeral as a tribute. The key phrase was *one last time*. So what if it had been twelve years since the heart attack that had claimed his life? The song still quickened those bittersweet memories of father-daughter bonding time. She wanted to keep that song hidden in a secret place in her heart forever.

Among the four daughters, Shari liked to think of herself as a bona fide daddy's girl. She and her father even shared his same rich dark skin, "the color of God's earth," as he had described it. And when she'd come of age to notice that a color divide still existed, even within black circles, her daddy had wiped away countless tears when she had been rejected, insulted, or frightened.

"Please, Sharmaine," John pleaded. "I—we—really do need you." He sounded drained. "Garrett is a perfectionist. I'm frantic now, having committed the band after hearing his desperation."

That song was a private part of her life that was not available for public viewing. It had sentimental value. She'd thought more about it, and her answer remained no. "If we're not wearing our robes, and the color scheme is black-and-white, I've sent everything to the cleaners and have nothing to wear. Sorry." She wasn't really, but she felt obligated to say it.

John mumbled something, and then his wife came on the line. "Pick your poison: I can go shopping either with you or for you," Rita said. "Sis, you really are one of the best on tenor sax. I was there when you broke down after playing that song at your father's funeral. I'm not insensitive. But I believe God will turn your midnight hours into joyful mornings if you play that song for a festive occasion. Do it for Brother Garrett and God will bless you."

God had already blessed her—with a career, a car, a healthy bank account. The only things lacking were a husband and children. Unfortunately, at twenty-nine years old and counting, Shari saw no relief from her singleness. Even the church busybody, Mother Stillwell, who took pleasure in tracking down sisters and proclaiming that they were next in line for a husband, wobbled in a different direction when she saw Shari coming. It didn't matter.

The older woman didn't even have a fifty-fifty accuracy rate.

The Whitmans were relentless as they took turns on the phone, chipping away at Shari's resolve. In the courtroom, they never would have won the argument; but, because she was hungry, Shari reluctantly caved in so she could go eat dinner.

But after the call, in the quietness of her bedroom, she wondered if she could get through the emotional song without breaking down. At a funeral, people understood her emotional state. A room of strangers definitely wouldn't understand. "And you call yourself a defense attorney," she scoffed. "You can't even defend yourself against those two amateurs." Then she stood and dragged her feet to her closet to begin a scavenger hunt for a dark skirt and a light-colored top to wear for her "showdown."

"Hey, sweetie." Shari's mother, Annette Carmen, knocked before stepping into her bedroom. "I didn't know you were here until I heard you on the phone."

"Hi, Mom. The Whitmans just ambushed me."

"Impossible." Her mother laughed. "They couldn't possibly take down a Drexel University Law School magna cum laude graduate."

"Don't underestimate those two," Shari said before rehashing their request.

Stretching across Shari's bed, her mother made herself comfortable. "Listen, baby," she said after Shari had finished her tale of woe. "Your father would want you to play the song to God's glory. For us, as saints of God, everything we do is about Him." She pointed up in the air. "It's never about us."

"I know that," Shari whined. "But that song has such sentimental value to me."

"Saul was larger than life sometimes, and our memories of him will never fade. But he was big enough to share that song with Brother Nash's grandparents. Plus, you don't need to spend your weekends stuck in the house with me."

Growing up, Shari had earned the nickname "house kid" because she'd always preferred claiming a cozy corner and devouring a book while her three sisters played with the neighborhood children. "I happen to like being a homebody," she good-naturedly argued.

There it was—the amused expression her mother displayed to convey nobody was going to win this argument but her. Annette Carmen had perfected the art of convincing her daughters to see things her way—telepathy or something.

The way her mother smiled, Shari almost wondered if she was in on John and Rita's scheme. "Seriously, I don't have anything to wear!" she protested, even though she knew the weakness of her rebuttal. After a long day in court defending those with colorful criminal portfolios and interviewing prospective clients, dealing with the Friday night crowds at King of Prussia Mall was not something she looked forward to.

Craning her neck, her mother squinted into Shari's closet. "I think I see a black skirt in the back on the right-hand side. It may be a little short, but I'm sure it's respectable."

Who said eyesight diminishes with age? Shari mused. At fifty-four, her mother, a former beauty pageant contestant, was as stunning as ever.

After a search-and-rescue in the maze of her clothes, Shari tugged the skirt off the hanger—it wasn't black but an indiscernible shade of dark brown. Close enough. It would have to do.

Shari manipulated the sleek fabric over her hips. She braved a glance in the full-length mirror, then patted her backside. "Yep, I see where the five pounds settled from Aunt Camille's earthquake cake, your pecan pie, and the cheesesteak from lunch."

"Ah, to be so generously endowed." Her mother released a

wistful sigh.

"It isn't always a blessing."

"Tell that to a skinny woman," her mother stated. "Speaking of food, I'll go warm up dinner. Leftovers okay?"

"Sure."

Left alone with her thoughts, Shari studied her reflection once more in the mirror. She would wear this outfit in the courtroom in a minute, but in church, the flared skirt, which hit just above the knees, would raise eyebrows, considering that her church clothes were always a little loose and inches longer. "It is what it is," she mumbled, not happy that Brother Nash wanted her to give up a piece of her that she held dear, even though he couldn't possibly know its value to her.

That night, Shari's sleep was anything but restful. When she awoke the next morning, she petitioned the Lord to keep her from embarrassing herself by crying. She grabbed her saxophone case and the garment bag containing her flirty cream ruffled blouse and brown skirt, then headed downstairs to say good-bye to her mother.

She found her in the kitchen, standing by the sink with a cup of steaming coffee. Wrapped in a long black satin robe, the woman easily could have been a stand-in for a movie scene as she strolled out of the kitchen. She turned to Shari and smiled. "Everything will be fine. I know you're not exactly happy granting this favor, but who knows? God has a reputation for giving back more abundantly when we give of ourselves."

Shari nodded, inwardly chiding herself for her selfishness. "I know, Mom. Thanks for the pep talk."

"It's called a love talk." Her mother gave her a kiss on the cheek. "I'll be praying for safe travels."

After the women shared a warm hug, Shari left. She made it to church in no time.

When she boarded the fifteen-seat passenger van, her best

IN DEFENSE OF LOVE

friend, trumpeter Faith Harper, gave her a brilliant smile. "Welcome aboard." Faith scooted over to the window to let Shari have the aisle seat. "I can't believe John and Rita talked you into playing that tune."

It was no secret among the band members how distraught Shari had been after performing the song at her father's funeral. Her sisters had needed to assist her back to the pew before she'd collapsed. "I'm still not sure about this." She groaned, once again regretting her decision. It felt as if she was getting on a roller coaster, even while knowing she was scared of heights. "I'm definitely losing my edge outside the courtroom to have been swayed."

Faith gave her a quick hug. "I'll be there for you, playing and praying."

"Why do I have this strange feeling that I'm being set up?" Shari asked her. "Of all the new and old songs, why that one? And Terrell 'just so happens' to get sick. Doesn't he have a prayer cloth?"

"Stop it." Faith grinned. "Only God knows why things happen the way they do."

As the van merged onto the New Jersey Turnpike, Shari closed her eyes and sank comfortably against her small travel pillow.

Just when she started to drift off, Rita began chatting away. "Brother Moses and Sister Queen Miller had seven daughters, giving them all biblical names, and those daughters went on to produce twenty-something children and even a few great-grandchildren."

What a tribe, Shari mused.

"Garrett and I go way back to when I attended BU in Boston," John chimed in from his spot behind the wheel. "I've met some of his family members. Many of them have exceptional musical abilities."

That part she could relate to. Who in the Carmen family didn't play an instrument? She smiled. As teenagers, she and her sisters had earned a reputation locally and in the surrounding cities for their musical talents. At various times, the Carmen sisters had tried to mimic the Clark Sisters, the Newell Sisters, and other family singing groups.

Her oldest sister, Stacy, who lived across town with her husband, Ted, commanded the keyboard like a pro, while Shari manipulated the high notes on the tenor sax—an impressive feat for a woman, as her two male cousins always reminded her. The two younger sisters could hold their own, too. Shae, a TV reporter/weekend news anchor who resided in St. Louis, had perfected her craft on the drums, admiring Sheila E. But it was Brecee who was out of control with her Chuck Berry antics on the guitar. Now the little fireball was pursuing her calling as a pediatrician in Houston.

Like Stacy, Shari doubted she could ever live anyplace other than Philly. She loved the feel of the historic city, she loved her home church, and she loved the local culture. Regardless of the city they now called home, she and her sisters had made their parents proud. Shari only hoped her performance tonight would be one that would honor her father rather than shame the Carmen name with another public meltdown.

Chapter Two

Shari hadn't realized she had dozed off until she awoke when their van arrived at the Doubletree by Hilton in downtown Boston. Once all the band members had gathered their things and strolled into the lobby, Shari s anxiety faded instantly, replaced by awe.

The grandeur of the entrance paled when compared to that of the ballroom. Festive gold helium balloons served as centerpieces, matching the ribbon that was tied into bows behind each chair. From the decorations, Shari deduced that no expense had been spared for this celebration.

An usher guided them to a small lounge where he said they could relax before their performance. According to John, they'd have just enough time to change clothes and freshen up before it was time to start playing. "Remember to keep the music going until every family member is seated," he told them. Then he gathered them together for a group prayer. "Lord, let us be a blessing so that we can receive one."

Shari and the others whispered, "Amen," although she continued praying silently for strength. She swallowed, anticipating the moment that would conjure up every emotion—

when she blew life into her sax. Her heart pounded heavily as they set up in the banquet room.

Some guests arrived as much as an hour early. Many of them seemed content to gather around the ivory linen-covered round tables, chatting. The women were wrapped in colorful lavish African garments; the men, from toddlers to overweight, cane-stepping elders, strutted in their black tuxedo tailcoats. Their excitement was almost palpable. The young girls looked picture-perfect with bows and baby's breath adorning their salon-curled hair. Shari remembered the days when her mother would dress her daughters like quadruplets. Yes, it appeared that the hundred-plus guests in attendance were in their finest apparel, fit for an audience with King Moses and his Queen.

She stopped gawking when Faith nudged her. She and her friend headed for the lounge.

"Aren't you glad you came?" Faith asked, her hazel eyes twinkling.

"I haven't played yet." Shari playfully scrunched her nose, a habit all four of the Carmen sisters had picked up in childhood.

John frowned. "I haven't seen Brother Nash yet."

Shari had been thinking the same thing but kept it to herself. John inquired of one of the ushers regarding Garrett's whereabouts, then trailed the man out the room.

When John returned, he had an apology from their sponsor. "Garrett said he appreciates that we came and he's sorry he couldn't meet us when we first arrived. He's trying to put out a fire. He seems flustered, so pray for our brother."

Murmurs of "Not a problem" and "It's okay" circulated around the room. Shari didn't reply. This was Garrett's shindig. The least he could do would be to extend a personal thank-you to her for opening her heart to share with his family.

Then Shari chided herself for her self-righteous attitude. She wasn't being fair to Garrett. The man had no inkling of her pain.

She lost track of time as a hush spread across the room, and the main double doors opened. Seconds later, the guests went wild, applauding the honorees and their dynasty as they made their appearance in a processional to the head table. John's fingers glided over the keyboard while the drummer tapped the cymbals. The horn section stood—Shari with her saxophone, Faith holding her trumpet, and Steve, an older gentleman, hoisting his trombone.

Taking a deep breath to calm her nerves, Shari closed her lips on the sax's mouthpiece as she blew the first notes of "Thank You." She fought back the tears, rebuked the sadness that tried to overpower her, and clung to the wondrous event that she had the pleasure of not only witnessing but also participating in. *Lord, help me not to fall apart—please.*

Shari didn't remember when her lids drifted closed, but suddenly she was transformed to another place and time where she played the piece with the same fervor that she had at her father's funeral. Time hadn't dulled her desire for the hugs her father gave every night at bedtime or for his encouragement and support on the dawn of her teenage years. The void he'd left in her life was still unimaginable. If only she could marry a good, godly man like her daddy one day.

With ease, Shari hit the notes she had mastered and manipulated her sax like a child skipping rocks across a pond. Claps, shouts, and whistles reminded her that she was not in a secret place. She dared to open an eye and was shocked to see the spotlight shining directly on her. Compliments to whoever was on special-effects detail for the event.

She eyed Faith, who nodded before joining her on trumpet for the chorus. Together they moved as if they were dancing the salsa, taunting each other with their instruments, until the last note was squeezed out from Shari's lungs and her heartbeat settled. She had peace.

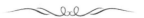

Wow. Never before had Garrett heard a woman take command of a tenor sax like that. To be honest, few male musicians played with that much discipline. Not only was her performance mesmerizing, but the saxophonist herself was stunning.

Shame on him that he didn't know her name. He couldn't even recall an introduction. Since he'd started attending services at Jesus Is the Way Church, he had been busy fending off what seemed to be an endless stream of sisters vying for his attention. After the relationship he had just escaped, Garrett was not looking for any new entanglements. But now, from where he was sitting, that self-imposed edict seemed too severe.

Joining everyone else on their feet, Garrett gave the band a hearty applause. He chanced a glimpse down the table at his grandfather. A Cheshire grin stretched across the old man's face beneath his trim gray mustache. Not many people impressed Moses Miller, but evidently this woman had.

Again, it wasn't only her musical ability that was the showstopper. Under the spotlight, her thick curls had bounced with each sway and dip. The richness of her dark skin reminded Garrett of his own. She was dark and lovely, like a goddess from Greek mythology.

But her assets didn't stop there. Even in a modest top and dark skirt, her allure could not be dulled. And despite the heels that supported her shapely legs, she moved with ease, despite gripping her ten-plus-pound sax.

If Garrett didn't force his eyes away, he would be drooling any minute. That was not good, for too many reasons. Lusting after a woman could cause a man to lose his morals and common sense. That had already happened. The scandal with Brittani had driven him from his homeland like Joseph in Genesis 39. But fleeing had been God's idea, and after his initial reluctance, Garrett had seen it for the opportunity it was and had run with it.

His heart had been like the heroes in the Bible that didn't yield. Joseph submitted to the Lord and resisted the devil's temptation from his queen's advancements. It was the other way around in the New Testament, where the devil fled if saints stood their ground as mentioned in James 4:7. So why hadn't that Scripture worked in this present situation?

He sighed heavily. Sound judgment and wisdom had been compromised after the demise of his last relationship. What really threw him for a loop was when some of the elderly church folks tried to convince him that marriage would clean up the mess. Had they lost their mind? The damage had already been done and he was walking away.

This is not the time or the place. Garrett shook his head. He was in Boston for a few days to celebrate bliss, not to dredge up past hurts and personal bitterness. He snapped out of it just in time. He was up next on the program with his nephew. Because of his on-again, off-again shyness, his nephew, Jamal, had asked Garrett to help serenade his great-grandparents. Grabbing his own tenor saxophone, Garrett escorted the boy to the front.

His eyes strayed to the saxophonist, but she barely acknowledged him, so he addressed the honorees. "Grandpa and Grandmother, throughout your marriage, you both have demonstrated a boundless love, an amazing ability to forgive, and a strong determination to walk with God. I pray that God will bless you with at least thirty more years of marriage."

He lifted his instrument and played as Jamal did his rendition of "You're My Hero" on the congas. The boy was impressive, and the audience agreed, judging by their thunderous applause.

Up next was his cousin Landon Thomas, who slid behind the keyboard, but not without first trying to get the saxophonist's attention—to no avail. At least Garrett wasn't the only guy she ignored.

All seventeen great-grandchildren were out of their seats for the next selection, dancing and singing the words to an old-time gospel favorite of his grandmother.

Midway through the song, Garrett strolled to the sexy saxophonist and looked her in the eye. Up close, she was even more beautiful, glowing and almost bewitching. And she wasn't wearing a ring. *Why did I go there?* "Play with me," he whispered.

Without hesitation, she reached for her instrument and stood. For fun, Garrett decided to challenge her musically, but she turned the tables on him, teasing him unmercifully with her performance. He could feel himself perspiring, and it had nothing to do with the lights or the energy required to blow his horn.

Together they held the last note to the max, as if testing each other to see who would surrender first. Garrett lost, gulping for air, and bowed to acknowledge her superior expertise. He grinned, knowing that the joke was on him, as the guests cheered the "battle of the sexes" on the saxes. To his amazement, the woman didn't gloat. With only a slight nod, she turned and started to return to her seat.

But Garrett closed the distance between them and escorted her. "Thank you, Sister...uh... I'm embarrassed that I don't know your name."

The cute trumpet player, sitting nearby, seemed more than pleased to answer, "She's Counselor Sharmaine Carmen, or Sister Shari."

Shari glared at the woman. "I can talk, Faith."

Faith grinned. "You were taking too long."

Garrett chuckled at their exchange as he stored away the information—Sharmaine, attorney, single, gorgeous, talented musician. As a child, he'd loved jumbo puzzles, and now, as an adult, the more complex the hundreds of pieces were, better the challenge. His sudden attraction to Shari was definitely complex, and contrary to the bottom line that he wasn't interested in another relationship for years to come. The challenge was to make himself believe it.

"What a beautiful name," he said, realizing he was practically cooing. "Hope you didn't mind being put on the spot." *Quit flirting.* His head needed recalibrating.

"I didn't."

With nothing more to say—at least, nothing that wouldn't cause him to come off as an idiot—Garrett excused himself and strolled back to the head table.

After that, several of his cousins performed another musical selection before the band resumed playing. Once again, Shari kept him distracted. Soon, John called for an intermission so the band could eat. Minutes after they had piled their plates with food from the buffet table and taken their seats, Garrett's nephew made a beeline to their table and nearly stumbled into Shari's lap, clamoring for her attention. Although Shari didn't appear to mind, Garrett decided to intervene.

As he approached the table, Garrett overheard Jamal saying, "You play better than my uncle."

"Traitor. You think so, huh?" Garrett directed his comment at his nephew but watched Shari for her reaction.

"Yeah." Jamal looked up at him and displayed an angelic toothy grin.

Winking at Shari, Garrett rubbed the boy's curly hair. "C'mon, let the lady eat."

"But she may need something to drink...or some napkins," Jamal protested.

"Her glass is full, and there are plenty of napkins on the table. Let's go, buddy—now," he repeated.

Twisting his lips into a frown, Jamal stomped away and trailed Garrett back to his seat.

All through dinner, Garrett chatted with relatives, joked with old friends, and embraced former church members who were still talking to him. Yet his gaze never wandered far from Shari. Finally, when he couldn't keep his distance any longer, Garrett strolled back over to the table where the band was seated.

Garrett tapped John on the shoulder, then leaned down and whispered into his ear, so that his wife wouldn't overhear, "I want to know everything about Shari when I get back to Philly. And I mean everything, even her shoe size."

The band director raised his eyebrows in a look of mild shock. "Uh...are you sure you want to pursue that already, man?" The two friends had reconnected when Garrett had relocated to Philly, and Garrett had confided in John the reasons for his sudden move.

"No," Garrett admitted. Being around Shari made him feel like he was having an out-of-body experience.

"Well, you'd better be certain, because the Carmens might do a background check—especially Attorney Carmen." John smirked, but Garrett didn't crack a smile. "All right. We'll talk when you come back."

"Thanks." Straightening, Garrett moved two seats down to Shari. "If you're finished eating, I would like to introduce you to the honorees."

Dropping her fork, Rita pushed back from the table. "I can't wait to meet them."

John stayed his wife's arm. "Not you, babe." He nodded to Shari.

Rita frowned at her husband, then squinted at Garrett. "On second thought, honey, I think I'd rather sample your dessert." She scooped up a bite of John's cheesecake. Her acting was terrible as she raved about the flavor.

When Shari stood, Garrett guessed her height at five feet five-or six inches tall without her high heels. He didn't try to conceal his assessment as he admired her flawless dark skin—not even a beauty mole. He wondered if her long hair was silky to the touch.

Everybody turned to watch as Shari strutted beside him to the head table. Garrett kept his hands to himself when he really wanted to brush against her arm—any point of contact that would confirm whether there were sparks that could ignite or whether he was losing his mind. "Grands, this is Sister Sharmaine Carmen, the young lady who played the sax so skillfully."

She extended her hand, displaying long, slender, manicured fingers—feminine fingers that didn't hint at their masterful skill on the sax. "Please, call me Shari."

"Then Sister Shari it is," his grandfather said. "You jammed, young lady. You really put a hurt on that instrument."

She lowered her lashes, clearly embarrassed by the accolades. "Thank you, and congratulations on your fiftieth wedding anniversary. You both look so youthful to have been together that many years."

Queen blushed. "Aren't you a sweet thing, and pretty too. I pray that God gives you fifty years of bliss, as well."

"Oh, I'm not married."

His grandmother's eyes sparkled. She shifted in her seat as a smile spread across her wrinkle-free face. "Well, dear, my grandson, here, is available." She leaned forward and whispered, "I heard he has a real good job in Philadelphia, too."

Garrett lifted his brows but didn't say a word. Evidently, the damage done by his ex-fiancée was fading fast if his grandmother felt so comfortable meddling. Queen had always been wary of women who were "sniffing" him out, as she said, especially now in the wake of what had happened with Brittani. On more than one occasion, Garrett had overheard her telling a woman, in her soft, sweet, grandmotherly tone, "Keep movin', honey," or "I'm watching you." Maybe he and his granny were of one accord that there was something special about this woman.

"Uh, thanks." Shari nodded, then excused herself. In her hasty departure, Garrett didn't miss that her shapely legs trembled, and her stiletto heels had nothing to do with it.

"We scared her off," his grandmother said, her tone pouty.

"Nonsense." Moses faced Garrett and looked him sternly in the eye. "God is stirring in your life. Pray fervently for wisdom, Grandson, and guard your heart."

"She's starting to show, you know," Queen interrupted her husband's counsel. Glancing over her shoulder, she scanned the room. "She seems remorseful, but to parade her condition around church...and sitting up front! I can't believe some folks still thought you two should have gone ahead with the wedding. If you'd stayed, no doubt they would have hounded you and made your life miserable. I didn't want that for you. Brittani was acting like a politician, drumming up votes, basically brainwashing people to pick sides."

"Sweetheart," Moses said gently, trying to hush his wife, "the boy didn't come home for an update."

Queen patted her husband's hand. "You're right, dear." Then she looked at Garrett. "At first, I didn't understand the reasoning behind God's directive for you to leave, but I have a feeling that everything is going to be okay." She batted her eyelashes.

Garrett took that as his cue to leave, since others had approached the table to vie for his grandparents' attention. Taking his seat, he studied Shari as the band resumed entertaining the crowd. Her magnetism wasn't limited to him. Other male guests were ogling her, including Landon.

He and his cousin were Moses and Queen's only grandsons. They had been born just five minutes apart. Sometimes it seemed as if he and Landon had a biblical Jacob-and-Esau type of relationship because they were complete opposites, from their appearances to their spiritual lives.

Landon charmed the ladies with his light skin and well-defined facial features—long nose, hazel eyes, and hairless face, except for a shiny goatee. Garrett had worn a mustache ever since he'd first grown one, at sixteen years old. He was an inch taller than Landon at six-three, and more buff overall, with deep sunbaked skin and dark brown eyes.

As far as Garrett was concerned, Sister Shari was hands-off to any male, including his little nephew, Jamal. Garrett was curious to find out what it was about her that made him forget his past. If any man was going to capture her affections, he wanted it to be him. *Devil, you've been warned.*

Chapter Three

Something had happened to Shari, and it was indescribable, unexplainable, and downright exciting! The Lord had given her incredible strength to play "Thank You" with such fervor that the invisible chains of missing her father had been broken.

That was huge. On days when her life seemed crazy and she longed for those special hugs or "daddy talks," Shari would pick up her sax, wanting to hold on to all the special moments she had played with her father, but before she could exhale the air into the mouthpiece, she would break down.

She deeply missed having her father in her life, even as a grown woman. Her uncle and two male cousins had always been there for her, but they couldn't fill the void. Her daddy had been her idol, and she didn't see any man filling his shoes—ever.

"See? That was a piece of cake. Aren't you glad you came?" John grinned in triumph as Shari boarded the van with the band for the return trip to Philly. He gave her an odd look, as if he was about to say more, but he didn't.

"Yes, I'm glad," she conceded. "But do you always have to be right? You win for ambushing me." Settling in the seat next to Faith, Shari was giddy with praise, which she'd had to restrain at the banquet for etiquette's sake.

Now she felt silly for holding on to something that had become a burden. She had been set free, delivered, and healed of the melancholy whenever she thought about her father. Suddenly, it was as if she could hear her mother sing the lyrics of "Look at Me," a popular old gospel favorite by Tramaine Hawkins. Closing her eyes, Shari began to hum the tune.

"That's why you're singing at my wedding," Faith said, nudging her. She picked up the melody, and soon the others on board joined in to sing the chorus. Needless to say, they had church on the road back to Philly.

It was after midnight when John steered the van into the parking lot of Jesus Is the Way Church. Shari yawned and stretched, then gathered her belongings and got out.

Faith walked with Shari toward their vehicles. "Hey," she said, coming alongside her, "I didn't want to say anything around the others, but did you notice Brother Nash checking you out?"

Shari frowned and studied her friend's face. She looked as tired as Shari felt. "You definitely need a good night's sleep, Faith. The only thing he was checking out was the fact that I could outplay him."

"Mmm-hmm. I spent half the night watching *him* watching *you*. He's a fine chunk of double chocolate. Girl, if I wasn't marrying Trask, I would definitely flirt with him, big time." She grinned. "Good night, sister," she added in a singsong voice.

Shari's father had always told his girls, "If a man is attracted in you, let him prove it." To date, no one had stepped up to the plate to prove his attraction to Shari. Dismissing Faith's erroneous observation, Shari got in her vehicle, buckled her seatbelt and drove off.

She was almost home when a what-if scenario stemming from Faith's comment came to mind. Maybe it was just her, but it seemed that most good-looking dark-skinned brothers like Brother Nash preferred a heavy dose of milk in their coffee when it came to a sister's outward appearance. Shari's long hair, smooth dark skin, long eyelashes, and even her "endowment," as her mother called it, couldn't hold a candle to fairer-skinned women like her beautiful sisters.

Since her skin was darker than a brown paper bag, she was encouraged not to affiliate with certain sororities and other organizations. It wasn't a myth. From slavery to the post-civil rights era, it was an unspoken truth that lighter-skinned black women enjoyed more inclusion, better positions, and the best-looking black men.

It didn't matter. Shari knew her worth, and she refused to use bleaching products on her skin in order to be accepted. She had other interests in life besides snagging the attention of a man, and she was open to any ethnicity, as long as he was a practicing Christian. Enough about letting Faith plant a tease seed in her brain. The real story tonight was what God had done for her. "Jesus, thank You for setting me free tonight," she prayed, praising Him as she turned the corner to her home.

You're welcome.

Her smile stretched wider. She loved it when God talked back.

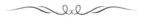

The next day, Garrett didn't bother attending Sunday service at his former home church, Blood Redemption Temple. If he ran into Brittani portraying herself as the victim, he would leave Boston on a sour note—again.

"What a joke," he mumbled, gritting his teeth. The only thing on his mind while he packed was Shari. His attraction was so sudden and so strong. He had to take deep breaths to slow his heart rate. Another relationship this soon was out of the question. Garrett wasn't looking, but his psyche begged to differ.

Garrett had more time to think once he got on 1-95 toward Philly. What a difference a day made. Months ago, he'd sat behind the same wheel, mad at God for sending him to a "foreign" land where he knew no one. The more he'd tried to trust God, the more bitter he'd become at the unexpected turn of events. Now, it was déjà vu all over again, except that this time, he couldn't wait to get back to the City of Brotherly Love.

Six hours later, Garrett pulled into his designated parking spot at his condo. He was barely inside his living room when he tapped John's name on his contacts list to call him. He took about twenty seconds for a greeting, then got to the point. "Before you tell me what I *should* know about her, tell me what I *don't* want to know."

"Hmm. Well, Shari's quiet, unassuming—"

"I figured that out, man," Garrett cut in. "But you can't hide beauty, and that woman is packed with it. She's gorgeous!"

"But she doesn't throw her looks or her business in folks' faces. She was very close with her father, and the last time she played 'Thank You' was at his funeral, over a decade ago. The song was a painful reminder of her loss."

Oh, no. The price of pain Shari had paid in order to bless his family was beyond measure. Garrett had both his parents and one set of grandparents still alive, and he couldn't imagine the void that her father's death must have caused. As a matter of fact, Garrett was closer to his grandfather than to his own father. His mother had always marveled at how closely he resembled his grandfather.

"Rita and I had to double-team her to get her to come, and we prayed she would get through it," John said. "And she did—very competently, wouldn't you say?" He chuckled. "Actually, I've never seen her so happy after a performance. If you think she can play, you should see her with her three sisters. The oldest, Stacy, is the church organist—"

"That's Shari's sister?" Now that Garrett thought about it, he realized there were similarities in their eyes and smiles. Come to think of it, he had also seen the two women talking together after church.

"Yep. Her other sisters are Shae and Brecee. Shari's an attorney...and, basically, that's it."

That definitely wasn't "it." Garrett was sure of that as he tugged on his mustache.

"You have your work cut out for you," John went on. "I haven't heard any rumors about her dating anyone in the church; given her strong Christian convictions, I doubt any man outside the faith could lure her into letting him buy her anything from a vending machine." John laughed at what Garrett assumed he had intended as a joke.

"I guess I'd better get plenty of change for the snack machines, because something tells me Sister Shari could be my sweet tooth." Garrett rubbed the waves in his hair. "I have really lost my mind. I can't believe I'm saying this."

"Man, unless you're a eunuch, one bad experience with a woman isn't going to stop you from falling in love again. Maybe next time—"

"Hold on. My love bank is empty. After Brittani, it will take a while for me to build it back up. But the more I say I don't want a next time, the more I feel God is telling me to be still."

"Then let God take the lead and see what happens." It wasn't long before John's wife summoned him away, and they ended the call.

Wife. Garrett grunted. He'd almost had one of those. What took him by surprise was that his instant attraction to Shari had become stronger than the love he had professed to Brittani before he'd proposed. In hindsight, he wondered whether he'd been so sure of himself that he'd assumed his choice of a wife was the same woman as God's choice for him. Boy, had he been wrong.

Chapter Four

On Monday morning, Garrett checked his Facebook account and found a rambling message from Brittani.

Garrett, I know you were in town last weekend for your grandparents' anniversary. I wasn't invited. That was disappointing. I was hoping that we would see each other at church on Sunday. You can't keep putting all the blame on me...

He deleted the message without reading the rest. He had heard it all before from her—the begging, the tears, the threats. His parents and grandparents hadn't raised any fools. Neither had the Lord.

Yes, he had loved Brittani like crazy and had strived to give her the desires of her heart, but it clearly hadn't been enough. Not when she'd slept with another man while wearing his engagement ring.

Note to self: Either block her or delete your Facebook account. He had moved on. Actually, it was God who had moved him—literally. His transfer from the U.S. Marshals office in Boston to the one in Philly had gone off without a hitch, considering that there had been two vacancies.

The hunt for housing had been just as flawless. Thanks to his savvy real-estate agent, he had put a bid on a pricey two-bedroom condo on City Avenue that was in pre-foreclosure. If that wasn't the Lord ordering his steps after an engagement debacle, then what was? Could Jesus be opening his heart to trust a woman again? Somehow his heart and eyes agreed that there was no comparison between Shari and Brittani.

The next day at work, when his smartphone played the familiar ringtone he'd chosen for his grandfather, Garrett put an end to his musings. As a deputy with the U.S. Marshal Philadelphia Fugitive Task Force, he had plenty of job security with the endless list of fugitives requiring apprehension. And here he was, daydreaming.

"Hi, Grandpa."

"I like her," Moses stated.

His grandfather never wasted time but always said whatever was on his mind. Garrett didn't have to guess who he was referring to.

"Funny, I do, too," Garrett seconded. He wasn't ashamed to be transparent with his elderly confidant. "As a matter of fact, I'll get to see her at Bible class this evening. But as a result, this day seems to be dragging. And I have plenty of work to do."

"Pray without ceasing. The Lord sent you there for a reason."

"Do you think Shari could be the reason?"

Moses didn't answer right away. "I won't assume anything, and neither should you. You've always been a praying man, which is why the devil targeted you with Brittani. Don't stop praying. If you get the right woman, you won't regret it."

Deputy U.S. Marshal Kyle Adams stuck his head into Garrett's office. "We've narrowed down two locations on Harris Forge—an ex-girlfriend's house or his grandmother's."

Nodding, Garrett pushed back from his desk. He had a good

excuse to end the call before his grandfather began to regale him with tales of the antics of his great-grandchildren, especially the boys. "I've got to go round up a bandit," he said, using the deputy U.S. marshals' term for a fugitive that was either suspected of or convicted of a crime and was hiding from the law. "Talk to you later. Love you, Grandpa."

Harris Forge was a suspected bank robber who had injured two security guards in his last holdup. The marshals had been hunting him for weeks.

Garrett and two other deputy marshals were stationed outside a home on West Huntington Street in the Strawberry Mansion neighborhood. Residents in that crime-infested part of North Philly rarely snitched.

While the lead deputy knocked on the door to serve the warrant, Garrett and the others were on standby at the back door and side door in the event that the fugitive tried to run or started shooting. To their relief, Forge came quietly. His eight-year-old daughter had opened the front door while he was in the bathroom. When he came out, he surrendered so not to alarm his daughter. Forge's grandmother didn't seem surprised to see them.

The day ended with one man in custody but thousands more on the run. Once Garrett got home, he had no problem switching his focus. He showered and dressed for Bible class. The more his eyes craved to see Shari, the more Brittani's face and expanding waistline competed for his thoughts. Why was the image of his ex-fiancée spiritually tormenting him? What happened to "out of sight, out of mind"? In all honesty, he was still trying to put back together all the pieces of his broken heart. Garrett was thoroughly confused.

Some answers come by fasting and prayer, the Lord whispered to his spirit.

"And I have been fasting twice a week," Garrett said, pleading for an understanding of this madness. "Lord, I asked You what I should do when Brittani became pregnant. I fasted and asked how I should handle that disgrace, and You sent me away from my family and friends. So here I am in Philly to regroup, start over, and enrich my spiritual life, not jump back into a relationship. Jesus, what is going on? Did You plant Shari in my life?" Garrett poured out his soul in prayer.

To everything there is a season, the Lord whispered. *Weeping endures only for a night.*

Garrett recognized the passages from Ecclesiastes and Psalm 30, and he paused to meditate on what God had said to his spirit. After a moment, he picked up his Bible and flipped through Ecclesiastes until he found the passage in chapter three, his eyes then falling on verse four: *"A time to weep, and a time to laugh; a time to mourn, and a time to dance."*

He had already mourned his loss in the love department. If Shari made him laugh, then he would truly have something to dance about, because Psalm 30:5—" *"joy cometh in the morning"*—had yet to be accomplished. When no other words came from the Lord, Garrett finished his grooming and walked out the door with more uncertainty swirling in his head. The primary question was had Shari gotten the same memo from God?

Once he arrived at the church, Garrett opened the door to the sanctuary and silently scanned those gathered there. It seemed as if his eyes guided him to Shari. She was seated with another woman, and Garrett slid into the pew behind them.

He knelt and prayed for thanksgiving to return to the house of God, then made himself comfortable on the padded seat. He leaned forward to make his presence known. "Good evening, ladies, and praise the Lord."

Almost in sync, the two women looked over their shoulders.

Whoa. John had described Shari's mother as "possessing

timeless beauty," and the woman looking back at him definitely had it. So, this was how the Carmen sisters would age to perfection. The mother had the same long lashes and flawless skin as her daughter, though her complexion was very fair in contrast with Shari's dominant African heritage.

Yet the resemblance was striking. Shari's sassy curls were gone, replaced by a long, thick silky ponytail that showcased her facial beauty even more. She was the type of woman who didn't need hair to enhance her looks. She'd be just as gorgeous without it. Still, Garrett preferred women with long hair—at least to the shoulders. Shari had that length, plus a whole lot more.

"Brother Nash." Shari's reception was pleasant, but there was no sparkle in her eyes to hint that God had spoken to her on his behalf.

Garrett pushed back a tinge of disappointment. It appeared he was going to have to work for her attention and affection. Was she worth the challenge? Time would tell. "What passage is Pastor Underwood teaching from tonight?" he asked.

"Galatians, chapter six," the duo responded in unison.

"Thank you." He twisted his lips in amusement as he sat back and opened his Bible. He flipped through the pages while his heart pounded faster with excitement of the unknown regarding Shari. For the next hour, Garrett listened to the Word but studied Shari's every movement—from the way she sat erect with her head tilted to the side to the moment she made a note on her tablet when God opened up her understanding about something.

"There are works of the flesh, which are worldly and lead to death. But with God, there are fruits of the Spirit..." For the next fifteen minutes, Pastor Underwood broke down verses eighteen through twenty-three from Galatians 6. Then he began wrapping up the message. "We'll end our discussion tonight on the attributes of a Christian, but remember, if you're ever in doubt on what is acceptable before God, it is right here." The pastor patted his Bible and concluded the class. Everyone stood for the altar call, then prepared for the offering.

After the service, Garrett inched forward again. Two distinct perfumes mingled for a unique blend. "Would you ladies care for an escort to your car?"

Shari's mother beamed. "Why, Brother Nash, isn't that nice of you? A sister can never be too careful. By the way, I'm Annette Carmen—Sister Carmen—Shari's mother." She needlessly identified herself as she extended her hand, which was incredibly soft. "My second eldest daughter, here, spoke highly of the party your family gave your grandparents in Boston."

Garrett thanked her but couldn't take his eyes off Shari. "She was definitely the highlight of the evening," he told Mrs. Carmen. "Trust me."

After the benediction, the three of them strolled out the sanctuary. Tonight, he was serving as bodyguard for two lovelies.

As they crossed the parking lot, Mrs. Carmen chatted away, while Shari said very little. What was she thinking? He never would've guessed she was an attorney. She appeared too timid to defend a case.

They stopped at a stylish black BMW X6. Garrett smirked at the similarities in her tastes and his as he held open the passenger door for her mother. Before he could extend the same courtesy to Shari, she was already behind the wheel and had started the engine.

Stuffing his hands in his pockets, Garrett stepped back and watched as Shari drove off, giving him a slight wave. As the taillights faded into the distance, a prayer came to him. "Lord, please don't let the reason for her presence in my life be for her legal services." Then, twirling around, he trekked to his vehicle and drove home.

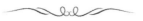

Shari shivered.

"Cold?" her mother questioned, turning up the heat in the car.

Goose bumps were spreading under Shari's wool coat faster than an allergic reaction, and it had nothing to do with the weather. It was Garrett. The night of the banquet, he'd been a blur, but tonight, it had been as if he was in 3-D without special glasses necessary.

Oddly, she had sensed his presence in the pew behind her before his deep voice had verified it. Maybe it was the scent of his cologne, the same type he'd worn the night of his grandparents' anniversary celebration. A detail she hadn't realized before that moment.

"I think he has a crush on you," her mother stated, as if Shari's thoughts were written on a marquee above her head.

"Huh?" Shari frowned.

"Brother Nash." She grinned.

Shari shook her head. "Right. First Faith, and now you're saying the same thing."

"And you don't see it?" Her mother *tsked.*

"I see he's a good-looking brother who was flirting with my mother," Shari teased. Then she sobered. "Seriously, I don't want to read more into his actions beyond face value. Not every man who offers to walk two women to their car has romantic intentions toward one of them. We're brothers and sisters in Christ, and fellow band members. That's all." She wasn't about to entertain the idea of being anything more.

Her mother silenced the radio. Shari started to protest, because gospel artist Tamela Mann's latest song had just started on 103.9, but it appeared Annette had an agenda.

"Sharmaine Lynn Carmen, when did you become so cynical?

You're young, stunning, and single. You're supposed to be hopeful and full of faith that love will come one day."

Resting her elbow on the armrest, Shari sighed. "Mom, you know I've had a few false starts when it comes to relationships, and there's always a reason. I've heard it all—men feel threatened by women who make more money than they do or who have more education... It's fine. I've worked and studied hard to make this career my companion."

"Sweetie." Her mother's voice softened. "I agree you don't need any insecure men in your life, but God has a standard of Christian men who aren't intimidated by strong, successful, independent women. I don't know what Brother Nash does for a living, but he can be my bodyguard anytime. He comes across as very confident." She giggled. "Plus, he is cute with his dark chocolate self."

"Mommy's drooling," Shari teased in a singsong manner. "But talk about a double standard. Skin color still matters. Our black men are marrying other races, and when they do marry African-Americans, the light-skinned sisters are the first pickings; we 'darkie' sisters are just a last resort." Shari swallowed. "I may be in that percentage of black women who never get married."

It always pained her to be called "darkie" growing up, but her father would ease the sting with his term of endearment— "My Egyptian ballerina." Even now, she cringed when men whispered behind her back that she was pretty...for a dark-skinned woman. What did that mean? That a woman couldn't be pretty unless she was white or fair-skinned?

She would never forget the hurt she'd felt when she overheard a boyfriend's mother say, "Do you really want to have children as dark as her, son?" The remark had resulted in a hasty end to the budding relationship. That had been Shari's decision. Why should she pine away for a superficial relationship with someone who had such a shallow mind-set?

For the most part, Shari had outgrown the pity parties of her childhood and adolescence. But it had never ceased to bother her that her skin tone still determined the way some people treated her and judged her character.

"You're simply beautiful!" her mother snapped. "Your sisters, especially the younger two, even envy your looks. Brecee still tries to wear fake lashes to make hers look as long as yours, and remember when she was a preteen?" She paused and chuckled. "I don't know how many times I had to stop her from walking around the house grinding pencils into her cheeks, trying to get dimples like the ones God blessed you with."

Her sisters. Shari smiled as she turned toward their home on West Gorgas Lane. "I miss that brat," she said, trying to steer the subject away from herself.

"Listen to me," her mother said, pointing a finger at Shari. "Men are like grass. They come in all different types of brands— Zoysia, the top of the line, all the way down to crabgrass. Every now and then, weeds try to camouflage themselves as real grass, but eventually, they get choked out."

"It seems like my relationship yard is mostly weeds," Shari mumbled, sounding pitiful even to her own ears. In the courtroom, Shari's colleagues called her "fierce" and compared her to a lioness fighting for her clients; but whenever it came to the subject of relationships, doubts crept in. Maybe she was going through a premature midlife crisis before she hit thirty.

"I'm just being honest, Mom," she went on. "I don't see a man, a marriage, or children in my near future. And I won't be disappointed if God doesn't see fit to bless me with a mate."

"Not even a little?" Her mother used her thumb and forefinger to indicate a tiny amount. "I think it'd be very interesting to see a man sweep you off your feet."

Shari grunted. "I haven't tripped over a man in a long time."

But, to be fair, bad relationships were equal-opportunity terrors that happened to women of all colors and ages. Her younger sister Shae was sweet and pretty, with skin the color of caramel. Yet that hadn't kept her from suffering through a horrible relationship. Because of that experience, Shae had uprooted herself from her first television gig in Nebraska and moved to St. Louis, where she was still recovering. As a favor to Shae, Shari should've sued the man for misrepresentation.

Their father had always said that when things seemed too good to be true, they usually were. Shari thought about Garrett. What was his story, really? Why had he relocated to Philly when all his family lived in Boston? Had it been for a job promotion? Or was he running away from something—or somebody?

Chapter Five

The next morning, Shari was back in her comfort zone, in her element—the courtroom.

"Your Honor, the alleged evidence against my client, Mr. Eric Smith, should be suppressed and thus thrown out," Shari argued. "His prospective employer, Network Security, conducted a botched Internet background check and retrieved the criminal court records of a distant cousin who bears the same name and date of birth. It was *that* Eric Smith who used his relatives' social security number when he was arrested for illegal possession of narcotics—"

Shari suddenly lost track of her rehearsed speech when she glanced away from the judge and her gaze connected with that of Brother Garrett Nash. In the blink of an eye, her heart skipped a beat, and everything blurred. It wasn't the first time she'd seen a familiar face in criminal court. What had he done?

"Counselor," Judge Dempsey warned her, "the court is waiting."

Regaining her composure and gathering her thoughts, Shari nodded. "My apologies. As I was explaining, in a rush to claim the ten-thousand-dollar reward on Eric Smith, the personnel manager contacted the police and set up a bogus interview for my client.

The sting operation landed him in jail. The authorities failed to conduct a full investigation, at the expense of my innocent client's liberty. That probe was stifled by the detective's willingness to accept the personnel manager's word without as much as a fingerprint analysis, which would have revealed a case of mistaken identity."

After making her concluding argument, Shari approached the judge and handed him a stack of information that was overwhelmingly in favor of her client. "Your Honor, please find attached Defense Exhibit 1, with exculpatory evidence completely negating my client's guilt."

The judge studied the documentation for a moment, then called for a month's continuance to review the papers. Shari countered with ten days. "Your Honor, it is no fault of his own that bad blood runs in his family and two cousins' identities were switched. Each day my client spends in custody, a grave injustice is allowed. Every minute he is deprived of his liberty as an innocent man, a miscarriage of justice is perpetuated. And every second he is permitted to be detained, justice is delayed."

As expected, the judge approved her request. Shari grabbed her briefcase and took a deep breath as she turned to leave, intending to ignore Garrett. Whatever he was doing there, it wasn't her business to inquire. Whatever it was, she could pray for mercy within the criminal justice system. She knew of too many Christians who lived double lives. But for some unknown reason, she would be disappointed if she found out he was one of them.

She could feel his eyes on her. *Don't look at him. Don't even peek.* Then she looked. Although no smile seemed forthcoming from him, there was gentleness in his expression. That was when she noticed his blue polo shirt and the badge hanging from his neck, and it clicked: Garrett was a deputy in the U.S. Marshals Service. They were very much part of the court landscape.

She exhaled with a smile and continued through the doorway to meet her next client in the hall. That was two days in a row that their paths had crossed. If she told Faith what had happened, her friend would be screaming in her ear before picking out a wedding gown, telling her it was "fate by faith." Shari didn't believe in coincidences. She had been taught as a child that God connects all the dots in people's lives for His divinely decided end result, which, in this case, was...what? She didn't have much time to dwell on that, as her next defendant stepped off the elevator, prompting Shari to revert to attorney mode.

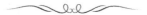

Now was not the time for Garrett to obsess over a woman, especially one who hadn't said more than a few sentences to him after Bible class.

He wasn't supposed to be in court that morning, but when another deputy had called in sick, and others were still on an early morning stake-out, he'd had to escort a drug lord to court. He smirked. *Thank You, Jesus.* He'd finally gotten a glimpse of the real Shari Carmen.

As soon as they'd entered Judge Dempsey's courtroom, Garrett's heart had leaped like a bloodhound picking up a scent when the object of his mental distraction had materialized. The shy, quiet band member had blossomed into a fireball, and her transformation had thrilled him as she'd commanded the attention of everyone in the room.

Shari's flirty banana-colored suit against her rich dark skin shouted, "I'm all about business, so don't mess with me"; her straight, trimmed mane hung down her back; and her stilettos showcased her well-toned calves. Evidently, she didn't follow the trend of nondescript dark suits that he had grown accustomed to seeing on other lawyers. She was creating a fashion mode all her own.

Against his better professional judgment, Garrett indulged, admiring her expertise in walking. She seemed to have a natural sway that he wished other women would try to emulate. Wowed by her confidence, beauty, and aura, Garrett almost wished he were the unfortunate client she'd been hired to defend. Shari was a tease, and unaware, which was why he'd kept refocusing.

The court proceedings for his client were conducted without any hiccups. Garrett was almost hoping Shari would return to the courtroom, but she never did, nor did she appear when he chaperoned the prisoner out the courthouse and loaded him in the armored car to carry him back to prison.

It didn't happen. Garrett supposed that if God was going to dangle this woman before him, he was obligated to kick his charm into high gear.

Chapter Six

A few days later, Shari had only one thing on her mind: finding food for her growling stomach. She'd already had two court cases that morning, and her next one was that afternoon, just a few hours away. A woman on a mission, Shari stepped out of the Criminal Justice Center on Filbert Street and prepared to search for some lunch.

"Shari!"

She twirled around and came face-to-face with Garrett. He closed the distance between them in a few long strides. His serious expression made him look lethal in contrast to his charming personality at Bible class.

"Hi, again." The warm gaze returned as his brown eyes seemed to dance. When he smiled, not one stain dulled his gleaming white teeth. *Nice.*

There went that chill that made her shiver. Just then, a slight breeze seemed to spin around them, and she caught a whiff of his cologne. *Ooh.* She loved the way he smelled. "We can't seem to get away from each other," she joked.

"And who would want to get away from the lovely Attorney Sharmaine Carmen?" Garrett lifted an eyebrow. "Not me."

Shari blushed and glanced away to gather her wits, then met his stare. "Believe me, there are plenty, mostly those who go up against me in court. I was shocked to see you there this morning. At first, I thought you were a defendant. I didn't know you were with the U.S. Marshals."

"Yes, and proudly serving for a couple of years." He playfully bowed. "But if I ever need a damsel to rescue me, you would be my one call from inside my cell."

Shari laughed.

"Seriously, you're an amazing musician, a stellar attorney, and you have the prettiest brown eyes."

His accolades, plus the compliment, rendered Shari temporarily speechless. When her voice returned, she thanked him. To stare boldly at him would be a challenge for him to say more, but she didn't find anything around them that was remotely interesting enough to warrant her gaze.

Shari had to scratch her initial assessment of Garrett Nash. Actor Lance Gross wished he looked as good. She snapped out of the trancelike state into which his magnetism had drawn her. "Uh, I'd better go grab something to eat. Enjoy the rest of your day."

"I will if you'll let me treat you to lunch," Garrett said, inviting himself along, then reached for the shoulder strap of her computer bag.

Putting up no resistance, Shari relinquished her briefcase. His initiative flattered her.

Garrett took the lead and guided her down the street. "I think eating at the Gallery will spare your feet from a lot of unnecessary walking," he suggested. The nearby mall extended four blocks and soared four stories high. Despite his long strides earlier, Shari couldn't help but notice that he'd slowed his steps, evidently to match hers.

The subtle gesture of chivalry was attractive, but the man

didn't know that she glided around in heels every day—and soaked her aching arches for almost an hour every night. That was the price she paid for wanting to add inches to her five-feet-five height.

"I have a burning question." He gently ushered her out of the way of approaching pedestrians with a slight touch to her arm.

"Okay." She swallowed, trying to act unaffected.

"Where did you learn to blow the sax like that?"

Unsure of what Garrett would want to know about her, Shari relaxed and laughed. "I learned from my father and cousins."

"That's right—your father. John told me what the song 'Thank You' means to you. I'm sorry for your loss. I can't thank you enough for sharing the piece with my family."

"It was my pleasure." Shari paused, then added, "Eventually."

They approached the mall entrance. Garrett opened the door, and she walked inside. She was accustomed to receiving this courtesy from male family members and colleagues, but the gesture felt different—almost personal—coming from Garrett.

In the Gallery food court, the two weaved their way through the maze of tables and chairs. Shari eyed the Saladworks menu. The thought of building her fruit salad sounded appealing. "Is this okay with you?" she asked Garrett. Judging by his build, he probably ate steak and eggs for breakfast.

"Sure. I didn't come just for the food but the company." He winked.

Once they had ordered, out of habit, Shari dug in her purse for money, but Garrett stayed her hand. "What man would ask a lady to lunch and allow her to pay?"

"I know a few," she answered without thinking.

"Well, I'm not one of them."

Shari thanked him, then looked for a place to sit while he paid the tab. She was still scanning the area for a *clean* vacant table when Garrett walked up to her with their tray and pointed to a square table for two in a cozy corner. She nodded and followed him there.

He waited for her to be seated first before lowering himself into his chair. After she silently blessed her food, Shari studied his salad. Was there any lettuce at all beneath the pile of ham and chicken strips? She hid her amusement. Between the crunches and chews, Shari caught him watching her as she observed him. What was he thinking?

More than once, the scent of his cologne drifted over and tickled her nostrils. She attempted to hold her breath, so that she wouldn't succumb to an attraction, but it didn't help. His dark face was clean-shaven, except for his thick black mustache, with well-defined features that were hard to resist. But she had to resist. There were no hints to suggest that he liked her as anything more than a sister in Christ, despite what her mother and Faith had said. *Bummer. That would have been nice.*

"What inspired you to become a Deputy U.S. Marshal?" she decided to ask.

He wiped his mouth with his napkin and took a sip of water. "The short answer is history."

Tilting her head, Shari studied him. "I like long answers."

He squinted as if concentrating hard on his response. "I'll never forget seeing the image of a brave little black girl named Ruby Bridges being escorted to an all-white school in the South by U.S. Marshal Charles Burks. It was at that moment I understood that 'protect and serve' meant more than being a police officer. That image changed history, and I wanted my purpose in life to be to make a difference. I started off in Homeland Security, which I enjoyed, but I was biding my time, waiting for an opening with the Marshals. It came more than a year ago. I certainly don't take my achievements lightly."

Passion. Shari was impressed, and that didn't happen often when it came to men.

Pushing his meal aside, Garrett folded his arms and focused on her. "Since we're talking about careers, was there a crime show that compelled you to become an attorney?"

"Justice in this life isn't a given. As long as man is in charge, life isn't fair. The color of our skin plays a major factor in whether we're a 'have' or a 'have not'—and not only in this country. More than once, I've been the victim of bias because of the way I look and a woman." She shrugged. "You're in law enforcement, so I know I'm preaching to the choir. Sorry."

"Hey, I invited myself along, so I'll listen to whatever you want to preach about. Being a black male in any profession has it challenges, too. For example, Bass Reeves was one of the first blacks to be appointed a Deputy U.S. Marshal west of the Mississippi River, way back in eighteen seventy-five. Now, fast-forward almost a hundred and fifty years, and out of ninety-four districts, our president has appointed twenty African-Americans."

Shari nodded as she stabbed her fork into her salad. "As long as there are minorities, regardless of their ethnicity, there will be racism and injustices that occur. That's where I come in. As a matter of fact, if I recall, there have been multiple class-action suits filed against the U.S. Marshals Service for denied promotions—" She stopped. Why did she always talk shop when she found herself alone with a man?

Because you're trying to mask your personal insecurities with your professional achievements. That was something her mother, sisters, or Faith might say.

Garrett was about to speak when his smartphone sang a tune played by Gerald Albright. The musician's mastery of the saxophone was unmistakable. "If you don't mind, let me take this to make sure everything's okay at home." He raised the phone to his ear. "Hi, Grandpa." He winked. The gesture was so sexy that Shari could have slid out of her chair. She shook her head, trying to unscramble her jumbled-up hormones. She didn't want to take his mannerisms personally. What she did find endearing was his concern for his loved ones, especially the elderly.

"I'm enjoying lunch with the most beautiful, fascinating creature God has formed." He nodded as his eyes sparkled adoringly at her.

Okay, I'm a goner. How could he say those things and she not take it personally? *Remember to breathe,* she coaxed herself.

Seconds later, Garrett handed her his smartphone. "It's Grandpa Moses. He wants to speak with you."

Me? Surprised, Shari blinked, then cleared her throat. "He—he wants to speak with me?" she stuttered before accepting the phone. "Praise the Lord, Brother Miller."

Garrett seemed amused at her discomfort. As a matter of fact, he began eating his salad with more gusto, as if her speaking to his grandfather was the norm.

"Praise the Lord, young lady. I hope my grandson is treating you to a fine lunch." The man's friendly tone relaxed her. "We plan to visit G—I mean, Garrett—soon, and we look forward to seeing you again. Then we'll treat you."

"Okay..." Shari didn't know what else to say. Her saxophone solo must have really earned her some fans. A smile tugged at her mouth. "Uh, would you like to speak with 'G'?" she teased, ready to hand him back his phone.

"Oh, I can speak with him anytime. Enjoy your lunch, and God bless you."

"Thank you. God bless you and yours, too." Shari exhaled once they disconnected. She raised an eyebrow at Garrett and gave him the stare that she usually reserved for her clients, daring them to come clean with the truth. "If I didn't know better, I would say you set me up."

Laughing, he shook his head. "Not guilty. My grandfather and I just happen to have a crush on the same beautiful sister."

Crush? Shari tried to maintain an unreadable expression as her heart fluttered. Finally she regained control. "Isn't it true that the same Moses Miller is married and has professed his love to his wife of fifty years?"

Garrett nodded.

"And yet, you accuse this wonderful husband, father, and grandfather of upstanding character of this indiscretion?"

"Well, Counselor, let me clarify my statement. It is a fact that he does like you." Garrett's nostrils flared, and she almost expected steam to pour out at any minute. "I'm the one with a crush."

Yes, he was handsome, a fine specimen of God's handiwork; but she knew little about him and wasn't about to be blindsided by his charm.

Leaning closer, as if the empty chairs nearby would eavesdrop, he lowered his voice to say, "You mesmerized me at the party, and my attraction has been growing ever since. We have other things in common besides my grandfather's affections. The most important commonality is that we've both been baptized with the Holy Ghost by fire and water in Jesus' name. Then, there is the fact that we both play tenor sax."

Shari didn't know what to make of the unexpected revelation. This was too serious a discussion over salad. She preferred to talk shop. She needed to keep a clear head and get back to her office.

"Ah, the counselor has doubts, does she? We both believe in law enforcement. You defend the laws of the land, and I make sure suspects pay for the crimes they committed by bringing them to court. And we have the same taste in vehicles. I, too, drive a black BMW X6."

"You're kidding me."

"It was the multi-contour power driver's seat and the premium audio sound system that sold you. Am I right?"

Uncontrollable giggles escaped Shari's lips. What script was this man reading from? How did he know? She couldn't let him think he had the upper hand. "Actually, it was the turbo engine and the all-wheel drive," she rebutted.

Their laughter mingled for a moment. Then Garrett reined in his chuckles, but his dark eyes continued to sparkle with mirth. "Thank God for dimples."

"Excuse me?"

"Your dimples. God made them to perfection." He kept staring.

As if she didn't believe him, Shari fingered the indentations. She hadn't thought about them since her recent conversation with her mother.

"There's more, Attorney Carmen. Our dark skins blend into a robust cup of Jamaican coffee. The aroma is so sweet that I don't care how the experts may try to duplicate the ingredients; only God got it right."

How was she supposed to respond to that line of poetry? Garrett closed his large hand over her smaller one, and she thought she was going to pass out. His was so warm, hers so cold. Her heart seemed to lose its rhythm. She didn't even know this man, and his well-rehearsed romantic lines were wreaking havoc with her peace of mind.

Withdrawing her hand, Shari scooted back in her chair, putting some much-needed distance between them. She was one of the best lawyers in the region, and no stranger to tense moments and quick-witted repartee, yet she found herself at a loss for words.

Shari took a deep breath to clear her head—and inhaled Garrett's cologne instead. Deciding it was time to prevent any further insanity, she steered the conversation away from the vulnerable party—herself. "Your assessment is duly noted and warmly welcomed, but I'm at a disadvantage. Somehow your presence in the City of Brotherly Love doesn't fit."

He frowned. "What do you mean?"

"It's evident that you are well-loved in Boston. What brought you Philly? It definitely wasn't family or career."

Suddenly, Garrett became tongue-tied. Her attorney instincts told her he was the one suppressing information.

"I have my reasons," he finally responded.

"I see." Shari wouldn't press him for more details. Everything within her shouted, *Watch and pray, and watch some more!*

When their salads were finished, they headed back to the courthouse. Garrett had done more than hint at his affections; he had stirred up a lot of questions—questions that would have to wait until after her next court case to decipher.

Chapter Seven

Although Garrett was enthralled with Shari and wanted to explore the fascination that God had instilled in him for her, he wasn't ready to bare his soul. He didn't want her pity for his humiliation. He had heard enough rumors circulating around the church: "Didn't you know better?" "She sure made a fool out of you," and the doozy: "You are going to give the other guy a beat down, right?"

The answer, of course, was no. Garrett had been too numb to lose it over Brittani. He'd opted for the default clause in Second Chronicles 20:17 and let the Lord fight his battle.

Despite her high heels, Shari quickened her steps on the return trip from lunch. He had laid it on kind of thick, which surprised him. But once he'd begun to speak from his heart, the more freely his words had flowed.

Silence had replaced their lighthearted banter from earlier. Shari must have sensed his discomfort, for she didn't press him. If only he knew what was going through her mind. She wouldn't be a great attorney if she didn't store their conversation away for future retrieval when necessary.

"I need to go to my office before heading back to court," she said. Garrett followed her as she detoured onto a different street a couple of blocks before the Justice Center. When they reached her office door, she turned and gave him a smile that seemed genuine. "Thanks for lunch."

"Thanks for letting me treat you." Garrett nodded and walked away without looking back. "Lord, I'm not ready for this," he prayed under his breath. "It wouldn't be fair to bring her my baggage."

Put your trust in Me, not in yourself. God had the last word on the matter for that day.

The following Saturday, Garrett was disappointed when Shari was a no-show at band practice. He had been curious to see how she would respond to him after the impromptu lunch date and his shutting down on her. Once rehearsal was over, he pulled John to the side. "What's the deal with Shari? Clearly, she enjoys playing. Why does she skip practice?"

His friend grinned. "Well, aren't we our sister's keeper?" When Garrett didn't crack a smile, John wiped the smirk off his face. "She wears a couple of hats here at Jesus Is the Way. Since Shari's an attorney, she lends her expertise to the prison ministry. They've been prepping and praying for their three upcoming prison missions trips, so her absences are understandable, considering she can pick up most songs with ease."

Tucking away that tidbit, Garrett thanked him and was about to walk away when John stopped him.

"I wouldn't move too fast, for both of your sakes. You need to make sure your head is clear, and Shari...well, let's just say she puts her heart into everything she touches. Don't break it, man. So, what's your game plan?"

Garrett glanced over his shoulder, then lowered his voice. "It's God's game plan. While I was praying, He basically told me Shari is the one." "All right." John lifted his hand for a high five, and

Garrett reluctantly tapped palms with him. "We're beating out Mother Stillwell."

"Who?"

"The church matchmaker. She's in competition with Rita and me, but we're on a roll." When Garrett didn't join in the celebration, John sobered. "Why aren't you happy about this?"

Garrett huffed. "I'm trying to figure out the intense feelings that sprang up in me without warning. It's a lot to process in such a short period of time, especially after being made a fool of by Brittani. The relocation has helped, although I miss being around my family. And then, to top it off, God is making me work for Shari's affections. I think she's clueless of what the Lord told me."

John nodded. "I see your point. Any other woman might be making wedding plans if a brother told her that God said she was the woman for him. Somehow, I don't think that would faze Shari."

"Yeah, I know." Garrett shook hands with his friend and walked out of the sanctuary, wondering if Attorney Sharmaine Carmen was worth it.

The next day, the morning sermon seemed to resonate with him. The title was "God Has Your Best Interests at Heart," and it was based on Psalm 84:11: *"For the LORD God is a sun and shield: the LORD will give grace and glory: no good thing will he withhold from them that walk uprightly."*

For the next couple of days, as Garrett spent more time praying and meditating on God's Word, one Scripture kept coming to his mind. It was James 1:4: *"Let patience have her perfect work..."*

God was surely asking a lot of him. "Lord," he prayed, "since You're orchestrating my life, please cue me when I'm supposed to make a move."

Since he'd missed Shari at band practice, he looked forward to seeing her at the midweek Bible class. She would be a breath of renewal after a day spent tracking down fugitives.

While two deputies stood guard outside the home of a convicted gang member of the 60th Street Posse, aka Six-O, in West Philly, Garrett and another deputy made an early-morning raid.

The suspect, William Truman, didn't seem surprised to see them when he answered the door. "Am I supposed to be in court?" he asked, as if he had missed a doctor's appointment.

Garrett hadn't dignified him with an answer as he'd snapped the cuffs on him. Although some felons were dangerous, evidently having a warrant out for his arrest was just a joke to Mr. Truman.

The two other fugitives they had tracked down during his shift hadn't been that easy.

When he got home from work, Garrett showered, dressed, and ate dinner in record time. As he was on his way out the door for church, his grandfather called.

"Hey, Grandson. My heart has been heavy about you lately. I've been calling out your name more frequently in prayer."

"I appreciate that, Grandpa. It's frustrating trying to figure out what God is constructing in my life. I didn't want to leave my family, but I was obedient. Twice, Shari and I crossed paths outside church. No doubt she's a beautiful jewel, but I'm battling conflicting feelings. If there had never been a Brittani in my life, I would pursue Shari the way I track down fugitives. But when I think about how clouded my judgment was in regard to Brittani, I kick myself for being so blind. While one voice is telling me that I'm not ready to pursue her, God is whispering, *She's the one.*"

"Don't you mess up this one by pushing too hard and too fast with Shari," his grandfather cautioned him. "Go at God's pace. Be patient with her and with yourself."

Garrett smiled. The Lord knew how to send the right person along to reinforce His message. "Thanks, Grandpa. I needed to hear that."

Moses chuckled. "If you open your spiritual eyes, you'll see what God sees in her that is best for you."

"I already do." Garrett glanced at his watch. "Grandpa, I need to head out so I can make it to Bible class on time. Love you, sir."

Traffic on the Schuylkill Expressway was not working in his favor. "Patience," he whispered as he inched forward along with other irritated motorists.

By the time he got to the church, the pew behind Shari and her mother was already filled. As Garrett moved to another section that still provided a view of Shari, he felt unexpectedly deep disappointment. He jotted notes during the lesson, but by the end of the class, none of the pastor's teachings had stuck.

Once the offering was taken and the benediction pronounced, he walked with purpose toward Shari and her mother. They were chatting with Stacy, the organist—Shari's older sister, John had told him—and a man who appeared to be her husband, judging from his protective stance by her side. Garrett waited impatiently to be acknowledged, but his feigned calm was impossible to keep up for more than a minute. He stepped closer to make his presence known. "Good evening, Shari, Mrs. Carmen."

"Praise the Lord, young man," said Annette. "Do we get an escort again tonight?" She looked hopeful.

He smiled. "Absolutely."

"Mother!" Shari balked, seemingly embarrassed.

"Mom, we can walk you to your car," the man next to Stacy was quick to offer.

"Ted, take your wife home. Brother Nash will take care of us." Annette beamed with the same bright smile as Shari, minus the dimples, as she plucked the Bible out of Shari's arms and handed it over to Garrett, along with her own, to carry.

Garrett was amused, as well as grateful, to have an ally in Shari's mother. With Ted and Stacy looking on quietly, Annette took the lead and walked ahead, leaving a distance for him and Shari as they followed. Her mother stopped numerous times to greet other people, and in several hushed conversations with other women, she glanced back at him, giggling like a schoolgirl.

Shari didn't even attempt small talk as she strolled beside him. Garrett was desperate to recover whatever camaraderie he'd built and then lost with her at lunch. After she deactivated the alarm on her vehicle, he opened her door. "You're participating in the prison team ministry this Saturday, right?"

Twirling around, Shari faced him for the first time. "How did you know that?" The element of surprise looked good on her as her seductive brown eyes widened. Her long lashes were another teasing asset.

He whispered for her ears only, "I make it my business to know things about you. Sorry I was late tonight and that my seat behind you was already snagged. It won't happen again. Until next time." Garrett meant it. He was going to woo her as if Brittani never existed.

Garrett watched as Annette buckled in and then Shari drove off without a word. Grinning, he strolled over to his SUV. "Oh, yeah. This time, everything's going to be different."

Chapter Eight

Shari had thought that music was her only addiction. Ever since Garrett had been making his presence known, things had been shifting. Tonight, she had expected to see him sitting in the pew directly behind her.

"That's two for two consecutive personal escorts, if you're counting," her mother said in a chipper voice, interrupting her reverie.

Why was her mother always so in tune with her thoughts? "I'm not counting."

"Why? Don't you think he's cute?"

After checking her rearview mirror, Shari turned onto the freeway. "No. Brother Nash is fine, but there's something about him that makes me uncomfortable."

Her mother released a laugh. "That's called attraction, dear."

"Hmmm. I won't deny that, but it's just something..." She paused to formulate her thoughts. "There are so many layers to a person. On the surface, people come off as solid, until you start to ask questions. Then their walls begin to crumble."

"And when did my daughter become so cynical?"

Shari shrugged. "It probably happened when I decided to

pursue a career in law. I see things in black-or-white. True or false. Innocent or guilty. The crimes that come across my desk sometimes take a toll on me."

"Leave those troubled spirits at work, honey. God gave you the Holy Ghost, and with that comes unspeakable joy, faith, and hope. As Pastor taught tonight, those are some of the fruits of His Spirit. Don't let the world's troubled spirits overtake you."

"I've learned to rely on prayer and spiritual discernment rather than a gut feeling in order to sense whether a prospective client is lying or telling the truth. But when it comes to men who are supposedly interested in me, I'm always suspicious, and Brother Garrett is no exception. I'm still asking the Lord what his deal is."

"Umm-hmm. Sweetie, the fun part about falling in love is peeling back the layers to uncover everything about a person. Believe me, the rules change, and exceptions are made, as part of the package."

Who said anything about falling in love? Shari wanted to refute that statement, but she decided to hold her tongue for now. As if taking her cue, her mother turned up the radio and belted out the gospel tune as if she were live on stage. She continued her impromptu concert, song after song, until Shari pulled up to the curb in front of their house. When her mother playfully bowed, Shari applauded.

On Saturday morning, Shari claimed a seat on one of two church vans filled with prison ministry volunteers. Today would be their third annual pre-Resurrection Sunday service in a jail, and this year, they were headed for Bayside State Prison in Leesburg, New Jersey. In total, twenty-five saints were on board, all of them either ministers or musicians. That was a record.

The prison ministry was one auxiliary within the church to which many members couldn't commit because of their hesitancy to evangelize "hardcore" prisoners. They usually couldn't stomach the restrictive conditions behind the prison walls. The legal system considered most of the inmates beyond redemption and rehabilitation. No wonder many of them felt hopeless—a disheartening reality for believers with loved ones behind bars.

Stretching her legs, Shari adjusted her body in a double seat for total comfort, then closed her eyes. She couldn't help but reminisce about the last time she'd ridden in the church van—the time when the Lord had delivered her from a self-imposed spiritual bondage.

She took a deep breath and began meditating on the Word when she recognized his voice—not God's, but Garrett's. His deep, velvety tone and strong, crisp enunciation drew her in whenever she heard it. What was he doing on board?

Shari slowly opened her eyes as his presence commandeered the van. She followed his steps until he stopped at her seat. "Shari."

"Garrett." She arched an eyebrow. "What are you doing here?"

"Remember when I said 'Until next time'? Well, this is my next time." The sparkle in his eyes caused Shari to wrack her brain until she recalled him making the same statement after Bible class that week, right after he'd asked if she was going on the prison trip. "Mind if I share your seat?"

Everything within Shari told her to say yes, but two things stopped her. First, she was a private person, and she could feel the curious stares of others around her. The second was that Garrett would be a distraction, and the ministry team had to be spiritually savvy to prepare themselves for entrance into the devil's playground at the prison.

"Um...I realize it's only about an hour's drive, you'll probably be more comfortable if you can stretch out," she told him.

"You aren't going to make it easy for me to get to know you, are you?" he asked quietly.

How did he read her so precisely? Garrett had no idea that he had her emotions all discombobulated. The man was a complete package: handsome, saved, and sanctified, and with a great career, to boot. And she was scared to tangle with the gift wrap.

Now she had another nagging question besides why Garrett had chosen to leave Boston: Why hadn't a woman snagged him yet? A few times, the Lord had used Shari to operate the gift of discernment through the Holy Ghost.

It would be a good time for that gift to manifest again. But since neither she nor anyone one else could control how and when God released His gifts, Shari could only hope that if there was something ungodly about Garrett, the Lord would let her know about it.

Another church member boarded the bus with much fanfare, saving Shari from confirming Garrett's question. Sister Xena Davis noticed Garrett and strutted their way. "Brother Nash, what a surprise. Looking for a seat? That's all right, you can sit with me." She tried, unsuccessfully, to steer him away from Shari.

Physically, Xena could stop traffic with her good looks. Any man would love to be seen with her, saved or unsaved. They clamored for her attention.

But then, once they had it, for some unknown reason, their interest seemed to wane. Or maybe it was Xena who became bored with them.

"Uh..." Garrett glanced at Shari with a silent plea for rescue. But Shari merely shrugged in amusement.

He might as well get it over with. Xena usually got first dibs on new brothers in the church, and it appeared Garrett was her latest prey.

"I'll probably be more comfortable alone...you know, with room to move and stretch. But thanks anyway, sister." Garrett backtracked to a vacancy near the front, apparently to escape Xena, who was moving toward the rear of the van.

Minister Terrence Wells, auxiliary chaplain and president of the prison ministry, was the last one to climb aboard. "Praise the Lord, everybody. As customary, let me go over the rules."

"We can repeat them in our sleep," Xena interrupted him, then released a loud sigh. She was echoed by a couple of "Amens."

"Great." He nodded, glancing around. "Then I guess you all fasted, anointed your heads with oil, and prayed this morning. This is a serious ministry. For those of you who might forget that, let me remind you of the witchcraft we witnessed last month at Curran-Fromhold Correctional Facility. Of the gang members who tried to intimidate other prisoners from coming to Christ. And of the time a man planned to escape by leaving with us.

"Remember, we aren't taking the gospel to these men but sharing a service with them. No touching. No accepting notes for families on the outside. Stay with the group, and be on alert for any mischief. As you know, we don't have any security chaperones, but we are blessed today to have Brother Garrett Nash, a Deputy U.S. Marshal, on the trip."

Shari smiled as a round of applause and a chorus of "Hallelujah" and "Amen" circulated around her. She, too, welcomed his presence—from a security standpoint only. It was the shivers he provoked that made her feel insecure.

She was going to have to get Stacy's take on Garrett. She was the only Carmen sister who was married, and Shari loved watching Ted treat her big sister with interest and admiration. Although Stacy wanted all her sisters to be happy, she didn't go out of her way to set them up on blind dates—to Shari's great relief. That had been her mother's department until Shari had threatened to move out for some solitude.

Once the team arrived at Bayside State Prison and had been cleared to meet with the inmates, they sang songs, shared testimonies, prayed, and distributed new socks, T-shirts, and underwear. Shari provided free legal advice for those who needed it. As a precaution, she always had a male team member and a prison guard present during her consultations. Without being asked, Garrett volunteered.

Prisoner #23987 nodded. "What's up, Sharmaine?" He was a short man with a large Afro and numerous tattoos from the back of his ear all the way down his thick right arm.

"How are you doing today, Leo?" She settled in an old metal chair across from him.

Immediately, Garrett expressed his displeasure with the inmate for not giving Shari her due respect as an attorney.

Shrugging him off, Shari closed her eyes, bowed her head, and began to pray. "Father God, in the name of Jesus, I thank You for this day and ask You to provide comfort and peace to my brother, here. Lord, we ask that You would forgive each one of us. In Jesus' precious name. Amen."

"Right," Leo said, grinning as gold flashed in his mouth.

Wrong. With so much demonic activity in federal penitentiaries, there wasn't a doubt in Garrett's mind that he was about to become a permanent member on the church's prison ministry team. He needed to monitor this Leo character, who seemed content to play church in order to have his legal needs met. While Shari closed her eyes in prayer, Garrett kept his wide open. Whether he was tracking bandits or fraternizing with prisoners, a Deputy U.S. Marshal letting a target out of his sight could prove deadly.

A few weeks later, the prison ministry was on the road again. This time, the trip was a short drive, to the local House of Correction. The team stood in single file awaiting their turn to be searched and to have their IDs checked against the list they had submitted to the director of chaplaincy services.

Within minutes, they waited in the hall outside a small chapel as dozens of inmates filed in. A few of them gawked at the female team members as if they were sheep ready for slaughter. One prisoner, a stout man who looked as if he used his daily half hour of free time to lift weights, watched Shari with more interest than Garrett cared for.

"If it ain't the great Attorney Carmen," he said as he passed. "You might not remember me, considerin' you didn't do nothin' to keep me from bein' locked up. I'm Calvin Brownlee. Now do you remember? I should kill you so that I'll have a reason to be in here."

Did he just threaten my woman—I mean, the woman God has for me? Yet Garrett felt the Holy Ghost holding him back.

Calvin sneered at Shari with calculated calmness before Xena managed to catch his attention or indirectly asked for it. He grinned, clearly enjoying the flirtation.

In Garrett's mind, Xena was playing a dangerous game. Surely she knew these men were not eligible, available, or Christ-centered. Most of them probably wouldn't be eligible for parole for decades.

When another mean-looking prisoner joined Calvin in returning Xena's flirtations, something didn't feel right within Garrett's spirit.

"What can you tell me about Jesus, pretty lady? Huh?" he whispered with a smile that quickly transformed into a devious grin.

By the time Xena sensed that something was wrong, it was too late. She tried to back away from the man as he approached. However, the sisters standing behind her, oblivious to the potential danger, didn't budge. In a flash, Calvin whipped out a long piece of cloth and tied her wrists. Garrett realized that Xena was about to be assaulted before his eyes. He moved with lightning speed to intervene, only to have Shari get in his way.

With strength he hadn't known she possessed, Shari shoved Calvin with her fist as she called on the name of Jesus. Startled, Calvin fell back, and two guards stepped in to restrain him.

A buff prisoner, twice as big as Calvin, grabbed Shari from behind. "Oh, baby, you want some, too?"

As one of the guards triggered the alarm to summon more help, Garrett put all his strength into his fist as it connected with the man's face. The jab didn't faze him. Laughing, he twisted Shari's arm. When she cried out in pain, the saints began to pray. Xena wept.

Garrett readied himself to deliver another hit, but before he could do so, several correctional officers rushed in and tased the inmate. Weakened by the electrical shock, he loosened his grip but didn't let go of Shari. With another jolt from the Taser, the inmate released Shari, and she staggered away.

Garrett caught her and helped her regain stability. "You okay?"

She grimaced as she rubbed her arm, but she nodded yes. The shock on her face faded quickly.

"Why did you do that? You knew you were no match for that criminal." Garrett tried to keep his voice steady.

Protecting judges and hunting down dangerous fugitives was part of this job, but this was the first time he'd actually been afraid—not for himself but for Shari.

"Xena would've been raped before our group knew what was going on. Jesus said, 'Greater love hath no man than this, a man lay down his life for his friends.'"

"I'm familiar with John fifteen, verse thirteen. But don't you ever try that stunt again." He frowned. "I mean it." *Whoa. Calm down*, he coaxed himself. Who was he to chasten Shari? Still, prison was the devil's sanctuary, and God's soldiers had to constantly be on watch. "Promise me."

I promise, she mouthed.

Garrett exhaled a sigh of relief. "Thank you."

"Thank God for His intervention," said Minister Wells, putting an arm around Xena's shoulder. "Now, saints, let's do the job God called us to do." Xena still appeared to be shaken as everyone started shuffling into the chapel, singing "He Wants It All."

He rubbed Shari's arm and squeezed her hand as they brought up the rear. Despite the fray that had just occurred outside the chapel, the men inside seemed eager to hear testimonies, to join in the singing, and to hear a short sermon within the two-hour time period the team was allotted.

At the altar call, one of the inmates, the grandson of a member at Jesus Is the Way Church, who had been incarcerated for drug possession and distribution, walked down the aisle to be reclaimed by God. His humble display of submission sparked three other inmates to seek salvation. They were baptized in Jesus' name, and two of them received the Holy Ghost, with the evidence of speaking in unknown tongues.

On the ride back to the church, Minister Wells instructed Xena to sit up front with him and his wife. Instead of giving her a tongue-lashing for provoking the prisoners, he simply told her and the rest of the team, "Good job."

Not waiting for an invitation, Garrett had snagged the seat next to Shari. Surprisingly, she had scooted close to him until their shoulders touched, which seemed to awaken every sensory in his body.

"You sure you're okay?" he asked her, thinking of the twofold nature of his question. He wanted to know how she was physically, after her contact with the inmate at the prison, as well as how she was emotionally, now that she had the faintest contact with him.

"Yes," she said, her voice barely above a whisper. "Thank you for being here."

"I'm supposed to be here." Garrett wanted to say something more, like *"God sent me here for you,"* but it didn't seem to be the time or the place.

She gave him a soft smile, then looked out the window until she began to doze. Before long, her head had found its way to his shoulder. He couldn't believe how right that felt as he relaxed and began to drift off, as well.

Chapter Nine

"You did *what?* Shari cast a suspicious look at Faith. They were at the church on a Thursday night for the first of two wedding rehearsals that Faith had insisted she needed because of the size of the affair. "And when did you decide to invite Brother Garrett to play along with me at your wedding? I thought I was doing a solo."

Her older sister's words from the other day came rushing to her mind. Stacy had warned her that if God intended Garrett for her, the more she pushed him away, the closer he would get. "Do you think his showing up at the courtroom and then taking you to lunch was a coincidence? Maybe, but sitting behind you at Bible class and being on the prison ministry team—now that is deliberate."

Even Ted had added his input to the conversation. "You're a marked woman," he'd said. "I believe that brother is serious."

Now Shari wondered if Garrett's participation in her best friend's wedding ceremony was another strategic move on which he and Faith were in cahoots.

Faith grinned. "Well, I got to thinking..."

"Which is so you—and very scary, I might add." Shari folded her arms and dared her friend to deny it. Faith embraced spontaneity and adventure—neither of which appealed to Shari. It seemed that even in friendships, opposites attracted.

"Who knows?" Faith shrugged. "Maybe you'll thank me someday. But when you mentioned that Brother Nash took you out to lunch, and I thought about the show you two put on at his grandparents' shindig, I thought, why not add him to the program? So, I asked, and he said yes!"

Shari rolled her eyes at her friend's deliberate play on a phrase commonly associated with marriage proposals. "It was an accidental meeting and an impromptu lunch—nothing more. Definitely not a date."

Faith snickered. "Not to mention Wednesday night escorts to the car and prison ministry trips together... Chance meetings are what great romances are made of! You know that's how Trask and I met—at that baseball game I hadn't planned to attend—"

"I was there, remember?" Shari said, cutting her off. "But you already had a secret crush on him. Will you stop keeping tabs on me?"

Shari waved her hand in the air. *Define "romance,"* she thought. Would she ever hear the words "I love you"? Feel the warm embrace of a soul mate? Experience the intoxication of a kiss?

"What are you, anyway, an aide to Mother Stillwell or Team John and Rita?"

"Neither. I'm just happy when I see others happy, especially my best friend." Just then Faith turned her attention to the wedding planner, who was approaching them.

"Right," Shari mumbled.

So, it was for Faith's happiness that she carried her saxophone case into the sanctuary. Garrett was already in the bandstand, adjusting his tenor sax. Taking a deep breath, Shari continued down the side aisle. She smiled at those in the wedding party she knew and nodded at those she didn't.

She had been a bridesmaid only once, at Stacy's wedding. The Carmen sisters had made a silly childhood pact that they would be bridesmaids only in one another's nuptials because theirs was a sisterhood like no other. Stacy had honored that vow when friends had asked her to be a bridesmaid in their weddings, and so, when Faith had asked Shari to be her maid of honor, Shari had graciously declined, instead volunteering to do anything else she could that would make the day memorable. Faith had asked her to play a selection at the ceremony and then supervise the gift table at the reception. That had seemed a simple enough request—until Faith had gone and complicated things for her "happiness."

Shari was almost to the altar when she heard a man whisper, "Ooh, she's pretty—for a dark-skinned girl."

The insult, poorly disguised as a compliment, made her lift her chin higher to mask the hurt that threatened to sink her heart. She was a career-success story, and that was what she always fell back on when someone tried to rattle her self-esteem. *Never let them see you sweat.* That was the phrase her father and two cousins, Dino and Victor, had drilled into her.

How many times would her beauty be defined by the hue of her skin? Even in this so-called modern age, skin was a deciding factor in so many situations, especially within the justice system. But winning cases didn't empower her nearly as much as the video clip of actress Lupita Nyong'o's speech at the *Essence* magazine luncheon.

Lupita had openly confessed that, as a child, she had prayed for white skin in order to be beautiful and accepted. She had finally embraced her dark skin before winning an Oscar for Best Supporting Actress for her role in the film *12 Years a Slave* and before *People* magazine had named her World's Most Beautiful Woman. Those were victories that couldn't be won in the courtroom—the acknowledgment of dark and beautiful sisters.

Shari lifted her chin even higher as she placed one foot on the first step to the pulpit. Garrett was there to extend a hand and assist her up the remaining stairs. His grip was strong but gentle. She whispered her thanks, then set her saxophone case on a chair.

"You look pretty," Garrett said softly.

Still distracted by the earlier comment, Shari glanced up and looked into his eyes. Sincerity stared back at her. She mustered a smile. "Thanks." *I needed to hear that.* She couldn't help but wonder if Garrett thought that she looked pretty "for a dark girl," too.

After taking her seat, Shari found herself staring in the direction of the offender. How could she be beautiful in one man's eyes and almost attractive in another's?

Favor is deceitful, and beauty is vain: but fear Me, and you shall be praised. The Lord whispered Proverbs 31:30.

Thank You, Jesus, Shari's soul whispered, strengthened by the Word of God.

"Ladies and gentlemen, let's get started," the wedding coordinator spoke into the cordless mic as she marched down the aisle like a staff sergeant.

As Shari watched the groomsmen practice escorting the bridesmaids with synchronized steps, she felt a sense of longing. Would she ever be the one whose wedding was being rehearsed?

According to her younger sisters, Shae and Brecee, she was supposed to be next, since Ted had taken their oldest sister off the market. That was easier said than done. Shari had yet to meet a man who would break down all her defenses to love, although every time Garrett was near, he gave her a glimpse of hope that love would find her.

When the coordinator called for the instrumental duet, Shari snapped out of her whimsical musings. Garrett was about to assist her to her feet, but Shari stood on her own. In sync, they began to play Antwaun Stanleys' "By Your Side." Cued by the coordinator, Shari lowered her sax and sang to serenade Faith and Trask at the altar. Garrett didn't miss a beat, following her notes high and low on the musical scale.

Once their duet had ended and they'd taken their seats, Garrett leaned over and whispered, "You are perfect, you know that?"

At that very moment, she didn't feel that way. But his glance, his statement, and his cologne mesmerized her to the point that she couldn't even respond. Meanwhile, somewhere deep within her, an alter ego reared its head and shouted to the insulting man in the audience, "Take that, dude!"

She would never admit it to Faith, but her friend had done a good job pairing her up without even making her a bridesmaid. Shari couldn't wait for the second rehearsal next Friday night.

Chapter Ten

Compliments seemed to surprise Shari—at least, that was Garrett's take. He had every intention to talk with her privately after the wedding rehearsal was over, but she packed up and slipped away without a good-bye while Garrett was speaking with a deacon. The brief moments they had shared that evening had been a mere tease.

At home later that night, Garrett studied the Word of God, then slid to his knees to pray before climbing in bed. Before he said "Amen," Jesus dropped Brittani into his heart, so Garrett earnestly petitioned God on her behalf. After experiencing so many emotions—hurt, bitterness, and even hatred—he could finally say with honesty that God had given him peace about what had happened.

His thoughts turned to Shari. "Jesus, I'm starting to care about her, not because You told me she's Your heart's desire for me but because she's becoming my heart's desire. You alone know what caused the light to dim in her eyes tonight, and only You know how to comfort her. Bless her, Jesus..."

I will accomplish all things I speak, God whispered from Isaiah 55:11.

With that reassurance, Garrett said "Amen" and got in bed.

A few days later, Shari made her first appearance at band practice since Garrett's return from his trip to Boston, and he felt starstruck. Her presence seemed to usher in an air of sweetness. Throughout the rehearsal, she was on key for every song, as if she hadn't been missing in action for more than a month.

At the Sunday service the following day, the Spirit stirred seven souls to repent and be baptized in Jesus' name at the conclusion of the sermon. Seconds after Pastor Underwood had given the benediction, Shari was making her way out of the bandstand. It was amazing to Garrett how a person so close—seated only two chairs away from him—could seem always just out of reach.

Garrett scanned the sanctuary, hoping to see where she'd gone, but the crowd had already swallowed her up as people greeted one another. "Not today," he mumbled to himself. He packed up his instrument quickly, refusing to partake in the conversations around him.

Finally he spotted Shari by the back doors. His jaw clenched when he witnessed two men he had never seen hugging her. He flinched when it appeared she was enjoying it. With determined steps, he headed toward the group to break up the cozy gathering. The more Shari eluded him, the more he desired her.

Right now, Shari exhibited yet another side of her personality besides her boldness in the courtroom and shyness at church. She seemed relaxed as she smiled and laughed. Her sister, Stacy, and Ted, her husband, were also snickering. He counted five times that Shari's slender fingers touched the arm of one of the men who had embraced her. Garrett quickened his steps before she could do it a sixth time. *Too late.* Why couldn't she keep her hands off the guy?

As if they sensed his presence on the outskirts of their cluster, the group ceased their conversation. All except for Shari's mother wore duplicate frowns at his impending interruption.

"Praise the Lord, Brother Nash." Annette Carmen smiled. "Meet my handsome nephews. This is Dino." She tilted her head toward one of the young men, who kept a straight face as he nodded his greeting. "And this hunk is his older brother, Victor. They fellowship at Greater Bethel Church of Christ, but they drop by every now and then to check up on us."

Family. Garrett exhaled, relieved that his fears of competition had been unwarranted. Once he let down his guard, he finally noticed the resemblance. Actually, the two could have passed as Shari's brothers because of their dark, wavy hair—gorgeous on a woman but too pretty-boy on a man, for Garrett's taste—and their rich brown skin. *The Carmens must have some strong genes*, he thought.

When Victor extended his hand, Garrett pumped it as they sized each other up. Victor was about the same height as Garrett, only thicker. That didn't matter. Garrett was trained as a Deputy U.S. Marshal, and muscle had its benefit. He squeezed the man's hand like he was making fresh orange juice.

"Stop it," Annette demanded of her nephew, unaware that it was Garrett who had the upper hand—literally.

Ted stood on the sidelines, hands shoved inside his pockets. "I need my hands to eat."

Good choice, Garrett thought as the group chuckled. "I'd like to speak with Shari for a few moments, if that's okay." Without giving her time to consent, he cupped her elbow and almost dragged her a few feet away. Once he had her attention, Garrett gazed at her appreciatively. "Have dinner with me...today." He didn't want to make plans for a date; he wanted her now. His grandfather had already ribbed him about him moving too slow with Shari, warning him that another man would soon step up to the plate.

He doubted his grandfather had been hinting at the situation with Brittani, but that was what it made him think about.

"I'm sorry. I can't." Shari gave him a slight pout, as if she was also disappointed.

Garrett kept his reaction in check. She owed him more than just a simple no. Folding his arms across his chest, he stared at her expectantly, waiting for an explanation.

She glanced around, appearing uncomfortable. "Uh, sorry. My family is going out to celebrate my uncle's birthday."

If it was the Miller family, Shari would definitely be extended an invi-tation. Evidently, Garrett wasn't on the guest list. "I'm looking for a commitment from you that you and me"—he pointed between them—"will happen. A dinner, a movie, a concert...you name it. Next time, then."

She lifted an eyebrow. "Next time?"

"There will always be a next time with us. Please tell your uncle happy birthday." Garrett turned and walked away, with every step devising another plan to woo her.

The following Friday night, before Faith and Trask's wedding, Garrett's jaw dropped at his first glimpse of Shari. She was stunning in a dress that hugged her curves. The color—orange, coral, or peach, or whatever it was called—never looked better on a woman with rich dark skin. Any woman who wanted to duplicate the effect would have to subject herself to a lot of sunbathing.

He couldn't keep his eyes from straying to her heels, which supported her shapely legs. Garrett doubted any bride could be more breathtaking. When she greeted him with a subtle smile, her beauty and perfume jumbled his mind. He hoped he would be able to play his sax on key.

Soon it was showtime in the sanctuary. The wedding coordinator cued Shari to sing "The Lord's Prayer" to start the wedding processional down the aisle. While Shari watched with a look of awe as the groomsmen escorted the bridesmaids to the altar, Garrett watched her. The woman was caught up in the hoopla, especially when the lights dimmed, and Faith appeared in the doorway of the sanctuary.

Garrett thought about his canceled nuptials and didn't feel even the slightest twinge of disappointment. As a practicing Christian, he knew that a wife was part of God's plans to complete his happiness, and that marriageable material was standing feet away, completely unaware. He planned to pursue her by any means necessary until she gave him a chance.

Once the bride and groom were standing at the altar, Garrett and Shari stood to serenade them with "By Your Side" before they recited their vows.

Shari's melodious voice, and the passion behind her words, mesmerized Garrett. Soon something stirred within him that made him lower his sax. She seemed to be calling out to him, and so he answered, his voice mingling with hers. It was a flashback to Boston as Shari looked shocked but quickly tested him, this time on his knowledge of the lyrics. He gladly accepted the challenge.

The guests became a blur as the two of them retreated into a special place. As they neared the end of the song, they both brought the mouth-pieces of their saxes to their lips and together blew out the last notes. *I'll apologize to Faith and Trask later*, Garrett mused, *but a man's got to do what a man's got to do*. And he did it.

Taking her seat, Shari breathed deeply—and he knew it had nothing to do with the effort of playing her instrument. She was just as affected, just as caught up in the moment, as he was. *Good*. Because if he couldn't get her to accept a dinner invitation, he could at least communicate his inten-tions to her through song.

Speechless. That was the first word Shari would use to describe what had just taken place. Wow was the second. Shari exhaled, still stunned. *Lord, help me to resist this man, because it feels like I'm losing a court case that I'm ill-prepared for.* But the brother could sing with his baritone voice. For the briefest moment during their duet, Garrett had almost convinced her that they were the two at the altar instead of Faith and Trask.

Shari was sinking into uncharted waters. For some unexplained reason, she wanted to cry. The moment was charged with emotion. Was this another one of Faith's surprise stunts? When she glanced at the bride, she had her answer in the twinkle in Faith's eyes.

Garrett touched her arm, reminding her of his presence. "That was a powerful song," he whispered, then gently wrapped her hand in his as Pastor Underwood initiated the reciting of the vows. "You okay?" His tone was soft.

Goose bumps made her shiver. Staring into his eyes, she shook her head but said, "I guess." Too lethargic to protest his touch, Shari settled back and watched the love scene unfold at the altar instead of in her head.

When Pastor Underwood said, "I now pronounce you husband and wife," Shari came out of her daze and snatched her hand back, playing it off as if she needed to applaud the newlyweds. She didn't dare look at Garrett, afraid of what he might say or do next. Instead, she kept her focus on the bride and groom and the rest of the bridal party as they processed slowly out of the sanctuary. When the last couple disappeared into the foyer, Shari stood and gathered her saxophone case.

"Wait."

"I can't," she said softly. She knew he wanted to talk, but she needed breathing space and had to put some distance between them. "I have to get to the reception hall to man the gift table."

Her heart pounded with a mixture of excitement and fear as she crossed the sanctuary to the exit. The vibes between her and Garrett were getting stronger, but he was the new kid on the block, and she knew so little about his character.

She could hear her mother saying, *"That's why you date, silly—to find out."* The thought made her smile.

At the reception hall, Shari wasn't surprised when Garrett joined her at the gift table, bumping her slightly with a killer smile, forcing her to make room for him. She didn't object, and honestly, she didn't want to, even though his closeness made her nervous. They worked as a team, he charm-ingly accepting cards and gifts from guests, then handing them over to Shari to tag them so that the couple would have an easy time of writing thank-you notes.

When there was a lull between guests, Garrett cleared his throat. "Can we talk privately?"

"Now?" Shari scanned the room to see if anyone was watching them. "We're among at least a hundred guests."

"Objection, Counselor." He arched his eyebrows. "Where you and I are concerned, whenever we're together, we're in our own private world."

Lost in the depth of his brown eyes, Shari was beginning to believe that. Someone cleared her throat. She turned and found herself face-to-face with Mother Stillwell. The elderly woman studied them with narrowed eyes, then nodded, tapped her cane once on the floor, and started walking away without leaving a card or a gift. Seconds later, she stopped in her tracks and glanced over her shoulder with an odd expression before continuing on her way.

"What was that about?" Garrett asked.

"Who knows?" Shari wondered at the woman's odd behavior too. "Mother Stillwell thinks she has the gift of matchmaking."

"Really?" He smirked, mischief dancing in his eyes. "I'll be right back."

"Where are you going?"

"To get on Mother Stillwell's good side."

Shari laughed to hide her uneasiness. The woman had never come to her with a so-called prophecy. "Go ahead. I'm sure she has your mate picked out for you with a red bow tied in her hair," she joked, wishing the church mother would add her name to the single-sisters-needing-a-mate prayer list.

Garrett's nostrils flared as he sent her a tender look that gave her goose bumps. "Maybe I should swipe a red bow off one of these gifts and tie it in your hair. Plus, I believe you would look fantastic in red," he teased.

Chapter Eleven

As Garrett walked away, Shari admired his swagger, thinking that if Mother Stillwell didn't already have her name on the list, the church saint had really better pencil her in. Shari's heart had nearly melted with Garrett's last words.

And the way he looked at her made her feel cherished. She immediately felt the loss of his presence, and he was right—somehow, regardless of who was around them, it always seemed like it was just the two of them in their own virtual world. He said the right words, but could she trust him with her heart? Scriptures seemed to flood her mind.

Lord, You say in Your Word that if I acknowledge You in all things, You will direct my paths. You say that if I delight myself in You, You will give me the desires of my heart. Lord, I don't even know what's in my heart, Shari prayed silently as the bridal party made their grand entrance into the reception hall to the sounds of cheers and applause.

Shari tried not to keep tabs on Garrett's whereabouts throughout the room, but it was useless. Ever since she'd been made aware of his closeness, she missed his absence as other women vied for his attention.

To wait for Garrett's return amounted to desperation. *Get a grip, girl, she told herself. You're caught up in the romance hoopla of the wedding.* After the personal pep talk, Shari refocused on the task at hand, double-checking that every gift had been numbered and recorded. When it looked as if no additional guests would be approaching the table, including Garrett, Shari decided that her job was finished.

She tried to circulate around the banquet hall and chat with other guests, but being in the same room with Garrett was distracting.

Soon Stacy waved her over to her table while Ted stood in the buffet line. Shari sat in Ted's vacant seat, and Stacy gave her a hug. "That was so beautiful. You and Brother Nash..." Stacy sighed and patted her chest just above her heart. "It took my breath away. Everything was perfect. I can see why Faith wanted two rehearsals. You two were such a great match on the saxes, and the vocal harmony—"

"Sis, we didn't rehearse the last part," Shari interrupted. "I had no idea Garrett was going to sing with me."

"Really? Hmm, I never would've guessed that." Stacy smirked. "Don't doubt God's hand in this."

Stacy always seemed to believe that, as the oldest sibling, she was charged with imparting wisdom to her younger sisters. And Shari, Shae, and Brecee always listened. At that moment, Stacy's morsel of wisdom scared Shari.

"I'm not doubting God," she confessed, "but I do have doubts about Garrett. He shows up out of nowhere and in short time begins to pursue me like I'm the only fish in the pond. What's that saying? When it seems like something is too good to be true, it usually is."

Ted snagged the empty chair on the other side of Stacy, bowed his head for a quick prayer, then stuffed his mouth with meatballs.

"Shari, why don't you join us?" he asked. "Mom Carmen already left with Sister Davis."

Shari's mother kept a busy schedule. She had attended a luncheon fundraiser earlier that day, followed by Faith's wedding, and she would end the day at a birthday party for a close friend. Annette Carmen's social calendar was always full, with events overlapping one another.

"No, thanks. I think I'm going to head home. I have some briefs I need to go over."

Stacy gave her a suspicious glance. "Umm-hmm. Don't leave until you get a slice of wedding cake. I heard it's from UNIK Cakes."

Cakes were the Carmen sisters' weakness. Ever since they were children, for every special occasion, the family would order a cake from one of the best bakeries in the area. That had always been the highlight of the parties.

"Well, in that case..." Shari grinned. "I guess I will wait around." The sisters laughed as they stood, and Stacy looped her arm through Shari's as they walked to the buffet table. As discreetly as possible, she scanned the room for Garrett. He was nowhere in sight. Why did her heart sink as it did?

"Stop looking for him, Sis," Stacy whispered. "If he's the one, I guarantee you, from his vantage point, he's checking you out."

Shari laughed. Sisters—what would she do without them?

The bride and groom cut the cake, and Shari sampled a mouthful before wrapping up her slice in a napkin. What she wanted was to yank Faith away from her husband's clutches and fuss at her about that singing antic with Garrett, but she didn't want to spoil her friend's happiness with a petty complaint. She would scold her later, when the couple returned from their honeymoon.

After hugging Ted and Stacy good-bye, Shari did one final

sweep of the room for Garrett, then left.

As she drove home in silence, she reevaluated her life. Faith and Trask had never looked so happy. She was convinced that the purpose of weddings was to make singles wish for their own happily-ever-after. "The satisfaction of being an independent successful woman is overrated," she grumbled.

Once home, Shari closed the front door and was surprised to see her mother seated on a chaise lounge in the living room. "You're back so soon?"

"Goodness, yes. Eloise had more people at her shindig than there were at Faith's reception, it seemed. I wished her happy birthday, gave her my gift, then left and dropped off Sister Davis at her house. I've been home for ten minutes, tops." Her mother scooted over and patted the spot next to her on the chaise. "Faith's wedding was so beautiful and romantic..."

Shari flopped down and kicked off her heels. She sighed happily and wiggled her toes as her feet enjoyed relief from the entrapment. "Yes, it was." "I took pictures." Her mother picked up her smartphone and showed her a series of photos.

"Mom, all these are of me and Garrett. What about the bride and groom?" She lifted an eyebrow.

"Oh, I snapped a few shots of them, when they got in the way." She chuckled, then beamed. "The highlight of the ceremony was your duet with Brother Nash. He likes you."

"And that's scary." Shari thought about the intense way he had looked at her. She shivered, recalling the sensation it had given her.

"What are you afraid of?" Her mother reached over and smoothed back a forgotten curl dangling above Shari's eye.

"That this utopia I felt today isn't real," Shari admitted with a shrug. She looked away. "His feelings, mine..."

"Something tells me Brother Nash is the real deal." Her mother leaned over and hugged her shoulder. "But, as with any man who comes within three feet—make that a yard and a half—of my daughters, I'll be watching and praying for God to give you wisdom."

Her mother smacked a kiss on her cheek and stood. "Sweetie, I feel this is your season for happiness. Some things in life are worth fighting for, Counselor Carmen. Love is one of them." She headed for the hall but stopped in the doorway and glanced back. "Oh, don't be surprised if Shae and Brecee call you, because I texted them the pictures."

Shari groaned and covered her face with both hands. With a smartphone now in her possession, her mother took a picture of literally everything, from a squirrel cracking a nut to random acts of kindness. "Who else?"

"Just your aunt, uncle, and cousins," her mother stated with no shame as she continued down the hall, humming "By Your Side."

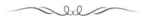

Garrett never should have walked away from Shari. That was how he'd found himself ambushed by John Whitman and the father of the groom. The two men had tapped him to help remove the decorations from the sanctuary because the regular maintenance man had taken ill. He wanted to get back to the reception hall.

It served him right for teasing Shari about Mother Stillwell's prediction. That woman's predictions had no bearing on his feelings. God was his matchmaker.

Now, on Sunday morning, he waited impatiently for Shari to take her place in the bandstand for praise and worship. Just in case he got caught up in the Spirit and missed her entrance, Garrett placed a sealed envelope on her chair, containing a letter asking her to wait for him immediately after the service.

The praise team had just finished a rendition of Hezekiah

Walkers "Every Praise" when Shari took her seat. He watched to see if she would open the envelope right away. She didn't but quickly prepared her sax to join in with the next song.

Concentrate on Me, the Lord whispered.

Yes, Sir, Garrett said silently. He refocused his mind as they played the last song, and then Pastor Underwood addressed the congregation.

"Good morning, saints and friends." He paused as the people responded. Then, after a few announcements, he began his sermon.

"In Ecclesiastes four, verses nine through twelve, the Bible speaks about the perks of being our brother's keeper. Verse ten is what I want to talk about this morning. It says, *'For if they fall, the one will lift up his fellow: but woe to him that is alone when he falls; for he hath not another to help him up.'* We have a race ahead of us today. Make sure you have a salvation-minded running buddy who will be your spiritual support system. It's not good for man to be alone..."

Garrett couldn't help but glance at Shari. She wore an intent expression on her face, as if she was soaking in the pastor's every word. She never looked in Garrett's direction. Then he remembered God's warning from earlier, and he deliberately blocked out everything and everyone, except for the pastor and his message. He didn't look at the object of his affections again until after the benediction.

"Shari," he said, getting her attention. "Don't leave."

She looked up and smiled. "I won't," she mouthed, and Garrett breathed a sigh of relief.

As the other musicians spilled from the bandstand, Garrett towered over Shari, still seated in her chair. It took several moments for him to register that she was calling his name.

"Are you all right?" she asked. "Why are you staring at me like that?"

Embarrassed, Garrett chuckled. "You wouldn't believe me if I told you."

Shari crossed her arms. "Try me."

"When I look at you..." He sat next to her. "You represent that priceless item I want so badly—a toy, a bicycle, a new SUV—that I'm willing to work two or three jobs to save up for it. Then, when I finally earn enough money, I want to put it on a pedestal so that nobody else will touch it."

"You think of me in that way?"

He nodded.

Shari blinked rapidly. "Wow. I'm honestly lost for words. I— I'm flattered."

"I'm hoping that since we don't have band practice next Saturday, you'll agree to go out with me. How about dinner and a movie? Or we could do something else...anything you'd like. There are plenty of places in Philly that I want to see but haven't gone to yet."

"So this would be a date." She lifted her brow in a teasing manner, which caused him to hold his breath, hoping she would say yes.

"Yes," she finally said. "I would love to."

Garrett pumped his fist in the air, then whipped out his smartphone from its holder on his belt. "Let's exchange numbers." Once that was accomplished, Garrett exhaled. "Let the countdown to Saturday begin." For once, she'd acted as if she was in no hurry to leave.

Chapter Twelve

*Y*ou are hereby summoned to a video chat with the Carmen Sisters, Counselor.

Shari chuckled as she read Stacy's group text. As she counted down the days to her date with Garrett, she also knew it was a countdown until the "snoop sisters" began their inquest into her personal affairs.

Shari didn't care. She liked being someone else's center of attention. The evidence was the fiery orange lilies that had arrived on her desk that morning as she was heading to court.

These flowers remind me of what you were wearing at the wedding. You're the perfect shade of dark chocolate. Can't wait for our date on Saturday, Attorney Shari Carmen.

—Garrett

Now, after a successful morning in court, all Shari wanted to do was to stay holed up in her office and admire the floral arrangement. But she couldn't keep her sisters from prying. She replied affirmatively to the text, and then, at the designated time, she signed on to her computer. Brecee popped up first, in Houston.

Stacy was second, and lastly, Shae joined in the chat from St. Louis.

"Look how you're smiling!" Brecee exclaimed, the first to jump in.

"I told you she was glowing," Stacy said smugly.

"He has to be special for you to go out with him," Shae said.

Shari felt herself blush. "He is."

"Well, details, Mimi!" Brecee demanded, reverting back to her childhood nickname for Sharmaine.

Biting her lip, Shari attempted to gather her thoughts. "I'm scared, excited, and happy. He's incredibly handsome—even more so than actor Lance Gross. He oozes with so much masculinity that I have to remind myself not to stare too long."

"Hmm." Brecee smirked.

"Okay, so he's good-looking," Shae said. "I'm sure there's more to him for you to give him the time of day."

"You're right, Sis. I'm comfortable around him, even though, at the same time, I feel a little unsure. He likes to remind me of everything we have in common, like the tenor sax. We even drive the same make, model, and color car."

"Get out of here!" Brecee said, crunching on a carrot stick as if she were watching a TV show instead of Shari's life unfolding before her.

"Somewhere I hear a 'but' in there," Shae coaxed her.

"Very observant my inquisitive little reporter sister." Shari smiled. "I do wonder why he isn't already taken. I mean, it's evident that he is sincere about his salvation, so why didn't a sister snag him in Boston? My spirit bears witness that Garrett is secure in his manhood and not a homosexual pretender. I have so many questions..."

"And you will get answers in four days," Stacy reminded her.

"Yep." Shari grinned. "Four days, and three hours...and I can't wait!" Her excitement was contagious as her sisters laughed with her. The conversation then turned to what was going on in the other sisters' lives, especially with Shae in her new role as weekend anchor in addition to being an investigative reporter for a news station in St. Louis.

When they finally said their good-byes, Shari's question remained: What was Garrett's story? Everyone had one. She planned to get answers to all her questions on Saturday.

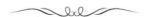

Friday night, Garrett opened his front door and blinked at the group of people standing in the hallway.

"Surprise!" the Miller clan shouted, grinning broadly.

"What are you all doing here?" Garrett asked as his parents, sister, nephew, and grandparents spilled over the threshold into his condo. Although they didn't need an invitation, apparently, they weren't waiting on him to issue one.

"To see you, silly." His sister, Deborah, elbowed him in the side before his nephew wrapped his arms around Garrett's waist.

Exhibiting his home training, he dispensed kisses, hugs, and handshakes to all. Although he was elated to see his family, the only thing on his mind was spending time with Shari the next day. As a matter of fact, they were fifteen hours away from their date. "How long are you staying?" he asked, hoping not to sound too eager to see them go.

His grandfather appeared to be the only one paying attention to him. Everyone else was exploring his condo.

"The weekend," Moses said.

Oh, boy. Garrett withheld his groan. What was he going to do? He didn't want to reschedule his date with Shari. All week, he had sent her reminders via text message to hype up the long-awaited event. On the other hand, he had missed his family so much, and he wanted to spend time with them. He had issued dozens of invitations for his folks to come visit, always boasting that he had a lot of space. But he could hardly host this many people at one time.

"Where's your luggage?" he asked his grandfather.

"At the hotel. We checked in at the Holiday Inn on Walnut, not far from here. We figured we'd do some sightseeing, take your nephew to this country's first zoo, and fellowship with you at Jesus Is the Way."

"Yay!" Jamal jumped up and down until Deborah gave him the look, which made him stand at attention as if he were a soldier like his father, who was deployed in the Middle East.

"How are you doing on food, Son?" his mother asked, finding her way into his kitchen and taking the liberty of opening one cabinet after another. "*Tsk. Tsk.*" She appeared in the doorway moments later, shaking her head and jamming her hands on her hips. "I'm going to stock you up on some food and home-cooked meals while I'm here."

"Mom, it's just me. I don't need to stock up. I buy food on an as-I-run-out basis. But I certainly won't turn down a home-cooked meal."

Like old times. Garrett smirked. But this was not a dorm room at Boston University. Besides cooking breakfast, his meals consisted of takeout from the local deli counters or occasional invites from John and Rita. He would rather eat Subway than accept dinner invitations from most of the sisters at church. That was how he'd met Brittani—at a church function where she had been helping serve the meal. Now, the only person he wanted to have dinner with was Shari.

"I planned to go sightseeing tomorrow with Shari," Garrett admitted hesitantly.

"Excellent." Moses beamed. "I can't wait to see that young lady again."

"Granddad, G and Shari might want to be alone," Deborah said, and Garrett nodded his thanks for stating the obvious. "We don't need a tour guide."

Then Garrett felt a tinge of guilt. His family had driven so far to see him; he couldn't push them away. Excusing himself, he went into his bedroom and closed the door to call Shari.

She answered in a sweet voice filled with excitement. He explained his dilemma and asked how she would feel about his family tagging along.

"Family is important," she affirmed. "And you haven't seen them in months. Spend time with them. We can reschedule anytime." Her voice was still upbeat, but he could detect an undercurrent of disappointment.

"Come with us," he insisted. "You're a local. You can be our tour guide. Plus, my folks think so highly of you."

But his pleas were to no avail. Garrett threw up an arm in annoyance. "How can I win a case against an attorney?"

"I don't always win," she said in a somber tone, which made him wonder if she was referring to her cases or their date. "There are two things in my life that I value more than anything: my close relationship with God and my family. I can't live without either. So, enjoy your weekend, and we can restart the clock again soon."

"Let's reschedule now," he pressed her.

"Let's talk about it later in the week," she countered. "In the meantime, I'm taking precious time away from your family visit. Tell them I said hi, and enjoy."

Garrett ended the call on a sour note. For the first time that he could remember, family was the last thing he wanted to see. He stepped out of his bedroom and broke the news.

His mother gasped. "Son, we're so sorry."

"We can entertain ourselves," his grandfather offered. "Maybe I can talk to her. She likes me, you know?" He appeared hopeful.

"She still likes me, too, I think." Shaking his head, Garrett tried to do damage control. "She's not going to back down." He took a deep breath to regroup his thoughts, then clapped his hands. "Well, why don't we get this Miller reunion started?"

Chapter Thirteen

*E*xhausted after all-day shopping and sightseeing—watching the Liberty 360 3D Show at PECO Theater and visiting the Liberty Bell, the Reading Terminal Market, and finally the Philadelphia Zoo—Garrett and his family returned to his condo early Saturday evening.

His sister, mother, and grandmother washed their hands and pulled out their newly purchased aprons. After a few hours spent in his kitchen, they made good on the promise of a home-cooked meal.

"I sure missed seeing Shari," his grandfather said between mouthfuls of his dinner.

"Not as much as me." Garrett didn't say anything more. He didn't want to make his family feel any worse than they already did, considering Shari's name had come up several times during their outing.

"We're sorry we messed up your date, little brother," Deborah apologized yet again. "I would have liked the chance to get to know her better." The other adults nodded in agreement. "My first impression is that she's stunning but doesn't flaunt what God gave her to get your attention...like you-know-who."

"Who, Momma?" Jamal looked up.

"Son...just eat," she said with a stern expression.

On Sunday morning, everyone was excited about attending Garrett's new home church. He reminisced about his lifelong membership at Blood Redemption Temple. Despite the warm welcome he'd received at Jesus Is the Way, and his relationships with John, Rita, the pastor, and his fellow band members, he had forgotten how much he missed attending a church where his family served in various positions, as deacons, missionaries, Sunday school teachers, ushers, and auxiliary presidents.

Because of the Millers' long-standing roots in his former home church, most of the older members had seen no reason why Garrett couldn't forgive "sweet Brittani" and go ahead and marry her. They based their warped thinking on the precedent of Joseph marrying Mary from the Bible. On more than one occasion, Garrett had needed to remind Mother or Sister So-and-So that he was not the father of Brittani's baby—and neither was the Holy Ghost.

Members of Jesus Is the Way Church greeted Garrett's family from the front door to the pews, with Garrett making introductions before taking his place in the bandstand. His eyes lingered on Shari before he leaned closer and told her, "Missed you yesterday." He owed her more apologies and many floral bouquets for canceling on her.

"Next time," she whispered.

He twisted his mouth. Was she throwing his words back in his face, or did she really want a "next time" as soon as possible, as he did? "I'm looking forward to it," he finally said. "My folks are looking this way, so you might want to smile."

She did so without hesitation.

After the praise and worship segment had ended, Pastor Underwood asked that any visitors stand to be acknowledged. "I understand Brother Nash's family is here today," he said. "Can we get a representative to speak for the family?"

"Grandpa," the group decided unanimously.

Moses stepped into the aisle and strolled to the podium. He still had pep in his step as he greeted the ministers in the pulpit before standing behind the microphone. "We are indeed honored today to be in the midst of the saints and in God's presence. I'm happy to see you're taking care of my grandson."

Garrett tried not to blush. Even Shari was clapping.

"I see some familiar faces in the band. My wife and I still talk about how some of the musicians got down at our fiftieth wedding anniversary, especially Sister Shari Carmen. That woman can play the sax."

This time, it was Shari who blushed as she bowed her head at the compliment. Pastor Underwood urged her to stand. Reluctantly, she did, and flashed a wave of her hand before reclaiming her seat. Her skin glowed against the backdrop of the band members' black and gold uniforms, which coordinated with the choir members' gold robes.

Once his grandfather had taken his seat again, Pastor Underwood shared the announcements and then opened his Bible. "Please turn with me to James, chapter one, verse four: *But let patience have her perfect work, that ye may be perfect and entire, wanting nothing.'* I like that the King James Version uses the pronoun 'her' when it refers to patience. Maybe it's because women are long-suffering toward their children, sometimes to a fault. They are the grace in the home, while the men—the fathers—dispense the law." He cited several other examples before continuing on to his next point.

"But we can't have patience without wisdom. In the Olympic Games, runners have to pace themselves to make it to the finish line. So, the gist of the message today is, whatever you want or need, ask God to settle patience in your heart, and when the timing is right, He will instruct you on how to."

The rest of the sermon was short and sweet, compared with the lengthy altar call, but it was well worth it. Twelve people made their way to the front—some with hesitation, others trekking with purpose—but they all came. Most requested prayer. Five repented and wanted complete salvation through baptism by water and by Holy Ghost fire in Jesus' name.

After the emotionally charged baptism segment, and offertory, Pastor Underwood pronounced the benediction. He had barely uttered "Amen" when the Millers filed out of the pew and headed toward the bandstand, intent on seeing Shari. Garrett watched the onslaught with amusement as he stood on the sidelines.

His grandmother had the first word for Shari. "Dear, we're so sorry we spoiled your plans with Garrett on yesterday. Let us make it up to you. Please be our guest at dinner tonight."

"Well, I...uh..." Shari glanced at Garrett, looking uncertain.

He feigned a pout, which made her almost smile.

"You're coming to Uncle G's for dinner, right?" Jamal prodded her. "You don't have to worry about his food. Granny Queen cooked," he whispered, "and her stuff tastes a whole lot better."

"You're a regular traitor." Garrett squeezed Jamal's shoulder, then looked at Shari. "You are more than welcome. Please join us." He winked.

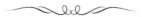

How could Shari refuse the invitation? She wanted to spend time with Garrett. Plus, she genuinely liked his family. Moses was most endearing. He had a way of making her feel as if he was in her corner like her own flesh-and-blood grandfather. She suspected he would deal with Garrett if he messed up. So, she grinned as she let Jamal tug her away from the bandstand.

Before leaving the sanctuary, Shari introduced Garrett's family to her mother and to Stacy and Ted. Her mother seemed to hit it off instantly with the women in his family. *Good sign.* When Queen recited the dinner menu, Ted licked his lips.

Shari smirked. Her brother-in-law looked as if wanted to raise his hand for an invite. The man was built like a tank. The way he acted when anybody mentioned food, one would think his wife didn't cook him hearty meals on a regular basis.

"You're welcome to join us," Queen said to Stacy and Ted, as if reading Ted's mind.

"Thank you. Maybe some other time." Stacy nudged her husband. "You're supposed to take Mom and me out to dinner, remember?"

He frowned. "I am?"

"You are," Shari's mother said, looping her arm through Ted's. She waved good-bye to Shari and the Millers as she led her son-in-law away.

Stacy winked at Shari, then took off after her mother and husband.

Minutes later, Shari strolled out to the parking lot with Garrett and his family. "Do you mind if I ride with you to G's condo?" Deborah asked her.

"Absolutely not. I'd enjoy your company," Shari said as she deactivated her car alarm.

"I guess great minds do think alike. You and Garrett drive the exact same vehicle," she said as she climbed in the passenger seat. Deborah snapped her seat belt, then faced Shari. "I'm so glad you came into my brother's life."

Shari smiled. "Actually, he came into mine." Yes, Garrett had an irresistible charm about him. Part of his allure was his white smile and the way it contrasted with his serious, dark eyes. And she felt so comfortable around his family, as if she'd always known them.

The two chatted about Philly's historic sites and discussed how they compared to Beantown as Shari followed Garrett's vehicle. Turning off the Schuylkill Expressway, they crossed into Montgomery County, heading for Bala Cynwyd, a trendy area known for upscale retail stores, restaurants, and hotels.

When Shari parked in the visitors' lot, Deborah thanked her for the ride, then got out and went to join Jamal and the others. Shari sat and stared at the impressive condominium complex. Without stepping one stiletto inside, she guessed that the residences were equipped with lavish amenities that weren't standard. Suddenly Garrett was outside her door, pulling it open.

"We should grab your saxophone," he said.

Shari frowned as she inhaled a whiff of his cologne as she got out. "Why would I need it?"

"You never know with my bunch." Garrett lifted the case out of the backseat, then shut the door, turned to Shari, and scanned her from head to toe, as if he hadn't seen her minutes earlier. "You are truly beautiful," he whispered. "I live on the second floor, but let's take the elevator anyway. It'll spare your pretty little feet."

Her eyebrows rose. "You don't think I can walk straight in these?"

"I never said that." He grinned and touched her arm, steering her toward the curb.

"Good, because, honey, I have perfected the art of *running* in three-inch-plus heels, so walking in them is a cinch."

They boarded the elevator in silence, Garrett carrying both their instruments. After stepping out on the second floor, they followed voices down the hall and around the corner to his condo where his family was chattering. Garrett unlocked the door and deactivated his security system, then ushered Shari inside.

A series of "wows" escaped her lips as she stood in admiration of the majestic open floor plan and stylish decor. For a man and a newcomer to Philly, he had rare skills—or knew someone who did. The dark mahogany furniture and dark accent walls were a testament to that.

Garrett set their saxophone cases along a wall that was lined with a dozen or more other instruments. *Just like the Carmens*, she thought. It didn't matter if they were at home or away, instruments were part of the luggage whenever her family traveled. Music was who they were. She could see why Garrett had insisted on bringing her saxophone inside.

The artwork adorning the walls drew her in, especially a series of African and African-American sketches. One of them featured a male jazz trio—a saxophonist, trumpeter, and a clarinetist—dancing on oversized piano keys against a backdrop of the New York City skyline. And on a bookcase was a telltale throwback to his childhood—a display of several remote-controlled race cars and motorcycles and model airplanes.

His nephew ignored the immaculate setting, making himself right at home as he grabbed a remote-controlled car and proceeded to run in circles around a leather ottoman and coffee table until his mother grabbed him by the shirt collar.

"The rules at home are still in force here, Jamal," Deborah said. "Now find a corner and sit down until dinner is ready."

"Next time, we'll leave them in Boston and have some real fun," Garrett teased his nephew.

"Yeah," Jamal cheered, provoking a stern look from his mother. Duly reprimanded, the boy sank into the nearest floor cushion and folded his hands in his lap like a diligent schoolboy. His pout was cute.

Shari saw Garrett's mother, sister, and grandmother head for the kitchen. "Do you need any help?" she asked the women.

"Absolutely not," Queen said, swapping her lightweight blazer for an apron. "You're a guest."

"And so are you," Shari countered.

"You'll never win a case against my wife," Moses said with a twinkle in his eye as he lay back in a recliner and folded his hands behind his head. "I think she was a lawyer in another life."

"While we wait, why don't we have a battle of the saxes?" Garrett suggested.

Moses beamed. "My money's on Shari."

Chuckling, Garrett offered Shari a place on a brown suede love seat, where he joined her. Although Shari did feel at home with the Millers, she really didn't like to be the center of attention unless she was in the courtroom.

Moses must have picked up on her hesitation, because he said, "Better still, how about I play a tune while Queen gets the food on the table?" He sat forward and sprang to his feet with the energy of a young man, crossed the room, and lifted the granddaddy of saxophones—the bass—out of its case.

Deborah walked into the room, wiping her hands on her apron. "Play, Grandpa."

"Yes, play, Grandpa!" Shari shouted before she could stop herself, caught up in the whirlwind of excitement.

At her outburst, Jamal raced to the love seat and squeezed into the space between her and Garrett. Instead of protesting, Garrett seemed amused.

Queen stormed out of the kitchen as Moses had just closed his lips over the mouthpiece. She stopped in front of Shari and planted her hands on her ample hips. "No, you did *not* just call my husband 'Grandpa.'"

Uh-oh. Shari swallowed. She had taken too much liberty and crossed the line. "I'm sorry—"

"If you're going to call him 'Grandpa,' it's only fair that you call me 'Grandma Q.'" She grinned and then strutted back into the kitchen, her laughter carrying out into the living room.

Shari breathed a sigh of relief, glad that she wouldn't have to file a lawsuit against Garrett's grandmother for assaulting her.

Chapter Fourteen

Garrett's grandmother's stunt had just put the fear of Jesus' second coming into everybody in the room. Garrett and Shari had sucked in their breaths of one accord, then exhaled together once his grandmother had made it clear she was teasing.

The Nefertiti beauty had won the heart of his whole family, and she looked especially gorgeous today with her hair brushed to the side and twisted up in a ball. Even without showcasing her long, silky tresses, the woman was stunning.

Her presence was becoming addictive. Shari possessed an innocence that drew everyone in, especially his sister and his grandmother. Those two had tolerated Brittani because she had been his choice. And his mother, quiet to a fault, liked everybody—unless he or she crossed her.

Soon, dinner was announced. After Grandpa Moses said grace, lively conversations mingled with the clatter of silverware on the plates. Music seemed to be the common theme of discussion.

"I understand you have other musicians in your family besides your sister we met earlier," his grandfather said.

Shari nodded, wiping her mouth with her napkin before responding. "Actually, there are four Carmen sisters, and each of us plays a different instrument: organ, sax, drums, and guitar. Our other two sisters live out of state. And it was my dad who taught me to play the sax." She paused, and Garrett reached under the table for her hand and squeezed it. The smile she gave him in return made Garrett feel as powerful as if he had just conquered a kingdom.

"My cousins helped me to perfect the sound," she finished.

His grandfather's eyes lit up. "Excellent. Sounds like our families need to have a battle of the bands, of sorts."

Shari's eyes sparkled with life as she turned and playfully wrinkled her nose at him. The trait was so endearing. "Challenge accepted."

"I can play the conga drums," Jamal announced.

"I know," Shari said with a smile. "And you're very good."

"Yep," his nephew said, not lacking self-confidence, and resumed eating.

Garrett knew it wasn't right to keep making comparisons, but the evidence sat next to him. He and Shari just fit together. In hindsight, Brittani had been all about getting her way. And Garrett had indulged her, even forsaking family events to be with her. *Thank You, Lord, for knowing who to set me up with.*

"That royal blue looks good on you," Deborah told Shari.

Shari seemed surprised. "Thanks. The saleswoman tried to talk me out of it. She kept arguing that soft colors went better with my dark skin."

His grandmother harrumphed. "I wish I'd been with you. I would have told her a thing or two—ending with a prayer, of course." She chuckled.

"My best friend, Faith, was with me, and she told that woman more about fashion than anyone cares to know." Shari smiled. "I purchased this ensemble, and several other items in the same shade, from another saleswoman. Clearly, the first saleswoman didn't want my money, so I had no problem not giving it to her."

Deborah reached across the table and gave Shari a high five. "That's what I'm talking about. We dark and lovely sisters have to stick together."

Now Garrett's attention was riveted to Shari's outfit, which had been hidden earlier under their band uniform: a blue shell and coordinating ankle-length skirt, which she had paired with a shimmery gold jacket. Simple, but Shari made the attire extremely fashionable.

From fashion to music to Scripture, their conversation was enjoyable. The time went by too quickly, and soon their plates were scraped clean, stomachs bloated with soul food. Shari announced her imminent departure, eliciting a groan of disappointment from everyone.

"Do you have to?" Jamal gave her a puppy-dog face that probably mirrored Garrett's expression.

Shari stroked the hair on his nephew's head. "Yes, sweetie. I have to review some documents. I have two big court cases tomorrow."

"You put bad people in jail like my Uncle G?" he asked.

Garrett was about to remind Jamal that a deputy U.S. marshal apprehended fugitives for the authorities to put in federal prisons, not in local or county jails, but Shari answered first.

"I try to keep good people out of jails and prisons," She told him. Then she scooted back from the table, stood, and stretched her body like a ballerina. "Thanks for inviting me," she addressed the family. "It was wonderful seeing all of you again." She exchanged good-bye hugs with everyone and then retrieved her purse.

"I'll walk you to your car," Garrett said, grabbing her saxophone case.

"Your family reminds me of the Carmens," she told him as they strolled down the hall. "They made me feel like one of them, and your grandparents...I really miss my own."

Family. Yeah, that was one thing Garrett missed, living in Philly. But Shari was slowly filling in the gap. Still, he and his grandfather were extremely close, mainly because Moses had only had two grandsons—his pride and joy after seven daughters and no sons. Every time another male was added to the Miller fold, he rejoiced. The new additions may not carry the Miller name, but they carried the blood.

"You can borrow my grandparents anytime," Garrett teased as he stopped at Shari's vehicle.

Shari snickered. "I just may take you up on that."

"I have no qualms about sharing." Garrett became serious as he studied her captivating face. "The pull between us is strong in every way, Shari. Physically, emotionally, intellectually—I'm not afraid of a smart woman; I'm surrounded by them in my family. And the main attraction between us is undeniably spiritual. You have no idea how you and your sax have messed with my mind."

"What's developing between us is still messing with mine," she admitted softly, as if she almost didn't want to.

Her vulnerability was safe with him. Garrett felt privileged that she would confide in him, and he felt it was incumbent upon him to return the faith and share about his past burdens—soon.

Garrett opened the door for Shari, then shut it after she climbed into her vehicle. Once she'd started the engine, she lowered her window, and Garrett leaned in, resting his arms on the door. Her beautiful dark brown eyes fascinated him, reminding him of melted chocolate, and her alluring lips beckoned. Unable to wait any longer, he inched closer, giving her a chance to refuse his next move. When she didn't, Garrett captured her lips in a sweet kiss. Man, her lips were soft. How could he stop at just one? He didn't, taking liberty with another one before calling on all his restraint and backing away.

"Nice," Shari murmured.

"Very," he agreed and leaned in again to brush several more soft pecks against her mouth. She was intoxicating. Reluctantly he pulled back once more, and his hooded lashes didn't obscure his view of her pout.

Garrett stood straight and patted her roof. "Call me when you get home." Then he stepped out of the way and watched her drive off.

As long as he had walked with Jesus, his praise had never included a shout; but as he headed back to his condo, Garrett could feel one coming on.

Chapter Fifteen

"So how was dinner with Garrett's family?" Shari's mother casually asked when Shari strolled into the kitchen. "You're glowing."

"Great company, great food..." Shari had known her mother would want all the details. *A great first kiss.* That particular aspect would remain a secret for now, even though she feared her mother would figure it out because Shari couldn't stop blushing. "I think I've been adopted as another granddaughter."

She couldn't help but smile at the memory of how, one by one, Garrett's family members had wanted to talk to her when she'd called from her car to let him know she'd arrived at home.

Anchoring her elbow on the counter, her mother clearly wasn't going to give up that easily on her quest for information. "And what about Brother Nash?"

There were so many things to say about him. "I don't know...he seems almost too good to be true. There are sisters at church chasing after him—Xena and Joyce, to name a few. I don't handle competition too well when it comes to vying for a man's attention. I'm sure that rumors are flying at church...other sisters are probably mystified by the fact that he seems interested in me."

"It seems to me that you've won the competition without entering and have already been crowned the queen," her mother said. "Let the Lord lead you, Shari. If Garrett has God's stamp of approval, then he's the man for you." She straightened and squeezed Shari's shoulder. "I'll go give your sisters an update. I know they're just as eager as I was to hear all about your date."

"Mom..." Shaking her head and rolling her eyes, Shari held her peace. Everyone was acting like she had never dated before. She supposed that, in all honesty, she hadn't. Not anyone like Garrett Nash.

Garrett was hyped about his first official date with Shari, and he was planning on pulling out all the stops. They had crossed paths once this past week in court, and it had taken every bit of self-restraint not to let his gaze linger on her but instead to focus on his job.

On Friday morning, he sent flowers to her office with a card that read, "A special night for a special lady."

When he showed up at her doorstep that evening, Garrett's knees almost gave way at the sight of Shari. Her hair was swept up on top of her head, her dress was simple yet flattering, and her smile was extraordinary, reaching her eyes, which sparkled with excitement and anticipation.

Since he had already taken the liberty of kissing her, he had no reservations about holding her hand once he was situated behind the wheel with Shari beside him. He craved that point of contact as he pulled away from the curb in front of her house.

He told Shari where he'd made their dinner reservations, at Avance in Rittenhouse Square.

"I've heard great things about that restaurant, but I've never been there," Shari said.

He grinned and brought her hand to his lips. "Me, neither. Should be a memorable first for both of us."

In no time, Garrett turned on Walnut Street and pulled up in front of Avance. Valet attendants were at their doors immediately. "I'll get my date," he informed them.

Hand in hand, they strolled to the entrance. Once inside, they were promptly shown to their table. Garrett barely heard the server rattle off the evening's specials, so entranced was he by Shari. As a matter of fact, his appetite was fading fast. Then he remembered what he was paying to woo her.

When Garrett asked the server to repeat himself, Shari giggled and took charge. "How about the Chef's Testing Menu? That way, we won't have to make up our minds."

"Excellent choice," the server said.

Once they were alone, Garrett reached across the table and linked hands with Shari. Her face continued to glow as she glanced around.

"So, do I have your stamp of approval, Miss Carmen?"

Shari studied him a moment. "You do." She exhaled. "So, what brought you to Philly?"

Garrett felt no hesitation about pouring his heart out. After all, he had God's blessing. "The Lord led me here to meet you." When Shari lifted an eyebrow, he chuckled before going on. "I know that sounds cliché, but I was—"

His phone chimed a familiar tune, interrupting his revelation. Too bad. He was determined to bare his soul to Shari tonight.

"At least see who it is," she urged him.

"I know who it is." He gritted his teeth. "My grandfather. He seems to have the uncanny ability to want to talk when I'm with you." He grunted. "Seriously? I'm not in the sharing mood tonight. I'll let it go to voicemail."

Shari grew visibly concerned. "No, you should answer it. What if something's wrong? It might be urgent. It's okay, really."

Reluctantly, he clicked the button to accept the call. "Hi, Grandpa." Garrett hoped he came off sounding irritated, because he was. His grandfather's constant interruptions were downright embarrassing.

"G, I hope you're not in the middle of anything. Are you?"

Watching Shari watch him, Garrett winked. "Actually, Shari and I are on our official first date. What's going on?"

"Oh, nothing. Call me back when you get a chance."

His grandfather's haste to end the call only made Garrett more suspicious. "Grandpa?" He tried to keep his voice steady, but his grandfather had him really alarmed.

"It's Brittani. She delivered twin boys last night—handsome fellows with strong lungs and Miller mouths. Their long heads reminded me of Jamal. A lot of your kinfolk were there, including Landon, your grandmother, and myself."

"Congratulations," he said dryly. Just like Brittani to double the trouble.

"Is everything all right?" She looked worried.

Garrett covered the phone mouthpiece with his hand. "It appears we just had two babies added to the Miller clan," he reluctantly explained.

Shari grinned. "That's exciting! Congrats!"

"I want those babies in our lives," his grandfather went on. "I've offered to set up a trust fund for them. Your grandmother is so upset—"

"We'll talk more soon, Grandpa," Garrett cut him off before ending the call. Yes, he was being rude and disrespectful, and he could tell that his grandfather was troubled. But he had other priorities at the moment. He would repent now and apologize later.

Closing his eyes, he bowed his head. *Jesus, help me to regroup. Shari is important to me, but I'm so mad at Brittani for her shenanigans, the only thing I want to do is throw a tantrum.*

Shari must have sensed the change in his mood, because he felt her hand tighten its grip on his and then heard her whispered prayer: "Jesus, whatever is wrong with the mother and babies, fix it, Lord. Give the Millers the comfort of knowing that You will make all crooked things straight..."

He recognized the references to Isaiah 40:4 and Luke 3:5. The more she prayed, the calmer he became. Despite the storm Brittani had tried to brew, Shari brought the sunshine. When she said "Amen," he echoed her, then looked into her eyes and thanked her sincerely.

"So, who in your family had the babies?" she asked, clearly unaware that it was a sore subject with him.

"My cousin."

While she'd been wearing Garrett's engagement ring, Brittani had gone and gotten pregnant by another man—Garrett's own flesh and blood. Landon was of the opinion that a little competition between family members was harmless. But he had crossed the line with Garrett's fiancée. Both his cousin and Brittani had tested his patience, his charity, and his ability to forgive.

For the rest of the evening, Garrett encouraged Shari to tell him about her childhood, her career, and anything else that interested her. He listened attentively, asking plenty of questions to keep her talking. His personal woes were the last thing he wanted to discuss right now, despite his earlier intentions of opening up to Shari.

Shari's heart bled for Garrett. She didn't want to pry, but she could tell that the phone call from his grandfather had upset him. So, she did what she knew to do—pray. And when he kept apologizing for his sour mood, she actually leaned across the table and pressed a kiss to his lips.

Their evening ended with plenty of hugs, mostly initiated by Garrett, and the sweetest kiss at her door.

Chapter Sixteen

$\mathcal{P}$rayer alone had kept Garrett s date with Shari from going downhill after his grandfather's phone call and the news about Brittani.

"I'll continue to pray for your cousin," Shari had said at her doorstep.

More than anything, Garrett had wanted to divulge the drama playing out in Boston. But it had been late when he'd dropped Shari off at home, and he had an early-morning surveillance on a fugitive. Rest was essential. "I'll talk to you first chance I get tomorrow," he'd assured her.

"I know," she'd whispered, giving his jaw a gentle caress before disappearing inside her house.

This has to be the worst day of my life! Garrett thought as he dragged himself back to his SUV. "No," he admitted aloud, "the worst day of my life was when I found out that my fiancée slept with another man, and that the other man was my first cousin."

Feeling mentally and emotionally drained, he refused to dwell on it any longer. Twenty minutes later, he arrived at his condo, not cognizant of how he'd gotten there. He'd made it by some miracle.

His alarm clock sounded at three the next morning. He groaned in agony at having to wake before the sun rose, but it was part of his job. Sliding out of bed and getting on his knees, he prayed for wisdom and peace, then jumped in the shower.

When he was about to walk out the door, he noticed that he had missed a text from Shari late last night. He must have been knocked out not to hear the notification.

Cast all your cares upon Jesus, because He definitely cares for you, and I do, too. 1 Peter 5:7.

Garrett smiled. The thoughtful gesture reinforced that Shari was the woman God had created after Garrett's own heart. When he got to his office, he was still grinning.

"What's got you grinning, Nash?" asked his partner, Kyle Adams. He knew that Garrett was smitten with an attorney, but that was all he was willing to share.

"A very special lady."

"Mmm-hmm. You can daydream about her later. Right now, the only 'special lady' in our lives is fugitive Janet Kobo. We've narrowed it down to three houses we can hit."

"Right." Garrett immediately reverted back to work mode as he tapped on his laptop. He had a knack for staying a step ahead of the fugitive they were tracking by getting inside his or her head. "If I were a woman wanted on child endangerment charges, where would I hide out?"

"Definitely not with someone who has kids," Kyle stated.

"But in this case, I think Kobo may be hiding in plain sight, especially if she has a sympathetic family member who doesn't believe her to be guilty of what she's been accused of."

The pair went back and forth for an hour, trying to put themselves in Kobo's shoes and making hypotheses about where she might be. Snooping around at the wrong house could tip off the fugitive, causing her to make a run for it. The woman in question was unstable. Catching her off guard in the predawn hours made it less likely she would react violently.

By five a.m., they decided to make contact at the home of Janet's niece, who was also the mother of two young school-age children.

"Let's wait until after the kids board the bus," Garrett suggested. "Then we'll make our move."

Kyle nodded his agreement.

The two of them watched the home from their parking spot at the corner. When the school bus drove off, Janet's niece looked up and down the street before returning inside and shutting the door.

"That was odd," Garrett said.

"Perhaps. You knock on the front door. I'll go around the back."

Moments later, Garrett prayed for safety as he climbed the porch steps and tapped on the door. The woman answered almost immediately.

"Yes? How can I help you?"

Garrett identified himself, then explained that he was looking for her aunt.

The woman's face took on the strangest expression, and then she whispered, "She's in the bathroom."

The wait gave Garrett time to signal Kyle for backup. When Janet came out the bathroom, the element of surprise worked in their favor, and they managed to arrest her without incident.

After booking her in the Montgomery County Correctional Facility to await her trial, they completed the paperwork to clear the felony.

With one fugitive down, they began working on two more cases from the most-wanted list supplied by the Bureau of Alcohol, Tobacco, Firearms and Explosives for a bond and a probation violation. The busy workload kept Garrett's mind off Brittani, but when his day came to an end, his personal life shifted to front and center.

Once he got home, he warmed up the leftovers from his dinner with Shari. Then he called his grandfather, bracing himself for whatever additional news he was about to learn. Garrett wasn't looking forward to hearing more about Brittani's mischief, but he owed his grandfather an apology, so he made that his first priority.

"Your frustration is understandable, Grandson. Apology accepted," Moses said in a voice that made him sound more in control of his emotions than he'd been the previous night. He clicked his tongue disapprovingly. "We've just learned that your cousin has two other children that we didn't know about."

Too many emotions battled for dominance for Garrett to choose one. Finally, he roared, "What?" Disgusted, he rubbed his face in irritation. Brittani was just a conquest to his cousin. He felt sorry for his ex, but that didn't change anything. She hadn't called on the Holy Ghost to restrain her from succumbing to the devil's temptation.

"Grandpa, I know you reared us to be forgiving toward each other, but right now, I wish I had beaten Landon like my flesh wanted to." He sighed. "But no, I stepped back to let the Lord fight my battles. And—"

"And God will continue to fight them," his grandfather reassured him. "Landon will answer to God, but Brittani is the one with two bargaining chips. She wants a husband."

"She and every other single woman." Garrett grunted and twisted his lips. "But I'm not the one for her."

"I think Brittani is beginning to realize that Landon is not going to step up to the plate. She's hoping that you will forgive her and come to her rescue."

Garrett almost laughed out loud. "Are you suggesting I consider agreeing to her nonsensical notion?" He was starting to question the sanity of the family patriarch. "I'm going forward, Grandpa. Not backward."

"Absolutely not!" his grandfather exclaimed. "I know God will work this out. Although I want Brittani's boys in our life, I want Shari in yours. Don't rush what you feel for her, and take your time to show Shari how much you care for her."

"Consider it done." Garrett relaxed and even grinned.

"Have you told Shari the whole story?"

"I was about to do that last night when you called. That woman is truly a godsend. She suspected something was wrong, but didn't pepper me with questions. She prayed for me instead, then last night, texted me a Scripture verse."

Their conversation ended with prayer that boosted Garrett's confidence that somehow, some way, God would work things out.

The next morning, Garrett stepped out of the shower to discover that he had missed a phone call from Shari. As her voicemail message, she had sung a few verses of "He Knows."

He called her back immediately. "The Lord knows I need you," he told her.

For the remainder of the week, Garrett and Shari's schedules were hit-and-miss. His working hours were erratic due to various fugitives he was tracking, and she was busy preparing for several major cases. As a result, their together time was limited to short phone calls or text messages.

Do you have any plans tomorrow evening? Garrett texted Shari on Thursday.

I hope with you, she texted back.

Garrett smiled as he confirmed they would do something special. Then he called John Whitman for a recommendation.

"Good to know you remember me, and not just at band rehearsal," John joked. "Seems like you and Shari are playing a different tune."

When he had brought his friend up to speed on their relationship, John strongly advised him to tell Shari what the drama with Landon was all about.

Right. Garrett exhaled, agreeing with him, but he still hadn't dealt with his outrage over the whole ordeal. "Can you believe Brittani's nerve?" he seethed. "I'm not the father, yet she's acting as if I am. Man, the night was going so good until my grandfather called, upset, and told me the news. Thank God Shari's a praying woman and that's why I want to redo our first date."

"Amen," said John. "Hold on a minute. Let me ask Rita what she would suggest." John gave a muffled shout for Rita, and she came on the line mere seconds later.

"If *my* husband were to take me out for a romantic dinner..." She cleared her throat. John must have been nearby. "It better be at Alma de Cuba in Center City. I hear the ambience is *very impressive.*"

He laughed. "Thanks, Rita. I plan to take her there tomorrow, so you guys can go any time after that."

The next evening, Garrett prayed as he stepped onto Shari's porch, *Lord, please let tonight be perfect.* He was seconds away from knocking on her front door when it opened and Mrs. Carmen hurried out.

"Oh! Brother Nash. You startled me. I'm running late for my dance class. Go on in and have a seat in the living room." She strolled down the steps and across the walkway, heels clicking on the pavement, then climbed behind the wheel of a Kia sedan and honked as she drove off.

Living room? Garrett had never set foot inside Shari's house before. Shrugging, he entered, stuffing his hands in his pockets. He peered down a long hall, then wandered into the first room on his right—and froze at the sight of the woman he wanted to be his wife.

Shari was seated on the couch, asleep, still dressed in her business suit, her feet soaking in a sudsy massage tub. The four-inch stilts on the floor nearby had to be the culprit. Why did she punish her innocent feet as she did?

Squatting in front of her, Garrett watched her long lashes fluttered open. Exhaustion draped her face. There was no way they were going out now. He didn't want her to feel obligated. He glanced down at the bubbles floating up from her foot massager. Shari followed his distracted gaze.

"Either you're early, or I'm really late," she said, shifting her body to sit up.

"It doesn't matter. I'm right on time. Do you have any blessed oil?"

She frowned. "Yes. Why?"

"I want to wash and anoint your feet."

"This isn't a Communion and feet-washing service at church. This is a simple home foot spa."

Garrett persisted until she relented, pointing to a small bottle behind a crystal vase on the mantel above the fireplace. He retrieved it, then knelt before her. Although she had beautiful feet, Garrett managed to keep his mind from wandering to the wrong places. He didn't want to act out of carnal motives. "Are you refusing prayer?"

"Of course not!" Her foot splashed a little water on him, and she quickly apologized.

"Good." He bowed his head. "Father, in the name of Jesus, we come before Your throne, thanking You for Shari's protection and for the blessings You have in store for her life. Give her peace, comfort, and wisdom. Bless her comings in and her goings out..."

As he continued to pray, he cupped her right foot with his left hand and used his right hand to scoop up the scented water and pour it over her foot like a gentle waterfall, after Jesus' example with the apostles in John 13. He did the same thing with the other foot, then ended the prayer and grabbed the fluffy yellow towel beside Shari. He lifted her feet out of the water, one at a time, and patted them dry before reverently lowering them to the floor.

Next, he rubbed a few drops of oil into his hands and massaged each foot, giving God praise. When he glanced up at Shari, tears were streaming down her cheeks. "What's wrong?"

She shook her head. "Nothing's wrong. That was so beautiful. Thank you for praying for me."

"You're welcome, but, baby, you need to stop torturing the gorgeous feet God gave you."

"But I'm short," she said softly with a pout.

"Five feet six inches is perfect," he told her.

When she exhaled, Garrett lifted her chin with his finger.

She blinked. "How did you know that was my height?"

"A man who cares about his woman makes it his business to know such things." He leaned forward and brushed his lips against hers, then pulled back. To tame his attraction, he searched for the button to turn off the massage contraption. After a few moments with no success, Shari giggled, reached down, and pushed a knob he hadn't seen. The smile on her face erased her weary look.

"I can be ready in—"

"Oh, no. Don't even think about it. You're tired." *Forget what it's going to cost me to cancel my reservation at the last minute.* "How about I go grab us something to eat and bring it back here? We can eat at Alma de Cuba another time."

"Alma de Cuba!" She jumped up, licking her lips. "You can't cancel."

"Shari—"

"That's my favorite place."

"I'm not surprised, but next time." He snatched his keys and trekked to the front door, dodging the sofa pillow she hurled at him.

Chapter Seventeen

Shari smiled, already looking forward to their next time. She ran upstairs to freshen up and change into something casual but nice—at least with coordinating colors. Glancing down at her feet, her eyes watered, and she lifted her hands in praise. "Jesus, thank You for a godly man. I love him."

Sucking in her breath, Shari held it. Had she just said that? She gulped. She was getting ahead of herself. She needed to slow down and take her time getting to know Garrett before making such a profession.

Whether she loved him or not, Shari enjoyed his company, so she hurried downstairs to wait for his return.

When he knocked on the door minutes later, she opened it and stepped back. Looking into his eyes, she was at a loss for words, so she simply whispered, "Hi, again."

"Hi, again." He brushed a soft kiss against her lips, then lingered there.

"I'm hungry," Shari fussed good-naturedly, then turned around and retreated into the kitchen.

Garrett followed her and unloaded his bags on the counter— cheesesteak sandwiches and a package of Tastykakes, a favorite of every Philly sweet tooth. She grinned when she saw the two bottles of Frank's Black Cherry Wishniak. Outsiders would call the drink "black cherry soda," but what did they know? Shari chuckled to herself.

She set the table quickly as her stomach growled. Once they were settled in their seats, she asked Garrett to say grace. As eloquently as he had prayed for her earlier during the impromptu feet-washing, he spoke in his deep voice, asking God to bless their food. She loved the sincerity and humility present in each word.

He seemed to be in good spirits, compared with their date last week. If Garrett didn't bring up his cousin's babies, neither would she. It was their night, and she didn't want anything to spoil it, even if they weren't dining at Alma de Cuba.

Seconds later, the front door opened, and her mother's heels clicked rhythmically down the hallway toward them. She frowned as she set her purse on the counter and peeked inside the empty bags. "You two must have eaten next to nothing at all at the restaurant to need this type of after-dinner snack."

Garrett wiped his mouth with a napkin. "Your daughter was tired, so I decided to grab something fast and stay in."

Shari was glad that his recap didn't include the consecrated feet-washing. "He'll make up for it." She beamed.

Her mother looked from her to Garrett, then shook her head. "That is the thinking of a wise man. I'll let you young people enjoy your date."

After their meal, Garrett stood up. "Well, I've fed you and enjoyed your smile, but let's call it a night so you can get some rest."

She wanted to protest, but her yawn popped up before she could stop it. It wasn't long until Garrett said good night and left.

As Shari watched him drive off, her mother reappeared. She came to stand next to her at the window, with her arms folded.

"Handsome, loves the Lord, well-mannered, and considerate...I wouldn't mind having him as a son-in-law."

"Mmm-hmm. Well, he would be cuter than your other son-in-law." Shari kissed her mother on the cheek before dashing upstairs. She wanted to be alone to savor the memories of her night in with Garrett.

He possessed all the qualities she could ever hope for in a practicing Christian man—quiet strength during the prison crisis, tenderness in the feet-washing, and, most important, the initiative to petition God on her behalf.

Not only was he concerned about her physical needs; he cared about her spiritual condition, as well. That was a man worth keeping. If Shari screamed her happiness, no doubt her neighbors might file a misdemeanor disturbance report.

She had never fought over a man in her life. Her cousins, sisters, and parents had always made sure of that. But if Garrett Nash were up for auction, Sharmaine Carmen would be the highest bidder. She shook her head in disbelief at the direction of her thoughts. *Slow down*, she reminded herself. "Lord, please don't let my heart lead me astray, in Jesus' name. Amen."

I will bless you, God whispered.

When the Lord spoke to her, she loved it and waited to see if He would say more, but He didn't.

She checked the clock to make sure it wasn't too late to call Stacy at home. Confident that her older sister would still be awake, she gave her a buzz.

"Hello?" her brother-in-law answered after the first ring.

"Hey, Ted. It's Shari. What are you guys doing?"

"If I told you, you'd blush. Seriously, hold on."

When she heard Stacy's giggles, Shari did blush. Stacy and "Theodore," his formal name he now detested, had grown up attending the same school, but Stacy basically hadn't known he existed until he came home from college. He had matured from a buck-toothed worry wart to a handsome, confident man. And for the past five years, they had been carefree lovebirds, committed to a happy marriage.

"Praise Him, my favorite sister," Stacy said when she came on the line. She sounded unusually upbeat. "How was the dinner date?"

Shari smirked. Every Carmen sister was Stacy's favorite. "The date and dinner happened here at home."

"Well, that wasn't very original or romantic," Stacy commented dryly. "I'm disappointed. He comes across as a type who would try to impress a woman."

"Oh, Garrett did impress. He prayed for me, fed me, and then—"

"Ouch!" There was a pause as Stacy muffled the phone, and then she came back on the line. "Uh, Sis? Can you hold the details until tomorrow? Ted just ran our—I mean, my bathwater." She cleared her throat.

The couple's antics amused Shari, but their deep love for each other also made her wonder how close she was to having someone to call her husband. "Okay," she said. "Talk to you—" She looked at the screen of her cell phone and chuckled. Her sister had already ended the call.

Days later, Shari strolled into her office after a crazy morning in court to find a box on her desk. She didn't try to contain her smile as she fumbled to open the card tied to it with ribbon.

I've washed many feet during many consecration services, but yours were by far the most beautiful—not just perfectly shaped but spiritually created for the path of God's work.

Always thinking about you.

—G

She opened the box to discover a smaller one packaged in gift wrap. Shari peeled back the foil and sucked in her breath as she fingered the miniature black velvet-covered stiletto shoe sprinkled with tiny rhinestones. The figurine was so beautiful, she wished she had a look-alike pair in her closet.

Shari's heart fluttered. Just like the man, his gift was unforgettable. She texted him to express her gratitude.

His response arrived several hours later: `Thank you for coming into my life.`

When they found a chance to talk, the first thing Shari asked him was, "Were you trying to tell me something by the shoe?"

"I'm pleading the fifth, Counselor."

"I have my ways to find the truth."

Their conversation was cut short when Garrett had to go. What he described as a "hit" would always be a police raid to her.

Although Shari preferred to settle cases out of court, she wanted to represent her clients in the courtroom in hopes of catching a glimpse of Garrett in uniform. But she had her work cut out for her with her newest client—a sixteen-year-old male who had happened to be riding in the backseat of a stolen car used in an armed robbery.

Cases that involved "being in the wrong place at the wrong time" were always tough to defend. They required convincing the judge and/or jury of the client's innocent mind-set at the time of the incident. Meanwhile, all that the prosecution had to do was prove that the defendant knew, or should have known, that the car was stolen, in this instance. After two days in court, the jury sided with her client, and Shari praised God for the victory.

On Tuesday, she couldn't wait to see Garrett at Bible class that evening, so she texted him right away to share the good news.

"How about dinner and a movie on Friday to celebrate?" Garrett suggested as they strolled hand in hand to his SUV after

Bible class.

"I can't." Shari sulked. "I'm the guest speaker at a Pretty Brown Girl Club meeting."

"A *what?*" He stopped mid-stride and faced her. "Is this an exclusive club for beautiful black women?" His eyes sparkled as he teased her.

Tilting her head, Shari thought about his question. "I guess it is. The Pretty Brown Girl Club is a national organization. For the past couple of years, their focus has been to encourage school-age girls to be comfortable in their own brown skin, regardless of the shade."

"Were you ever uncomfortable in your beautiful brown skin?" His voice was barely a whisper.

I still am, at times, she thought, recalling a recent event. Rumors had begun to circulate at church that she and Garrett were a couple, and some sisters seemed mystified that he was interested in her. Shari had been like a fly on a wall one Sunday in a bathroom stall when she'd overheard two sisters talking.

"Shari has the hair and the body, but I'm surprised he's attracted to her. She's so dark. Can you imagine her kids?" one sister said.

"Maybe it's because she makes a lot of money. In the end, dark-skinned brothers go for the white or light-skinned sisters," the other offered her take before the two exited the restroom.

Why did it always come down to skin color? White men were attracted to black women, as were men of other races. Regardless of the disparaging comments, she was comfortable in her skin— most of the time. She could have confronted those women with her attorney persona, but what would that have accomplished? Only God could change their hearts.

Shari bowed her head and swallowed before meeting his eyes. "I do struggle with being a dark African American woman," she finally admitted to Garrett. "That's why it's important to build self-confidence in girls while they're young, so they will make good choices in life from careers to positive relationships."

"I happen to like dark skin beauties. I'm dark and I look forward to having all shades of brown babies." He smiled. "You're something special, woman. You wow me with your obvious commitment to God, your humble shyness is sweet and refreshing, and you're beautiful."

His praise and assessment made Shari's heart soar. She did have confidence, which stemmed mostly from her success as an attorney that was magnified in the courtroom. Little did most people know that, deep down inside, she hadn't felt pretty all the time as a young girl—not when almost every commercial on television used white women as the standard of beauty. Any African American women who were featured on TV and in print were so fair-skinned that a person might question their ethnicity. Shari cleared her throat. "I was Daddy's little girl, and he played a major role in helping me to understand my self-worth."

"Well, Miss Carmen—or should I say Attorney Carmen?—I know your worth to me."

His voice—or maybe it was the way he said the words—convinced her she was falling in love. The thought both scared and excited her.

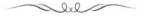

On Friday night, Garrett opted to stay at home while Shari spoke to a bunch of girls at the meeting of the local chapter of the Pretty Brown Girl Club. He couldn't help but wonder who had rocked her self-confidence—and when and how. Had she been overweight as a child? Had she worn braces or suffered from severe acne?

All Garrett could imagine was a gorgeous chocolate baby doll with eyes the color of brown marbles that reflected the sunlight and chubby cheeks that invited endless kisses. With each moment he spent with her, he craved more of her presence.

He sent her a text message, asking her to let him know when she had made it home from the meeting.

OK, she answered minutes later. Two hours passed before she let him know she was home safe and sound.

If you're up to it, how about going to the gospel fest on Penn's Landing with me after band practice tomorrow?

She replied, Sounds great. Can't wait!

Me, neither. That was why, the next morning, Garrett drove up to the curb in front of Shari's house more than ten minutes early. Although his body was conditioned for self-defense, his knees almost weren't sturdy enough to hold his weight when she opened the front door. With the lightness of a feather, Shari had overpowered him with her magnificent allure.

How was it possible for a beautiful woman to become increasingly stunning in his eyes? How did God do that?

As if Shari had signaled the wind, a breeze ruffled the hem of her tan dress, teasing his vision as she stepped onto the porch. Garrett's breathing stilled while his eyelashes provided cover for his assessment that continued down to her feet, where a recent pedicure was evident. Polished pearl-white toenails were accented with a trio of tiny gold rhinestones on both big toes. He released a weak sigh. His heart needed a pump to maintain the blood flow.

"Woman, you're trying to slay me. You look incredible."

"You make me feel incredible." She blushed.

At that moment, Garrett was aware of the seduction of her bedroom eyes that she probably had no clue she possessed. "You were incredible the very day the Lord molded you."

He took another peek at her pedicured toes—and her high-heeled sandals. "You might want to bring a pair of flat sandals to wear after band rehearsal so your feet won't get tired. I made dinner reservations at Ristorante La Veranda, and I thought we could stroll along the bridge and then board a ferry to Susquehanna Bank Center."

Shari furrowed her brow. "I thought we were just going to see Hezekiah Walker at the Gospel Explosion. I haven't been to Penn's Landing in years. My sisters and I used to attend events there all the time."

"I wanted to give you some options." Garrett lifted her hand and placed a soft kiss on one finger. "I'm still a newbie here, with lots of exploring still to do."

"If you really want to play the tourist, we might as well visit Adventure Aquarium across the river and see the exotic fish and animals."

"You're the most exotic creature I've ever seen," he said as he waited for her to grab her flat shoes, then he helped her into his vehicle. As they drove to the church, Genesis 50:20 ran through his head. *Yep, despite Brittani and Landon s deceit, God has turned it around and used it for my good.*

Chapter Eighteen

After they placed their orders at La Veranda, Shari glanced around to take in the ambiance of the restaurant when Garrett's smartphone played a tune, and he reached for it. Even Shari was beginning to recognize the familiar ringtone.

Keeping a smile on her face, she groaned inwardly. Now what? Did his grandfather have a satellite tracking device that notified him whenever the two of them were together? His frequent calls, which she initially found endearing, were becoming annoying. Couldn't they just have a normal date without interruptions or the need to reschedule?

"I'm turning off my phone," Garrett told her. "I want this time to be about us."

Shari exhaled and repented for her resentful thoughts. After all, she did like his grandfather. Now her smile became genuine.

"A while back, we were discussing bad relationships," Garrett began. "Well, I was engaged once, but I broke it off when my fiancée got pregnant."

She must have frowned or otherwise made her hurt obvious, for he rushed to add, "Before you jump to any conclusions, you need to know that the babies aren't mine."

Shari couldn't help herself. "Excuse me if I step out of church mode and put on my attorney suit. The only way you would know that the baby—babies, rather—aren't yours is if you didn't sleep with her." She knew it sounded bad.

Practicing Christians didn't fornicate. But she had to make sure he didn't play church on Sundays and role-play as a saint the rest of the week.

Garrett didn't seem intimidated by her questioning. "Shari, I'm pure. I've never touched a woman. Christian ladies aren't the only ones who strive to keep their virginity until marriage. She slept with my cousin, or my cousin slept with her—however one wants to phrase their sick behavior."

Shari gasped and then covered her mouth. "Your fiancée and your cousin? *Their* babies?" Her eyes watered with compassion for his situation, then she chided herself for questioning his character. "Oh, no. I'm so sorry." She sniffed.

Save yourself from this unruly generation, the Lord whispered.

How many times had her mother drilled Acts 2:40 into her daughters' heads as they were growing up? While Shari had been saving herself for her future husband, Garrett had also been saving himself for his future wife. It was a welcome affirmation that not all God's people yielded to the temptation of premarital relations. "Praise Jesus for His keeping power."

"Amen." Garrett exhaled and looked around before meeting her eyes again. She liked the gentleness staring back at her. "The Lord saved me as a boy. I think I was seven, maybe eight. My grandfather read countless stories to my cousin and me from the Old Testament about kings who pleased God, only to have their descendants do evil in the sight of the Lord.

"My grandfather and my parents practiced holy lives—they were living examples of what it means to walk with God. While I took that to heart, Landon must have been biding his time to be the generation that messed up." He shook his head. "If I had known that Brittani wasn't God's choice for me, I could have saved myself from a lot of grief."

Shari gave him a grim smile. "I don't say this lightly, but she was a fool. A good man is hard to find—"

"But a great woman is no easy catch," he interrupted her, reaching for her hands. She easily surrendered them, only to have to let go moments later when their meals arrived.

After thanking the server, they both bowed their heads, and Shari listened as Garrett said grace. Once Shari sampled her Filetto Di Salmone, she dabbed the corners of her mouth with her napkin. "So, you broke it off with your fiancée. What about your cousin? How did you handle that?"

Garrett remained silent as a series of different expressions flashed across his face. Shari felt bad for asking. Finally, he huffed before responding, "Landon knows how to play the game. He asked me for forgiveness. I went ballistic, but my family was there to restrain me." He gritted his teeth. "Some of my friends who knew the truth said that Landon deserved a beat down for his betrayal, and they told me I should give it to him and then repent. The devil taunted me, telling me that I was a wimp if I didn't lash out in retaliation."

Shari admired his self-control. "You have such long-suffering patience." She reached out and rubbed his hand.

Garrett didn't respond. He seemed to struggle with her assessment. "I've never felt so many emotions at one time. I actually entertained..." He paused. "Let me just say that, without the Lord, I might have needed the services of a criminal attorney. But God..."

"Yes, but God," she whispered.

"Yes, thank God for Jesus. I think Brittani was counting on not only my forgiveness but also my love. She wanted me to completely overlook her sin. But only God can do that. I fasted, prayed, and read the Word to find comfort and forgiveness. Then I did what God required of me—I forgave her and Landon. It wasn't long after that when Jesus moved me away, literally, from the situation."

Shari nodded. "The way we're inclined to respond to so many situations is rarely God's way. Although God took 'side streets' instead of the direct route to get you here, I'm so glad you arrived when you did."

"Me, too." Leaning closer, he brushed his lips against hers. Shari wanted more, but he pulled back. "It's important for you to know that you don't have just the remnants of my heart, Shari. You have all of it."

When he explained that Brittani had started a smear campaign against him in the church, declaring that Garrett was the father, Shari couldn't contain her indignation any longer. "Do you need representation?"

Garrett smiled until his eyes seemed to dance. "No, my little spitfire. What bothers me the most is how upsetting this is for my grandparents. They want to be a part of the babies' lives. But Brittani is being difficult, making outrageous demands that she be married to a Miller before the babies 'change hands,' so to speak."

"It may be worth securing immediate counsel to advise you whether it's worth filing a petition for visitation rights," Shari suggested.

"Or we can just pray, baby," Garrett said softly. "I put my trust in First Corinthians six, verses one and two: *'Dare any of you, having a matter against another, go to law before the unjust, and not before the saints? Do ye not know that the saints shall judge the world, and if the world shall be judged by you, are ye unworthy to judge the smallest matters?'* I believe prayer can turn any situation around, and I need a woman in my life who believes it, too. If God intends for me to go to court, I trust Him to steer me in that direction."

"You're talking with an attorney who makes her living in the courts, defending the law that God established for the lawless—" She held her tongue. Although she could argue any case in the courtroom, she couldn't go up against God, so she held her peace.

"Baby, let's change the subject," Garrett suggested. "This is exactly why I held off telling you about the babies. When I'm with you, I want everything to be about us."

"You're right." Shari sighed. "It's just that it's in my blood to fight injustices. If my daddy were here, not only would he like you, but he would say that you have wisdom beyond your years."

Their server appeared, as if to remind them that they had a sumptuous meal to enjoy, so they floored the conversation and enjoyed their food. Garrett did so with more gusto than usual, as if the discussion had caused him to work up an appetite.

"This is excellent." He licked his lips. "I'm sure Mr. Carmen would be proud to know that you've become the princess he groomed you to be. I hope that I'm the type of man you pictured when you were little and wanted to marry somebody just like your daddy."

"You are," she whispered, blinking away a tear.

Chapter Nineteen

The next morning, Shari awoke earlier than usual, replaying Garrett's bombshell in her mind. She couldn't begin to fathom that type of betrayal within a family. When she and her sisters had started dating, they'd been on the lookout for signs that the guy was trying to hit on another Carmen. The few times when that had been the case, the guys were history, and Shari's cousins, Victor and Dino, had enforced the edict.

Garrett was more complex than she'd first thought. Only God could have given him the kind of peace he exhibited after having been wronged so deeply. The biggest revelation had been his desire to remain pure and to foster faith among the men of his generation. His faith was most evident in his obedience when God told him to pack up and leave Boston, removing him from the situation instead of taking away the problem from his life. Talk about completely trusting in the Lord. Wow.

Shari slid to her knees to pray. "Lord, in the name of Jesus, I thank You for opening my physical eyes this morning, and for opening my spiritual eyes, too, so that I am able to see the man Garrett really is. You have to be proud of him. I am, too; but, Lord, we know that the fallout is far from over. Lord, please move in the lives of the Miller family, so that the situation would resolve itself and there would be no need for legal services..."

Jesus moved in her spirit until He took control of her mouth, causing her to speak in other tongues. Once she quieted, Shari waited to see if God would give the interpretation of His words.

In this life, one's faith is tested, sometimes with fire. Go through it with praise and honor until I return. The voice of the Lord was clear as He reminded her to reread 1 Peter 1, which she did when she got up off her knees.

"Lord, increase my faith in You," Shari uttered as she closed her Bible. She showered, dressed, and was eating breakfast when her phone alerted her that it was time for a video chat she'd scheduled with her sisters. She quickly logged on to her laptop.

Not surprisingly, Brecee didn't waste any time starting the conversation. "I heard a U.S. Marshal has you under private protection, Shari. I woke up just for this chat after a fourteen-hour rotation, so give your snoop sisters the latest scoop."

The others laughed, and Shari smirked. "Correction—it's *Deputy* U.S. Marshal, but I'm not running away from him. I really like him, and I'm one hundred percent committed to see where this relationship is going."

"Ooh, the prince has arrived on his white horse," Brecee cooed.

"Nope." Shari shook her head. "Garrett's my black stallion. My Holy Ghost confirmed that his Holy Ghost was the real deal."

"That's good to know." Stacy cast her a suspicious frown. "Okay, spill it. What happened for you to be so sure of Brother Nash?"

How could she convey to her sisters the type of man Garrett was without breaking his confidence? "We had a heart-to-heart over dinner last night. I know Daddy would approve of him."

"It's about time," Brecee said. "This means Shae is next."

Shae groaned. "You can take me off the 'available' list,

Brecee. I'm so through with men."

Everyone's heart ached for Shae, who was still recovering from a disastrous relationship in Nebraska that had almost pushed her to the brink of insanity. The Carmen men had threatened to pilot a fighter jet to take him out. And Mother Ernestine Stillwell, who had prophesied that Shae's husband was within reach, had amassed a contingency of senior members from Jesus Is the Way Church to board a bus and travel to Nebraska to defend her honor.

In the end, Shae had requested that her family back off and let the Lord help her work it out—and He had, landing Shae a far better position at a more prestigious TV news station in St. Louis.

"If the Lord can make dry bones come alive, He has a special someone for you," their mother said, startling Shari as she stepped farther into the kitchen. She stood behind Shari, peeking over her shoulder into the computer camera. "Jesus will resuscitate your heart, too, Shae."

"Definitely," Shari affirmed, knowing whenever there was a sisters' chat, her mother would be nearby to comment on whatever topic was under discussion.

"Maybe Shae's special someone could be a baseball player." Brecee grinned.

"What's the medical code for delusional? I think our baby sister needs an evaluation," Shae stated.

The sisters stared at their computer monitors, waiting for Shae to come clean. Finally, Stacy took control. "An athlete? Okay, you'd better spill it." Her tone was the same authoritative, big-sister voice she'd used with them all her life.

Shaking her head, Shae shrugged. "Brecee's referring to a thank-you note I received from a viewer, and she's acting like it was an application for a marriage license."

"Speaking of marriage..." Brecee grinned. "Since this is your fairy tale, I have to ask: If your Secret Service Brother Nash asks you to marry him, what will you say?" She merged the multiple topics with ease.

"Fairy tale or not, I would most certainly entertain his proposal," Shari said softly, realizing she hoped that would be the case.

"So, as we close this chat, would you confirm that you're falling in love with him?" Stacy asked her.

Shari smiled. "I have fallen, and I don't want to get up. Good-bye, ladies. Love you," she said before signing off.

Chapter Twenty

*S*hari had planted the seed. Now Garrett debated if he should mention to his grandparents the idea of filing for visitation rights with Brittani's twins.

Although they had every legal right to do so, as blood relatives of the babies, Garrett didn't feel in his spirit that it was the right direction to go. Regardless, he hoped whatever God's intentions this time, they didn't involve him.

I know the plans I have for you, the Lord whispered.

Yes, You do, Lord. When he first relocated to Philly, Garrett had reread Jeremiah 29:11 countless times, wondering what good could possibly come of the situation. He was so thankful that God had made Shari a part of the plan. He smiled as he thought of his lady. Shari had called him twice to see if he was doing okay. What man wouldn't fall for her?

At church on Sunday, after Pastor Underwood had dismissed the congregation, Garrett was chatting with Shari in the bandstand when John and Rita walked up to them with grins as wide as their faces. "We one-upped Mother Stillwell," John said, turning to give his wife a high five.

Garrett chuckled. When Shari didn't react, he wondered what

had her distracted. Glancing over his shoulder, he spied Mrs. Carmen and Stacy signaling Shari with their hands. Caught in the act, the women froze. Ted, standing behind them, grimaced at Garrett while moving his finger in a slicing gesture against his throat.

Shari leaned over and told him, "You've been summoned to dinner at my aunt and uncle's." She wiped off her serious expression, then turned back to the Whitmans and smirked. "We have no statement to release at this time," she said, somehow keeping a straight face.

Laughing, Garrett couldn't help but put his arm around her shoulder.

"Right," he said before he and Rita walked off, still grinning.

"I wouldn't want your family to issue a warrant, so I eagerly accept," Garrett told Shari.

"Good answer."

He grabbed their saxophone cases and followed her to the parking lot. Since the band members had to report to the church over an hour before the service started, Garrett had made a routine of picking Shari up on Sunday mornings. Once they were in his vehicle, they linked hands and enjoyed a blissful ride to Mt. Airy, with Shari giving him directions as he drove.

When Garrett parked in front of the two-story house on Seymour Street, instead of getting out of the vehicle, he turned to Shari and studied her. Staring deep into her eyes, he saw all the love she had for him—a reflection of his love for her. Empowered by her affections, he took a deep breath and exhaled. "I love you, Shari Carmen. And although I've said that to another woman in the past, I know in my heart that you are God's choice for me. When I look at you, I forget that I ever uttered those words before."

Shari reached up and stroked his jaw. He captured her hand and kissed her palm.

"I love you, too, Garrett Nash, and I have never said that to another man."

They were about to steal a kiss when someone whistled to get their attention. Annoyed, they faced the house, where three men stood imposingly, their arms crossed like guardsmen. Shari's two cousins, who'd stared him down at church several weeks ago, bore an uncanny resemblance to the older man frowning at their side. A petite older woman with a bright smile forged an opening between them.

Shari sighed. "That's our cue." Once outside the SUV, Garrett took Shari by the hand again as they strolled up the walkway. He gave it a squeeze as he nodded to the welcome committee.

"We've heard so much about you, Brother Nash. Well, actually, it was through the grapevine with my sister-in-law." The woman gave him a bashful look. "I'm Camille Carmen, Shari's aunt."

Garrett extended his free hand to her. "It's nice to meet you, ma'am." Her giant sons, who were anything but jolly and green as the one plastered on vegetable cans, begrudgingly stepped back, creating an entrance. As Garrett passed, they grunted. Did they expect their stony expressions would intimidate him? He withheld a smirk. For a Deputy U.S. Marshal, backup was only a phone call or text message away. At least Stacy and Ted would be there, adding to Garrett's friends among foes. He saw them getting out of their car.

"I hope you two brought your appetites," Camille said as she led them inside.

"You know it, Auntie," Shari said. Then she disengaged their hands and disappeared into another room, leaving Garrett to fend for himself.

He attempted to follow her, but a large hand landed on his shoulder. "Not so fast. Have a seat. Let's set the rules first."

Bring it on. No one—family, friend, or foe—could keep him from the blessing God had given. Sinking into an off-white leather sofa, Garrett stretched his legs and gazed around the room at the array of framed family photos that adorned the walls, shelves, and tables. He heard the front door open and saw Stacy and Ted walk past, Ted pausing in the hall just outside the living room to make another slicing motion across his neck.

"Let me formally introduce myself," Shari's uncle said. "I'm Bradford Carmen, the patriarch of this family. It's my responsibility to cherish, instruct, and protect every woman who bears the Carmen name."

"Yes, sir." Garrett nodded, avoiding eye contact with Shari's cousins, who were seated on either side of their father.

"You recently moved from Boston. You're thirty years old. A Deputy U.S. Marshal. You play the tenor sax—though I doubt better than my niece." Bradford grunted. "Your parents are Gary and Phoebe. One sister, Deborah; she has one son, Jamal. Her husband is stationed in Iraq..."

It didn't take much to find free or paid-subscription information off the Internet these days, so Garrett didn't flinch. Bradford seemed to be enjoying his oration, and he happily yielded the floor to his rhetoric.

Once the summary was over, Bradford narrowed his eyes. "What doesn't my niece know about you?"

Glad he had already come clean with Shari, he looked the man straight in the eyes. "Absolutely nothing."

Folding his hands, Bradford didn't seem satisfied. "It seems to me that Boston is a great place to live, work, and worship. What prompted you to move to Philly?"

Garrett considered saying that the Lord had sent him there, but Bradford didn't strike him as the type of man who would appreciate a response like that. "I needed a change of scenery, and the Lord opened up doors for me to relocate here."

Shari appeared in the doorway, along with her aunt. *"Sorry,"* she mouthed before striding into the room and reaching for his hand. She tugged him to his feet. "C'mon, let's eat." She wrapped her arm through his.

Bradford cleared his throat as his sons flexed their muscles. "Nash, our conversation is far from over."

"As it should be, Mr. Carmen. With a jewel like Shari, I completely understand your desire to protect her." For the fun of it, Garrett flexed his own muscles.

In the dining room, the scent of lemon furniture polish lingered beneath the aroma of fresh-baked food in various dishes spread out on the table. Meat piled on oval platters served as the centerpieces, with several vegetable sides strategically placed around them. Each place was set with fine china.

Once everyone had taken a seat, Bradford said the blessing, then proceeded to stuff his mouth with creamy mashed potatoes. "What's the name of the church you're from, again?"

As if the man didn't know already. He had probably phoned every pastor from downtown Boston to the outskirts of Dorchester, Roxbury, and so on. And if he'd gotten ahold of the church secretary, then he'd spoken with Brittani's aunt through marriage.

"Blood Redemption Temple," Garrett replied.

"Ever been married? Fathered children? Backslidden from the Lord?"

Shari seemed to sense the tension brewing. "Uncle Bradford, please stop this inquisition."

"She's right, dear." Her aunt tsked. "He's a guest in our home, not a thief breaking into it. I don't think you've allowed him to swallow even one mouthful of my delicious dinner."

Bradford nodded at his wife in a show of humble submission. He waited until Garrett had taken a bite of green beans, chewed, and swallowed before saying, "Explain—"

Camille silenced her husband with a warning glare.

"So, Garrett, man, what college did you attend?" Victor asked, seeming to pick up the interrogation where his father had left off.

"BU," Bradford put in, proving he had all the answers—and then some.

"Boston University is good school, honey," Camille told him. Then she turned to Garrett. "Brother Nash, my niece told me how you two met, but I would love if it you would indulge me with your version."

Victor folded his arms across his chest, and Dino copied him. "Yes, indulge us," Victor echoed.

Garrett stopped eating and met every gaze in turn, then wrapped his hand around Shari's, thankful for its soft warmth. "Shari and I met through the praise band at church. We had been to only one practice together before God put her front and center at my grandparents' anniversary celebration. The way the spotlights reflected off her skin, it was as if the presence of Nefertiti was being announced. I was wowed first by her beauty and talent, and, soon after, by her spiritual commitment."

When he'd finished, Camille sighed wistfully, Stacy smiled, and Shari sniffed. Victor, Dino, and Bradford helped themselves to dessert—pecan-topped sweet potato pie.

Despite the barrage of questions, Garrett connected with the Carmens' sense of family ties. He even appreciated their nosiness, to a point. Yet he was glad when Shari announced that it was time for them to leave. The mystery was whether he had passed or failed.

At Shari's doorstep, he lifted her hands to his mouth and brushed his lips against them. "I don't mind the tough questions," he told her truthfully. "If they keep watching me, all they'll see is how much I truly love you."

She gave him a tender smile. "I'm the only one whose opinion matters."

Garrett guided her chin closer to his face. "My proof will always be in the way I treat you with respect." After kissing her, Garrett pulled back. "'Night, baby."

Chapter Twenty-One

Rain wouldn't damper Garrett s plans for a picnic the following Saturday. After a week of busy days spent capturing more than a dozen fugitives, he was ready for some downtime. He stopped by BoDacious Baskets, a well-known gift shop in West Philly, then headed to Shari's house as the first raindrops spattered on his windshield.

She was waiting on her porch, umbrella in hand. Garrett didn't give her a chance to rescue him as he bounded up the steps with his white wicker basket large enough for a small load of laundry. The boutique owner had assured him that it was jam-packed with delectable items that would delight any lady.

Shari s bright brown eyes, wide smile, and glowing face were all the sunshine he needed on this dreary day. Her sweet perfume tickled his nose. Even casually dressed, she was still as alluring as ever. It didn't matter that he had seen her just hours earlier at band practice—Garrett couldn't get enough of her. Each sighting was fresh.

"I came bearing gifts."

"You must be hungry." Shari giggled as she held the door open for him.

"I brought enough in case Mrs. Carmen wanted to join us for an afternoon snack," he told her as he stepped into the foyer.

"She's visiting the next-door neighbor."

Inside, they created the perfect setting for a picnic by arranging a blanket on the living-room floor. "This is exciting," Shari said. "I've never had an indoor picnic before."

"Neither have I, but I wanted to be with you—rain or shine."

"I love you. You know that?" Shari leaned closer and puckered her lips for a kiss.

After a few moments of bliss, they began their exploration of the basket's contents.

"Ooh, chocolate-covered blueberries and sparkling vanilla pear cider," Shari recited from several labels.

Garrett shifted the fresh fruit around, looking for the meat. "Aha! Sausage and smoked salmon. That's what I'm talking about." He scrutinized the crackers. "Where's the bread?"

Shari laughed. "Evidently, it's a gourmet basket. What did you expect, a sit-down dinner? I'll go grab a couple slices of wheat bread from the kitchen." She returned as he was twisting the cap off the cider bottle. He poured them both an equal portion in the plastic stemware provided in the basket. Once their plates were filled, Garrett took Shari's hands in his and bowed his head.

"Jesus, thank You for this moment with this incredible woman You kept just for me. Thank You for Calvary and for the blood You shed to sanctify our lives. Now I ask You to sanctify our food for the nourishment and enjoyment of our bodies. And, Lord, please remember my grandparents. In Jesus' name, amen."

"Amen," Shari repeated, watching him as she stole the first bite. "How's Grandpa Moses?" she asked softly. A frown etched her brow.

Liking the sound of "Grandpa Moses" on her lips, he couldn't stop his smile, despite the touchy subject she wanted to discuss.

"Brittani's mandate is taking an extra heavy toll on him and my grandma."

"I noticed that your grandpa hasn't called lately during our times together, and while I've appreciated that, I worry about him."

"If Brittani has repented, she needs to do the right thing. As does Landon." Garrett could feel his nostrils flare involuntarily with irritation at hearing his cousin's name, so he took a few moments to inhale and exhale, choosing his next words carefully. "How can this situation have closure unless he steps up and takes responsibility for his actions?"

Shari dabbed her mouth with a napkin, then reached out and patted his hand. "Ecclesiastes four, verse nine: *'Two are better than one.'* I'm here to hold you up because I love you. I'm your prayer partner, your shoulder to lean on."

"Yes, you are, and a beautiful one at that." Garrett snickered, then winked. "I love you far beyond my heart's capacity."

"And you have a big heart."

They ate and chatted a while longer while listening to some gospel music Garrett played on his phone. When they were stuffed, they cleaned up, and then Shari tugged him toward the side patio, where they cuddled together on a porch swing, watching the clouds roll by.

Life is good, Garrett thought, and he believed that Jesus would calm the storms brewing within the Miller family.

Chapter Twenty-Two

After an enjoyable weekend, Shari sat on her bed on Monday evening, reviewing the three-hundred-plus-page file on Jean Pickett. The case was an example of the increasing identity theft epidemic. To date, it was the biggest case Shari had ever taken on. Law enforcement agencies and the IRS had failed her client.

Combing through stacks of paper, Shari learned that Miss Pickett's privacy had been compromised when her social security number had been used to create fake IDs that were sold at flea markets. She was determined to win this federal case, which would mean going up against an attorney from the Department of Justice.

The next morning, Shari dressed in one of her power suits, this one melon-colored with a double-breasted jacket, and her three-inch heels that crushed the pavement as she walked to the Criminal Justice Center. She wished Garrett would be in the courtroom to see her. Then again, maybe not. He would probably fuss at her later on about her shoes. At least she had reduced the additional five inches to just three. She was getting there.

Once she cleared the metal detectors, Shari opted to climb the three flights of stairs instead of squeezing onto a crowded elevator.

It was as if her bouncing curls kept time with each step. Slightly winded, she exited the stairwell onto the third floor seconds before the elevator doors opened and spewed out a slew of riders. She scooted around the sea of colleagues and yanked on the heavy door to Courtroom C.

It had become a habit to check the side seats for any U.S. Marshals. None were present today. It didn't matter. Whether or not she and Garrett saw each other in passing, they would manage to steal a moment to say "I love you" through FaceTime or text messages.

As she walked in, her client stood in the back pew. "Attorney Carmen, I'm ready to put this behind me."

"Me, too," Shari said. "Let's get it done." She conversed with Jean for a few minutes before proceeding past the bar.

When the judge called the Pickett case from the docket, Shari prayed for guidance and justice, then began her show. "Your Honor, our investigation has uncovered at least eighty-three people in twenty-three states using Ms. Pickett's social security number. Sixty-nine of them are illegal immigrants. My client has continued to suffer because the government didn't do its job of tracking and prosecuting these cases. It wasn't until the IRS sent her a bill for seven years' worth of back taxes that she initiated her own probe— a task that the IRS, SSA, and Department of Homeland Security are highly paid to do."

The agent took the stand to defend the procedures of his department, and Shari didn't back down, peppering him with yes or no questions.

"In conclusion, Your Honor, I'm requesting that the Social Security Administration make an exception and issue Jean Pickett a new number. The IRS should pardon all back taxes, clear her credit report, and erase the criminal charges she has incurred due to the fraudulent activities of others operating under her name. I'm asking that Miss Pickett be awarded actual damages of seventy-five thousand dollars for her time and injury to her character and punitive damages of three hundred thousand." Shari was pushing it by asking the government to pay punitive damages, because they normally enjoyed immunity from civil suits, but there were exceptions to every case, and Shari believed in going after every possible loophole.

After Shari spent two days presenting evidence and arguing her point, the court recessed for deliberation. *The* next day, the judge returned with a decision, awarding Jean Pickett the full amount of actual damages and two hundred thousand dollars for punitive damages.

Shari congratulated her client and thanked God for the victory, then texted Garrett to share the news. It felt good to have someone who was excited about what was going on in her life. Within the hour, a stunning arrangement of flowers arrived at her office, along with a card that read,

Victory! I'm sure God was pleased as much as I am proud of you.

—G

Staring at the note, Shari smiled. Garrett's praise was priceless. It meant more to her than the pats on the back from colleagues and even her family's bragging.

At home that evening, it was business as usual: Shari sat on the sofa with her eyes closed, soaking her feet and enjoying some much-needed relaxation. She didn't realize she had dozed off until a husky voice whispered, "Hi there, Sleeping Beauty," in her ear.

She smiled before her eyelids fluttered open. The cologne that tickled her nose was proof that she wasn't dreaming. Shari met Garrett's gaze. "Hi. You caught me again." She sat up and quickly lifted her feet out the tub, then dried them off with a towel, before he could assist her. The consecrated feet-washing he'd given her had been special. She didn't want to diminish the gesture to simply a massage every time he saw her feet soaking in water.

Garrett presented her with a beautifully gift-wrapped box that she hadn't noticed.

"What's this?" She frowned up at him. "You already sent me flowers."

"I sent them only because I couldn't deliver them myself. Now, open this," he ordered her, feigning a threatening voice that only prompted her to smack a kiss on his lips.

Then she did as he'd requested. After parting the layers of red tissue paper inside the oblong box, she gasped as she unearthed a striking figurine. She fingered the outline of the beautiful, classy woman—with skin the shade of chocolate—sitting alone on a bench. Draped in a red fitted dress with ruffles at the knees, the woman sported matching high-heeled shoes that completed her ensemble.

Lifting the foot-long sculpture from its resting place, Shari then picked up the card that had floated to her lap. It was a certificate of authenticity that read, "*Vision in Red*, Limited Edition."

"It's beautiful," she whispered. She leaned closer and kissed his cheek. "Thank you."

His gifts were one-of-a-kind and personal, always calling attention to her appearance or character. They weren't the types of things she ever saw on store shelves. He either must shop at specialty boutiques or order online from stylish websites. Either way, he was far more thoughtful than most men. Shari's eyes watered with emotion as she stared into his.

Reaching for one of her curls, Garrett twisted it around his finger. "I remember one morning when I saw you in the distance, making your way to the courtroom. You were gorgeous in your red suit and rocked your stilettos with every strut. I watched in amusement as other men gave my woman a pause of appreciation. Unfortunately, I couldn't leave my post to greet you. Not long after that, I stumbled upon this piece online, and I ordered it immediately because it captured the image of you that I had seared into my mind."

Shari inhaled deeply to keep from crying as she reflected on the day he had just described. "I haven't worn that suit since, because I lost the case." Bowing her head, Shari exhaled. "I was representing the man who threatened to kill me when we visited the House of Corrections with the prison ministry. It wasn't my fault he failed to appear in court and went on the run, allegedly committing additional crimes, after a warrant was issued for his arrest."

Garrett lifted her chin with his forefinger. "No sad stories today, Attorney Carmen."

"You're right." Despite her losses, she still had more than her share of victories.

They were a breath away from indulging in a kiss when his smartphone played a symphony melody. It wasn't his grandfather's ringtone, and they both sighed with relief.

Huffing, Garrett detached the device from his belt. "Hold that position, baby," he mumbled. "It's my sister."

Shari was about to stand, anyway, but Garrett tugged her back down onto the couch. As he listened to Deborah, he frowned, and then his eyes glazed over before an expression of panic raced across his face. "I'm on my way." He ended the call and jumped to his feet.

Shari's heart sank. "What's wrong?"

"Grandpa was rushed to the hospital with chest pains. He's...in a coma." Frantically, he dug in his pant pocket for his car keys. "I'm catching the next flight home."

"Book two tickets," Shari told him. "I'm coming with you."

Chapter Twenty-Three

*I*t took Garrett half the usual time to get back to his condo. His packing consisted of stuffing pants and shirts—hangers and all—into a duffel bag, whether they matched or not. His mind raced as he logged on to his iPad and booked two flights to Boston. He had no idea whether Shari could stay for the whole weekend, but it didn't matter. He simply appreciated her presence.

Shari was the bright spot in the middle of his chaos, and she was willing to put everything on hold in order to support him and his family as they dealt with the stress of Brittani's shenanigans.

"Jesus, I don't have the right mind-set for prayer right now, but please send Your angels to my grandfather's side to minister to his needs. Lord, show up and show out in that hospital room, so that folks will know You are a healer. In Jesus' name, amen."

There is a time and a season. Circumstances happen to all, but I will deliver My people out of all of them. God reminded him of Ecclesiastes 9, which gave him comfort.

Mrs. Carmen dropped Shari off at his condo an hour later. Garrett did his best to keep up the pretense that he had his emotions under wraps.

Standing in the doorway with a small carry-on, Shari took a

deep breath, then exhaled. "Ready."

When he stepped back to let her in, Shari wrapped her arms around his waist and snuggled her head beneath his chin as he just held her. "Jesus, please give him strength," she whispered.

Shari offered to drive his SUV to the airport, and he accepted. As they rode, he called his parents for an update but was sent straight to voicemail. He tried his sister—voicemail. Next, he was able to reach his uncle.

The grief-stricken tone to the older man's voice got to him. "Moses has been drifting in and out of consciousness, but he's still alive, praise Jesus." He paused. "He's still alive. He keeps mumbling, asking for the twins..."

Garrett gritted his teeth. *Not the twins again.* It took all of the Holy Ghost within him not to yield to a fleshly outburst. He wanted to wring Brittani's neck and repent later. But scheming about and practicing premeditated sin wasn't part of his lifestyle. This was simply another test whose outcome was known by Jesus.

"Moses is also asking for Shari," his uncle stated.

Really? That was a shocker. He glanced at the woman who had captured not only his heart but also his grandfather's. It was bittersweet to see her concentrating on the road ahead, having no idea that she had been summoned. "We're on our way, Unc. See everybody when we get there."

Once Garrett ended the call, he closed his eyes and buried his face in his hands. Thank God he had a strong heart, or he might be lying in the bed beside his grandfather's. Without saying a word, Shari rubbed his back with soothing strokes whenever they were stopped at a red light.

"All this is happening because I let that woman into my life," he mumbled.

"Sweetie, everyone has thorns in life. Brittani was one of yours, but God already has the end planned out. It will be okay," she said softly.

Garrett nodded, trying to believe in his heart what he knew in his head. He couldn't comprehend this turn of events. Hours earlier, he was happy and in love, looking forward to a blissful future. Now, it felt like he had been tossed in the middle of a hurricane that was building to a category ten.

This can't be happening. Even though he was well into his seventies, Moses Miller was strong and in good health with a never-ending supply of wit and godly wisdom. Garrett couldn't fathom a life without his sidekick and spiritual advisor. *Lord, I'm not ready for him to leave us yet...*

"Babe, we're here," Shari whispered.

Garrett blinked his eyes open as they turned into the long-term parking lot at Philadelphia International Airport. She eased the car into a space, turned off the ignition, and handed him his keys.

Taking a deep breath, he nodded and went through the motions of getting out, retrieving their bags from the backseat, and linking hands with Shari for the walk to the terminal. She had to remind him to lock the car and activate the alarm, which he did like a zombie.

Garrett was glad that Shari had chosen low, sensible heels as her footwear as they hurried toward the check-in line.

The nonstop flight to Boston took off without delay. Shari was silent, allowing him space for his thoughts. He glanced over and saw her watching him. As always, Garrett was struck by her beauty and by the calming effect of her presence. "I love you."

"I know." She rested her head on his shoulder, and he returned to his thoughts.

Lord, if my grandfather dies as a result of this mess, help me to refrain from committing double murder.

Chapter Twenty-Four

Shari could empathize with Garrett s anxiety over the prospect of losing a loved one. When her father had died instantly from a massive heart attack, eliminating the chance for anyone to say good-bye, the sudden loss had forced her into a state of deep depression for months that had turned into years.

She blinked, realizing that it wasn't until she played "Thank You" for Garrett's grandparents' anniversary celebration that the hairline fracture that had lingered in her heart had finally healed. Without realizing it, she'd been praising God for the blessing that she hadn't yet received.

When U.S. Air Flight 1715 landed at Logan Airport and had taxied to the gate, Garrett leaped up before most of the other passengers had unbuckled their seat belts. He was already inching down the aisle away from Shari when she called out, "Uh, Garrett?"

He whipped his head around, looking annoyed that someone was interrupting his mission, until his eyes connected with hers. He hurried back to her with a sheepish expression. "Sorry, babe. Forgive me?"

"Forgiven and forgotten for always." Unbuckling her belt, she reached for her things as Garrett tugged her out of her seat.

"C'mon." He nudged her forward, barely offering apologies to the passengers he urged to get out of his way. They hurried through the airport terminal as if they were trying to catch a connecting flight instead of a cab to the hospital to join his family in their prayer vigil.

Before the taxi came to a complete stop at the curb, Garrett was already opening the door for Shari. "Brookline Ave., Beth Israel Deaconess Medical Center," he told the driver. "As quick as you can get us there."

The taxi lurched away from the curb before they were settled. The ride was uneventful—if they didn't count the three red lights the cabbie ran, the two pedestrians he nearly mowed down, or his constant conversation with himself. Clearly, he had missed his calling as an Indy car driver.

Shari snuggled closer to Garrett as they flew past a series of historic landmarks. She hoped that Garrett would one day bring her back here for a tour. "I know this is tearing you apart, but I'm here to help put you back together again, if I can," she told him. "I love you, G, and everything that's connected with you—especially your family."

"I know." He kissed her hair.

Despite the harrowing ride, Shari and Garrett arrived at their destination in one piece. After collecting the fare, the driver dumped them and their luggage at the curb, then sped away. Garrett's mad rush to the hospital suddenly came to a shrieking halt. He took a deep breath as he gazed up at the imposing complex of buildings.

Shari leaned into him. "Ready?"

Although he nodded, Garrett didn't make a move, so Shari gently tugged him toward the historic-looking entrance, which clashed with the modern additions and renovations. They walked through the lobby to the bank of elevators and joined others waiting to get on. Once they stepped inside, Garrett pushed the number seven.

As he and Shari exited the elevator, the gleaming white floor tiles almost blinded them. The corridor was deserted. Without moving another step, Garrett took a deep breath. "Baby, let's pray." He took Shari's hands in his. "Lord, in the name of Jesus, once again I'm trusting You. Help me to accept Your will in our lives. I thank You for blessing me with Shari to love. I love Grandpa, too. Prepare us, prepare me..."

No sooner had they said "Amen" than several people spilled out from a door at the end of the hall. Once they spotted her and Garrett, they raced in their direction.

Shari's heart sank as they hugged Garrett and wept. They barely acknowledged her, but she wasn't offended. She understood. *Lord, please tell me Moses hasn't passed away.*

"I want to see him," Garrett demanded.

At that moment, the Holy Ghost stirred within Shari, advising her to proceed with caution. With Garrett's hand gripping hers, she counted the steps to the double doors of the ICU. Inside the private room, at least ten people were gathered around Moses's bed. Her heart ached for the family. Queen sat beside her husband, clinging to his hand. Deborah and several other faces she didn't recognize were clustered on either side. Jamal and a few other cousins were posted at the foot of the bed.

One of the family members—a good-looking young man—turned to Shari and gave her an appreciative perusal. He seemed detached from the anxiety in the room. She remembered seeing him at the anniversary celebration. That had to be Landon, Garrett's unscrupulous cousin—the Judas of this precious family.

"Ah, just in time for prayer," said a thin man with a well-groomed mustache and beard standing next to Landon. He wore a white minister's collar, which contrasted starkly with his pecan skin and piercing dark eyes.

"With bowed heads, let us call on the Almighty," the man instructed the group.

Seconds into the prayer, Shari felt that something wasn't right. She listened a few moments longer before popping her head up. "Stop the chanting," she ordered with authority.

"What?" The word rippled through the group as all heads turned to Shari, their faces showing shock and frowns of displeasure at her untimely outburst.

Even Garrett gave her a questioning expression. "What's wrong, baby?"

"Do not lay hands on him!" Shari could feel the spiritual tug-of-war between the man's dark spirit and hers.

"What do you think you're doing?" Landon demanded. "You have no right to come in here and speak with Minister Bey—"

"Shut up, Landon," Garrett practically growled as he balled his hands into fists.

"Shari, what's going on?" Queen asked her.

While she was praying, Shari had sensed the presence of shadows circling the minister, and she'd watched without opening her eyes as dark, formless figures had attempted to attach themselves to Moses. She lifted her chin regally and narrowed her eyes at the minister. "He's not a man of God. The blood of Jesus is against you, demon."

All eyes glared at the man with Landon, whose expression never changed. His hands were still folded in prayer. "I'm a licensed minister."

"Who ordained you?" Shari demanded.

"I received certification online."

Gasps echoed around the room. Then chaos exploded, prompting two nurses to show up and hush them.

"Why would you bring such a man in here?" Garrett's uncle demanded of his son. "Haven't you wreaked enough havoc in this family?"

Landon shrugged. "I didn't know."

"The anointing of the Lord is against you and all the demons that accompanied you here," Shari told him. "Let the saints begin to pray." She closed her eyes, but her spiritual vision was vigilant as she stretched forth her hand toward Landon and the decoy minister.

In full force, their voices rebuked any demonic spirits that lingered. As the prayers grew louder, the children began to scream, "Send him back! Send him back!"

Shari heard God say to her, *You wrestle not against flesh and blood, but against principalities, against powers, against the rulers of the darkness of this world, against spiritual wickedness in high places.*

Ephesians 6:12 was manifested before their presence as they all witnessed the Lord's angels pushing the dark forms away from the bed and forcing them out the room. Calmness descended around Shari as she opened her eyes. Landon and his friend were gone— MIA. She placed one hand on Moses's chest and continued to call on the name of Jesus. Others followed her lead until she whispered, "In Jesus' name, amen."

The prayer was then transformed into praise and worship.

Several minutes later, Deborah planted her hands on her hips and scowled. "We chase off one devil, and another walks in." Shari turned to see a tall and very pretty woman who glided into the room with a grand entrance like it was her God-given right. The only clue of her identity was the double stroller she pushed with two identical infants inside. *Brittani.*

Shari held her breath. No wonder Garrett had fallen for her. From her innocent look, there was no hint that she could have been the mastermind behind Garrett's heartache. Shari didn't know whether she should begin to pray again in defense of the love she had for her man. And for now, God was silent on the matter.

Paying no mind to the motionless figure in the hospital bed, Brittani scanned the faces of those standing around her until she met Garrett's gaze. He was watching her but hadn't said a word. His expression was unreadable as he squeezed Shari's hand so hard, it nearly cut off circulation. When she gasped, he loosened his grip.

"Sorry, baby."

Brittani glanced at Shari with a sneer before returning her eyes to her ex. "I'm sorry about Papa Moses," she said softly. "I brought the twins in hopes that their presence would help him mend faster."

As if the moment had been staged, a faint moan escaped from Moses's lips. His groans grew louder as he struggled to lift his eyelids. Squinting, he tried to focus, his eyes moving rapidly.

"Dad," "Grandpa," and other terms of endearment were shouted around the room as everyone clambered closer for a better view.

Moses gripped the sides of his bed, trying to sit up. Evidently, he was too weak. Several family members tried to assist him, but Queen shooed them away. Then, sniffing, she bowed her head. No one had to guess that she was sending up prayers of thanks. Tears fell from her eyes.

"You gave us a scare, old man," Moses's younger brother mumbled.

"Honey..." Queen sobbed as she stroked her husband's hand and arm, both of which were severely bruised from the numerous IVs that had been unmercifully implanted in his veins.

There was not one face that wasn't wet with tears. Shari cast a peek at Brittani and saw that even her eyes were misty. Garrett relaxed his shoulders and the creases that had marred his forehead vanished. He studied his grandfather and smiled, then glanced over his shoulder at Brittani and scowled.

Shari cleared her throat. The fireworks had been lit. "I'm going to find the ladies' room," she said, wanting to escape before an explosion erupted. But then she had second thoughts.

As if granting her permission, Garrett released her hand and dismissed her with a nod. His nostrils flared as he jammed fists on his hips. His family members stood motionless, their eyes on Brittani, evidently waiting for her to advance her agenda. Shari silently prayed that the showdown between Garrett and his former fiancée would exorcise his demons and end his heartrending torture.

So what if women like Brittani graced the covers of glamour magazines? So what if Brittani stood regally. Her figure was shapely, even after spitting out two sons. So what if short, sassy hair highlighted her exotic features? So what if Garrett had proposed to her? Shari couldn't stop her heart from pounding, but she could clear her mind. Straightening her shoulders, she quietly excused herself again and focused on finding the ladies' room, refusing to let the devil suck the joy out of her.

Chapter Twenty-Five

Garrett had to gather his thoughts before speaking. He had already said everything he needed to say to Brittani the night he'd confronted her about the affair—the night she had "explained" her compromising position in the affair.

"I'm surprised to see you here, considering..." He walked slowly toward Brittani, forcing her into the hallway. "You need to repent on the spot. Refusing to allow my grandfather the courtesy of seeing his great-grandsons unless they were Millers...how mean-spirited can you be?"

She looked wounded. "I'm not a bad person, Garrett."

"You're just not faithful."

Pouting, Brittani shifted her stance. "You never gave me another chance. It just happened—once. I was never attracted to Landon. I never wanted him. I still don't, but my sons need a father. And Landon...well, he's not father material. I've already begged you to forgive me and asked you to spare me the shame of my indiscretion."

Garrett couldn't mistake the pleading in her eyes. But all he felt was compassion—none of the attraction or love he'd once had for Brittani. His heart had room for only one woman, and Shari now occupied that space. He lowered his voice. "Brittani, don't make your sons pay for your sins. I'm not the one to rescue you. Only Jesus can do that."

"And you said you would love me no matter what," she muttered. "Liar."

He grunted. The woman was delusional if she thought he was going to allow her to flip the script on him. "Although you were once my choice for a wife, you were never God's choice for me. The Lord has since sent me a beautiful woman whom I plan to ask to marry me and to have my babies."

"Shari," he heard his grandfather mumble faintly.

"Excuse me." As Garrett went in search of Shari, he thanked God again for sending him the right woman. Telling someone that you no longer loved them was hurtful, and he'd felt bad to be the bearer of that news to Brittani, but he no longer had feelings for her. His only prayer was that she would do right by her twins and by the Miller family. Landon was another story.

Garrett overheard Shari and Landon talking before he turned the corner. He was about to intervene, but the woman who was a spitfire in the courtroom was holding her own with his cousin. So, Garrett folded his arms and stayed on the sidelines.

"You're incredible," Landon said, trying to flirt. "I had no idea that—"

"Save it." Shari lifted her hand. "Evidently, when you backslid with Garrett's fiancée, you didn't repent, because seven-plus demons now possess you."

"Wait a minute—"

"No, time's up. In the name of Jesus, I bind the spirits that have overtaken you—lust, sexual perversion, defiling God's temple with drugs and alcohol..."

What? Garrett blinked. How did she know the dirt on Landon? Then it dawned on Garrett that his baby was operating under the influence of the Holy Ghost.

"Repent, Landon," she ordered him.

Before his eyes, Landon's body shook with convulsions as if something from within fought to escape. Suddenly, the trembling stopped. Landon composed himself, and had the nerve to smirk as he relaxed against the wall. He folded his arms as if they had been involved in a pleasant conversation for the last few minutes. "Hmm. So, you have the gift of discernment," he stated in a mocking tone.

Shari frowned. "I have received power from the Holy Ghost, and, as you are aware, with that comes many gifts, including the discerning of spirits. Repent, Landon, because those demons want to destroy you. Talk to your pastor and live."

As Shari tried to step past Landon, he moved out from the wall and blocked her path.

She balled her hands into fists. "You do not want to mess with a Carmen. Trust me."

"Or with the man who loves her," Garrett said, making his presence known. He had seen enough. "You and Brittani are a piece of work. God spared you a beat down once before, but I can't guarantee He'll help you this time."

"Babe," Shari said softly, touching his shoulder.

Garrett curved his arm around Shari's waist and brushed his lips against her hair, all the while keeping an eye on his cousin. This woman belonged to him. "Are you okay?"

"Yeah, I'm fine, Cuz," Landon joked. "Can you believe that guy? I escorted him out—"

"Not you, Landon. My baby. Speaking of babies, I think Brittani is looking for you."

Landon held up both hands. "Oh, no. She seduced me—"

"Do I look stupid to you? I'm no fool, Landon. But you are a regular whoremonger. Instead of preserving yourself for marriage, you're making women's lives miserable with your lust," Garrett snarled in disgust. This time he was ready for a fight.

Shari calmed him by rubbing his back. "You won, G. The Lord fought your battle and won. Your cousin is just the remnants. Let God finish the cleanup."

Shari was right. Garrett nodded and took his eyes off Landon for the first time in several minutes. "You're right. C'mon, Grandpa wants to see you."

"Cool." Landon stepped forward. "We'd better—"

"Wrong again." Garrett scowled at him. "Not you but Shari."

There was a haunting undertone to Landon's laughter. Despite the Lord's having called him out using Shari as a mouthpiece, his cockiness had returned, magnified. He acted like he hadn't a care in the world.

"You really have no fear of God, do you?" Garrett shook his head. "There's a chapel somewhere in this hospital, Landon. Find it and stay on your knees until God delivers you."

Then he and Shari wrapped their arms around each other, turned their backs on Landon, and started back to his grandfather's room.

At the door, Jamal raced to greet Shari as if she was his hero. His face was bright with excitement. "He's going to be okay." He dragged her to the bed.

Moses's eyes flickered as he appeared to gather strength. "Th...thank you," he said, pointing to Shari. "I heard you...praying." His voice faded. The family remained silent, waiting to see if he would speak again. Moses's speech was slurred, but he struggled to get the words out. "The devil had me bound... Couldn't move... The doctors gave me up, but God's army battled with the devil's angels for my soul."

"And we won, Grandpa!" Jamal shouted, his wide grin showing his missing tooth. He jumped up and down, pumping his fists in the air.

Shari patted the family patriarch on the shoulder, then began massaging his arm, careful of the IV tubes. "I'm glad I could be here for you, Grandpa Moses. Now get some rest."

"I've rested enough. Garrett?" He strained his voice as he squinted, focusing on every face.

"Yes, sir. I'm right here." He bent and kissed his grandfather's forehead.

"You pro...prose to her yet?"

Shari blushed as Garrett glanced over his shoulder. "No, sir, any minute now."

"Good," his grandfather mumbled before drifting back to sleep.

Chapter Twenty-Six

Shari's heart fluttered, not so much because of what Garrett said but what his grandfather had asked. How had she managed to be so blessed to have found favor with his family?

She and Garrett followed the others to the family waiting room in order to give Queen some quiet time with her husband. Feeling drained, Shari sat next to Garrett on a sofa and snuggled under his arm. She smiled to herself. Any minute now she would be an engaged woman. How long would that take? She was still wondering to herself as she drifted off.

When Garrett disentangled himself from her and stood. She blinked, then stretched.

"Babe, let's go," he suggested. "I was going to check you into a hotel, but Deborah has offered her spare bedroom. I would prefer that."

It didn't matter to Shari. All she wanted was a bed. "Okay."

After checking on Grandpa Moses, Shari and Deborah walked ahead of Garrett, who carried his sleeping nephew in one arm and his carry-on in the other.

By the time they arrived at Deborah's house in Roxbury, Shari was wide awake. Garrett hugged and kissed her good-bye, then left for his parents' house. Deborah showed Shari to the guest room, which was decorated like a scene from a bed-and-breakfast magazine, with a tall four-poster bed, a mahogany side table and coordinating chair, and an upholstered bench at the foot of the bed.

Before retiring, Shari left a voicemail message for her law clerk to ask for a continuance on a case she was due to represent in court. When Shari said the words "family emergency," she paused. Garrett's family had become hers, even without an engagement ring. "I plan to be back in the office on Monday," she said before concluding the message.

After getting ready for bed, she climbed under the downy-soft sheets and grabbed her Bible. The Lord led her to read Matthew 12:29-31:

Or else how can one enter into a strong man's house, and spoil his goods, except he first bind the strong man? And then he will spoil his house. He that is not with me is against me; and he that gathers not with me scatters abroad. Wherefore I say unto you, all manner of sin and blasphemy shall be forgiven unto men: but the blasphemy against the Holy Ghost shall not be forgiven unto men.

"Jesus, what are You trying to tell me?" Shari wanted to make sure she had a complete understanding.

No man can steal from you unless he binds you, God whispered.

Sliding to her knees, Shari petitioned Jesus on behalf of the Miller family—including Landon that he would repent. She finished and was about to climb in bed again when Garrett texted her.

I just wanted to thank you for coming and to remind you how much I love you. Sleep well. Hugs and kisses, G

Shari grinned. Love you, too. More hugs and more kisses.

As soon as her head hit the pillow, she started dreaming about Garrett until she heard a noise. It sounded like an animal, but Deborah didn't have any pets.

The night-light in the corner gave the room a soft glow. She scooted up and looked to the right, where a hissing sound seemed to come from. A dark figure was standing over her. It wasn't an outline of a person but a formless spirit—maybe the same one she had cast out of Grandpa Moses' hospital room.

Whatever the thing was, it was powerful as it tried to bind her to the bed, immobilizing her body. Then she remembered the Scripture God had given her earlier. The only thing she could move was her mouth.

"Satan, I bind you in the name of Jesus. The Lord rebukes you, so flee..." She continued calling on the blood of Jesus until the spirit loosened its hold and vanished before her eyes.

Some demons come out only by fasting and prayer. God's words seemed to rattle the windows like thunder as He spoke Matthew 17:21.

Shari blinked as she registered what had actually happened. It definitely hadn't been a dream, because she was wide-awake. Immediately, she thanked the Lord for sparing her life and that of Garrett's grandfather. But the demon Landon had brought to the hospital was strong, and if she hadn't acted as God had instructed her to when that man had been chanting, then he probably would have taken Grandpa Moses' life.

She decided to fast, which would mean forgoing the big breakfast Deborah had promised in the morning before heading to the hospital. "Jesus, thank You for leading me on this battlefield." She looked over her shoulder one more time. Even though her rebuke had caused the demon to flee, the encounter had her shaken up so that she couldn't fall back to sleep right away. As she lay awake, Shari debated calling Garrett. While she didn't want to wake him, she needed to hear his voice.

"Hey, baby," he said when he answered, his speech slurred with slumber. Now she wished she hadn't disturbed him. "Is everything okay?"

"It is now." She went on to explain in detail what had happened.

"Do you need me to come over there?" Now his voice was strong and fully alert.

"No, but we need to fast and pray without ceasing. Your grandfather isn't out of the woods yet. In the morning, I'll call my mother and tell her to activate the prayer band and to notify my sisters. The devil is about to go down!"

Garrett chuckled. "I love my little spitfire. If I were a demon, I would be very, very afraid. Okay, we've got this. I'll be praying for you to get some rest. See you in the morning, babe."

"Yes, in Jesus' name. Night." Shari rolled over. She drifted back to sleep with one eye open.

After Shari's phone call, Garrett couldn't sleep. He blamed his cousin Landon for bringing the seven demons around his family. He was not about to let them win by taking his grandfather *and* his woman. Getting out of bed, Garrett grabbed his Bible and began to read, rebuking the devil. When he couldn't keep his eyes open any longer, he climbed back in bed and fell fast asleep.

The next morning, Garrett prayed while he showered and dressed, then called to check on Shari. She assured him that she'd slept like a baby. En route to his sister's house, he called Deborah and told her what had happened.

"What! You mean the devil had the nerve to enter my house while I was there? Shari should have come and awakened me."

"She handled it with prayer, but the Lord told her that the only way to fight this is with prayer and fasting. That means Shari and I will be skipping breakfast this morning. Sorry."

"I'm in," Deborah told him. "I'll just fix Jamal something light. Once you get here, we'll pray and then head to the hospital."

"Sounds like a plan."

Garrett grinned. His sister was probably already on the phone, calling or sending texts to other family members and telling them to pray and fast. Shari was right—those demons were going down. Twenty minutes later, he pulled in front of Deborah's row house and parked. He jumped out of his SUV and hiked up the front steps two at a time.

He didn't even knock, because Jamal had already opened the door when he reached the porch. "Hi, Uncle G. Momma and Miss Shari are in the back praying." He took a bite of toast smothered with jelly.

Garrett's stomach growled, but he shook his head, summoning his resolve. He planned to punish his flesh today. After closing the front door and locking it, he headed to the family room to join his sister and Shari. The sounds of voices lifted in prayer drew him closer. He didn't waste any time falling to his knees and crying out to Jesus. Soon, he felt Jamal's body slump against him.

"Jesus, please make my great-grandfather better," Jamal interjected his own prayer request, evidently recognizing the seriousness of his relative's condition.

They lost track of time as God descended in their presence and filled their mouths with holy language until they all were speaking in other tongues to Jesus. No interpretation was necessary; they all were of one accord in their intercession for Grandpa Moses.

Chapter Twenty-Seven

*A*t Logan Airport the next morning, Shari lost track of the number of times Garrett hugged her and told her how much he loved her as they said good-bye. He probably would have felt no shame at all if she missed her flight home because of her insistence on stopping by the hospital one more time to check on his grandfather. Grandpa Moses had been resting comfortably and looking better.

"Any minute now," Garrett said, his eyes reflecting all his love for her.

"I'll be waiting." She tapped a kiss to his lips, waved good-bye, and entered the security check-in line. "God, You are truly great."

It's because of Calvary that you have the victory, Jesus whispered as she boarded the plane back home.

Already dressed for church, Shari arrived in Philly with plenty of time to make it to church for the morning worship. Stacy, Ted, and her mother met her at the airport. They exchanged hugs, and Ted took her carry-on.

"You did the right thing, going with Brother Nash," her mother told her. "How is his grandfather this morning?"

"Mr. Miller is greatly improved, to the rejoicing of his family, praise God." Shari lifted a hand in the air. "He's out of the ICU and in a private room."

"Yes!" Stacy and Ted exchanged a high five.

Looping her arm through her mother's, Shari followed her sister and brother-in-law to their vehicle.

"Judging by your smile and glow, Brother Miller must be as good as healed," Ted stated as he maneuvered his car out of the parking garage.

When Shari looked up, she noticed him eyeing her in the rearview mirror. "Let's hope so. Plus, Garrett is going to propose." Shari squeezed her eyes closed at the thought, feeling excited beyond measure.

"'Going to'? Why didn't he already?" Ted demanded. "Do the Carmen men and I need to have a talk with him?"

Her brother-in-law took his role as protector of the Carmen sisters very seriously, although she found it quite comical. "There's no need." She chuckled. "It will happen *any minute now*."

"We have good news all around," Stacy said slyly.

Frowning, Shari leaned forward. "What's going on?"

Stacy shrugged. "Oh, nothing. Just don't miss our sister video chat tomorrow. Now we can add your being almost engaged to the agenda. Maybe you'll be betrothed in a few days and married in a week."

"I doubt if Garrett is going to rush it."

"He's saved, isn't he?" Ted asked.

Shari nodded. "But what does that have to do with it?"

"Then he won't be able to wait."

Stacy slapped her husband's hand. "Dirty mind."

"Just keepin' it real." Ted smirked as he chauffeured them the rest of the way to the church, humming an off-key rendition of "Here Comes the Bride."

Chapter Twenty-Eight

$\mathcal{W}$ith his grandfather on the mend, Garrett was ready to get back to Philly. His job could wait, but he had to see Shari. She was too far from his reach.

For the first time since he'd relocated, Garrett planned to attend his former home church, where he would give thanks to God for His mercy and grace and for the gift of the Holy Ghost. Whether Brittani or Landon decided to make an appearance at the service or not, Garrett would have praise in his mouth.

Surprisingly, more than a few members welcomed him back with open arms as they asked about his grandfather. Some were the very people who had cast judgmental glances at him when the rumor had surfaced that his fiancée was pregnant with his baby, despite his denial. What a difference a few months made! None of them asked for his forgiveness, but Garrett was at peace enough to forgive them in his heart, anyway.

Settling in the pew with several other family members, Garrett pre-pared to hear the Word preached by his former pastor, who was already standing at the podium, welcoming visitors.

"Today's sermon comes from First Samuel fifteen, verse twenty-two," Bishop Jackson announced. "God makes it plain that obedience is better than—preferred to—any sacrifice. The trade-off is that He will not withhold any good thing from us. He loves us too much. At times, however, God does require a sacrifice on our part. We must not be selfish by refusing to part with anything we hold dear. There is nothing we have that is greater than His sacrifice on the cross for us..."

That passage seemed more relevant this morning than Garrett remembered when it was preached years ago. Without knowing what blessings awaited him in Philly, he praised Jesus that he had been obedient to His voice.

He shuddered to think what turn of events his life might have taken if he had stayed in Boston, expecting God to remove Landon and Brittani from his life. In hindsight, that had been a ridiculous assumption, considering that Landon was family.

When Bishop Jackson closed his Bible, the congregation stood for the altar call, a summons to those who knew they weren't saved and who wanted to accept the Lord's salvation. His former pastor's plea was just as passionate as it had always been when Garrett had attended here. Souls repented and requested baptism by water and fire in Jesus' name.

Garrett didn't linger long after the benediction. The only thing on his mind was picking out an engagement ring for Shari that was as exquisite as she. For the next two days, he split his time between the hospital, monitoring his grandfather's recovery, and several jewelers, shopping for a ring.

The search proved more challenging than anticipated. He visited three respected jewelers in the Boston area, but nothing caught his eye. Frustration began to nag at him. He didn't want to return to Philly empty-handed.

As he was parking his mother's car in the driveway of his childhood home, his smartphone played its generic tone. He smiled when he saw John Whitman's name on the caller ID.

"What's up, bro?"

John said, "I'm calling to check in on your grandfather, on your reception at Blood Redemption Temple, and on Bishop Jackson. I wasn't the only one missing your presence in the bandstand on Sunday. Under her smile, Shari looked lost without you, so I advise you to hurry back." He chuckled.

"I miss her, too—one more day, and then I'll see my lady." Garrett smiled. "My Grandpa is steadily regaining his strength." He paused and twisted his lips. He was still exasperated over the fruitless ring search. "I'm a little bummed, though, because I've been shopping for an engagement ring, and nothing seems to hold my attention."

"Man, I'm sure you'll find something on Jewelers' Row on Sansom Street here in Philly. It ranks up there with New York's Diamond District. Even Edgar Allen Poe's engraver resided at seven thirty-two Sansom." John sounded like a sales rep.

Although Garrett had wanted to buy the ring in Beantown, where he'd grown up, he figured the Philly jewelers were worth a try. "I'd rather have the ring in hand when I propose, but if this place is what you say it is, per-haps Shari and I will just go there together. One thing is certain: By this time next week, I plan to be an engaged man."

John grunted. "What took you so long? Rita and I saw it coming all along."

"Sure you did," Garrett joked.

Once they had ended the call, Garrett reflected on the amazing sequence of unpredictable events in his life. Who would have thought that he would be asking two different women to marry him, and within the span of two years?

Of course, Brittani hadn't had a clue that a proposal was coming. They were strolling through Morris Arboretum, admiring the colorful foliage along the trail, before stopping at the waterfall.

Garrett suggested they rest, and when they settled on a stone wall, he got on one knee and proposed.

"I guess this time around, it could be fun to do it differently," he said to himself as he grabbed his Bible. Although he had heard various people claim to have found their "soul mate," he hadn't understood them until now, knowing that God had caused their paths to intersect at a designated moment—not a minute too soon or too late. God's timing was perfect.

Garrett flipped the pages until he reached the book of Proverbs. He skipped over the popular eighteenth chapter, where it stated a man who finds a wife is a good thing. Finding a wife was the easy part. He should know, having had two chances. Now he was searching for something deeper. He flipped back a few pages and found it in Proverbs 5:18: *"Let thy fountain be blessed: and rejoice with the wife of thy youth."*

He studied each word. He wanted a consecrated life and a long marriage with Shari. His parents had been married for thirty-five years, and his grandparents were going on fifty-one. He reread the passage, then meditated on it, trying to apply it to his own life.

Finally, he knelt by his bed and prayed. "Lord, thank You for walking with me throughout my life. I know it was You who changed my course. Help me to be the head that my wife can honor. Guide us to give You the glory through our marriage. Bless us with many children to come through her womb. In Jesus' name, amen."

I will bless you. I will bless her womb. I will bless your children, God whispered to his spirit.

Although God's presence made Garrett tremble in reverence, he smiled. He couldn't wait to be a married man.

Shari's heart pounded as she stepped into the courtroom. Garrett wouldn't be there; he was still in Boston. Her focus was to keep her two clients, both young black nineteen-year-olds, out of jail. They had told her that they had been the victims of police profiling because of their race.

Once they had explained the situation in detail, Shari had come to believe them, and now she hoped to convince the judge to reach the same conclusion. Her mission was to save innocent black men from entering the prison system.

When the bailiff called her case, Shari approached Judge Halston with confidence. "Your Honor, my clients' civil rights were violated when officers Campbell and Brown used the 'jump out' tactic to intimidate the defendants because they believed the two looked suspicious by the way they were dressed."

The "jump out" ploy was supposedly successful in snagging unsuspecting drug dealers, catching them off guard. Officers would cruise up in an unmarked police car and ask for drugs, weapons, or cash. But the scheme also sometimes framed innocent citizens such as her clients.

"The police had no probable cause to believe these two defendants were drug dealers or criminals of any sort. They simply saw two young black men standing outside and targeted them..."

The judge called for an hour recess and then returned with a verdict: case dismissed. Shari silently praised God for the victory. Two down, thousands more innocent people to go.

Although it had been a long day in court, she smiled when she checked her phone and saw Garrett's text.

Landed.

Chapter Twenty-Nine

*A*lthough choosing between Gods business versus personal business was a no-brainer, Shari would have preferred to be anywhere except on the church van with the other prison ministry members.

Shari had pouted when she'd broken the news to Garrett that they would have to reschedule their weekend date. "Saturday is our last prison ministry outing of the season," she'd explained. "It's been a couple of years since I've been to the Edna Mahan Correctional Facility in Clinton, New Jersey, but the women there are hungry for self-help books and inspiration."

"Okay. At least after Xena's incident at Bayside State, I'm glad Pastor Underwood banned you and the other sisters from setting foot inside another all-male prison," Garrett had admitted. "Be careful just the same. Men aren't the only violent offenders."

"I will be careful, and prayerful, too," Shari had promised him before they'd said good night.

Now, settling into her seat for the hour-and-a-half ride across the state line for their final mission of the year, Shari stared out the window at the passing scenery as they traveled north on Route 31. She had a lot to be thankful for, including Grandpa Moses's improving health. She had seen firsthand how the devil had afflicted Landon and Brittani's minds. No wonder God had removed Garrett physically from the situation.

Garrett. Despite the chaos around him, he had found a way to love again, and he had chosen her. "God had handpicked you for me before I even opened my eyes to see you," Garrett had told her during a late-night phone call.

She had never been happier. Her eyes filled with tears of gratitude. *Thank You, Jesus, for looking out for my behalf,* she mused.

Since Garrett's return four days earlier, she had been waiting for him to hint at when he might propose. If she hadn't needed to fulfill this commitment, would today have been the day? Nothing would keep her from saying yes. One perk of marrying Garrett, besides getting a praying husband, would be to gain praying in-laws.

She wanted to text or talk to Garrett, but he would only serve as a distraction, and she had to deny herself that pleasure for now. Going into the enemy's camp required fasting, prayer, and spiritual discernment if she wanted to expect God to manifest wickedness before her eyes as He had at the hospital. Refocusing on the mission at hand, Shari opened her Bible and began to study the Scriptures.

Soon the van turned off 1-78 onto 30 County Road. An antiquated-looking brick mansion came into view, with wide stone front steps and twin gaslights offering a mock warm welcome to visitors.

The grounds resembled the campus of a small rural college, and anyone who didn't know better might have wondered if he had stumbled upon the nearby Beaver Brook Country Club. But Edna Mahan was New Jersey's only all-female correctional facility.

"This is one cool correctional palace if you have to serve time,"

Xena mumbled as the bus pulled to a stop.

Lord, give this woman a mind to fully serve You, Shari silently prayed. It was a known fact that Xena liked to be seen doing things in the church, but her mind was usually elsewhere rather than on the task at hand.

"Any way you look at it, freedom is denied," Shari responded, but Xena had already vanished down the aisle to exit the bus.

The glamorous exterior of the building did nothing to camouflage the downcast spirits of those awaiting them inside. As the prison ministry team cleared security, Shari's spirit confirmed the presence of gloom. They were led into a chapel that had about fifty benches.

She and the other musicians pulled out their instruments while the ministers counted and separated the prayer cloths for distribution, then unwrapped the small vials of holy oil for use during prayer. They were ready for fellowship to begin within minutes. As the inmates dragged themselves into the chapel, the spirits of oppression, despair, and hopelessness followed them and lingered.

Shari swallowed. What really broke her heart were the young inmates who looked barely old enough to drive.

Once the women were seated, an evangelist slapped her tambourine while another band member stroked the keys of a portable keyboard. "We come to glo-ri-fy His name. We come to praise His name. We come to magnify the name of the Lord. Glorify His name. It's good to lift up Jesus..."

Many of the inmates stood. Others remained in their seats, some praying or observing; but one young girl caught Shari's eye. She sat in the back, away from the others, sobbing. She was pretty—as pretty as one could be dressed in the orange prison-issued uniform.

What could she have done to land her in here? Shari supposed the possibilities were endless. Judging from her distress, the woman was probably afraid to be in this place.

The praise was a fifteen-minute prelude to a brief sermonette on John 16. Evangelist Anita Cecily was known for getting to the point without much fanfare. She concentrated on one verse of Scripture and expected the hearers to do their own research. "Although ye shall be sorrowful, God commands that your sorrow shall be turned into joy. Joy is the ammunition to build your strength. I'm appealing with you today that if you desire prayer, come to the altar. Joy? God's got that, too. Deliverance? Come on down."

One by one, the ladies crowded the narrow aisle under the watchful eye of the correctional guards, both of whom were male. Shari had always had a problem with men guarding female prisoners, knowing some of them took advantage of their charges.

"C'mon, there's always room at Calvary for us," the evangelist continued. "Lift your hands as a sign of humility."

Those who didn't move watched with intense curiosity. Ministers were then dispatched throughout the room. Working in pairs, one member would anoint a woman's forehead with a dab of holy oil while another prayed.

"Mind if I sit down?" Shari said after making her way to the young inmate seated in the back. The childlike woman didn't look up or respond. Shari sat anyway and began to hum the tune of the song that sounded like a lullaby. Soon the woman's tears were dry, replaced with sporadic sniffs. "Thank you."

"You're welcome." Shari smiled. "What's your name?"

Facing Shari for the first time, the woman squinted. "My name or my prison number?"

The first despair of being incarcerated was the loss of identity behind bars. A woman was no longer who she used to be but a faceless number. "Let's exchange names," Shari suggested. "I'm

Shari Carmen."

"Karyn. Karyn Wallace."

"Nice to meet you. If you don't mind my asking, how old are you?"

"Almost twenty-one." She twisted her lips and shrugged. "Yeah, I know I look younger."

"And could be my little sister."

That made Karyn smile. Soon she began to share about her concerns, which would have seemed unimportant to most outsiders. She talked about the number of years she had yet to serve for the crime she had admitted having committed. Karyn never elaborated on the nature of her offense, and Shari never pushed her to.

"Can I ask you a favor?" she finally asked.

Shari tried not to tense. *Lord, help me not to be swayed by a pathetic face.* What did Karyn want—a pack of cigarettes? Money? A jail break? "As long as it's legal."

"Could you write to me?" Karyn's eyes pleaded more than her voice.

Shari relaxed. "Absolutely."

"Then you'll need my prisoner number."

After giving Karyn her office address, Shari debated whether she should drop money into her account for incidentals. If the woman was a hustler, Shari wasn't about to become her prey. So, to start off, Shari would simply pray for her.

When the service concluded, Karyn fell into step with the other inmates as the correctional officer corralled them back to their cells.

Remember those who are in prison as if they were you, God whispered, reminding her of Hebrews 13:3.

The words stung as they digested into her spirit. *Yes, Lord.* As the team gathered to leave, Shari deposited fifty dollars in Karyn's account. Back on the van, Shari smiled. Working in God's vineyard had its benefits—including giving others the hope that came from knowing the Lord was on their side. It was even more satisfying than Garrett's love.

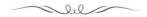

While Shari was in New Jersey with the prison ministry, Garrett was on his own mission at Jewelers' Row, hunting for the right engagement ring. As startling as the duck in the Aflac TV commercials, a display in a store window almost slapped him to grab his attention as he passed.

Freezing in his steps before backpedaling was a big mistake. Garrett nearly tripped over the walking cane of an elderly lady. He apologized, but Granny wasn't hearing it, as foul language discharged from her mouth.

When he reached out to steady her, she yelled, "Get your hands off me," then wielded her cane as a weapon. Too bad he wasn't wearing his badge. Though he doubted the woman knew that it was a federal offense to assault a Deputy U.S. Marshal.

And he doubted the senior citizen would listen to reason as he sought refuge inside the jewelry boutique. The lone employee laughed at him, which further humiliated him.

"If you spend a lot of money, I won't tell the police what I saw," said the overfed, toupee-wearing man, snapping his red suspenders on his wrinkled dress shirt, which Garrett thought probably hadn't seen an iron since the day he purchased it.

He decided not to inform the man that he was guilty of trying to bribe a federal agent and instead took it in stride, rubbing his forearm. "I'd like to see that hand sculpture in the window that led to the assault in the first place."

"My merchandise is worth fighting over, yes?" The salesman grinned and unlocked the case. Then he lifted the figurine, cradling it.

Garrett studied the work of art. It was nearly a foot in height. "I'll take it." Here he was supposed to be buying a ring, yet he was purchasing a statuette instead. But he couldn't resist the allure of the piece. He only wished that a diamond ensemble would grab his attention in the same way.

"You don't know the cost yet," the salesman said tentatively.

What did Garrett care about the dollar amount? Shari was priceless. "Love doesn't have a price tag. Can you engrave it with the words 'Marry Me for Life'?"

Grinning, the man stood straighter. "Yes, sir."

Back in his condo, Garrett rubbed his arms, still aching from the wounds that elderly "bat woman" had inflicted on his limbs. Then he roared with laughter as he imagined the scene as it must have appeared to any bystanders.

The following morning, the Sunday church service was charged with the presence of the Holy Ghost. The message, which emphasized that Jesus was looking for recruits for His army of soul-savers, kept the praise flowing throughout the sanctuary.

That didn't stop Garrett's heart from pounding whenever he snuck a glance at Shari. He could tell by the glow on her face that she was as excited to see him as he was her. She had arrived at church early for a meeting; otherwise, he would have picked her up, as he usually did.

Once Pastor Underwood had pronounced the benediction, Shari stood first.

Garrett jumped to his feet. "Do your plans today include me?" He grinned and wiggled his brows mischievously as he took in her every detail: her rich, dark skin; her cute dimples; her long, thick eyelashes; her full lips; and her jet-black hair that was silky to the touch. Every time he looked at her, it was like seeing her for the first time.

"I think I can pencil you into my schedule." She playfully

wrinkled her nose.

His nostrils flared at her teasing. "If we weren't standing in church, I would smack you with a kiss for that one."

"Actually, I have a big court case to prepare for tonight. How about tomorrow after work? I can't wait." She smiled as her eyes glistened with excitement.

"Little woman of mine, I don't want to wait until tomorrow. But I will."

"I love you," she whispered.

"And I love you, too." Garrett hadn't bothered whispering. His feelings were no secret as he escorted her out of the sanctuary.

Chapter Thirty

This was it. Garrett swallowed. The dim light from Shari's living room window served as a beacon in between the dark houses on either side. He was seventeen minutes early. Stepping out of his SUV, he adjusted the strap securing his saxophone on his shoulder. Although he wished that he had a ring box in his pant pocket, he had come bearing gifts: a fragrant bouquet and the exquisite figurine.

Creeping up onto her porch, Garrett knelt and lifted the saxophone, bringing the mouthpiece to his lips. The first note of Karen Clark Sheard's "Jesus Is a Love Song" filled the air. The mellow serenade intensified as he closed his eyes in order to conjure up all the moments they had shared together—the first time he laid eyes on her. Their first kiss. Their first declarations of love.

He grew breathless as he concentrated on the music, momentarily transformed into a Romeo professing his love to his Juliet from outside her window. After he released the last note, Garrett felt drugged as he opened his eyes. He didn't remember hearing the door open; neither had he inhaled Shari s favorite scent. Yet his Egyptian queen stood in the doorway, leaning against the frame, her saxophone in her hands. Their eyes connected, then she began to play the tune again and he joined her.

The final note faded in a moment of surrealism, and Garrett stood to greet her. His trance was shattered when applause erupted from several neighbors as porch lights flashed on. Garrett actually felt himself blush at the hearty round of catcalls. He had been trying to play quietly, but his emotions must have gotten the better of him, because he had evidently blasted his love throughout the neighborhood. "Sorry."

"Go on, Sharmaine," cheered a woman to the right. "You know how to pick 'em."

"I give you credit, young man, because I would be stuck on my bad knees," shouted a male neighbor on the other side.

"Shut up, Milton. We know Marge's got you trained," yelled a big, tall woman across the street, provoking snickers from the others.

Any other time, Garrett would have laughed right along with them, but his heart and his eyes were focused on the love of his life. After swiping up the gift and the flowers, he stepped into the foyer, and Shari backed up into the house. "We need to talk." He scanned her appearance—glowing, beautiful, and sophisticated. He had expected nothing less.

"I thought we just did," she said softly.

"We did with music, but I need to say something—and listen to your response." He handed her the flowers.

She shut the door and buried her face in the bouquet. "Thank you." Then she left him in the living room while she went to the kitchen for a vase.

Thinking back to the neighbors, Garrett wouldn't be surprised if the entire saxophone scene was playing on YouTube by now. He shook his head in amusement. Thanks to Mrs. Carmen, they had the house to themselves. Once Garrett had informed her of his intentions for this evening, her mother had happily agreed to visit a neighbor before he arrived.

When Shari returned, Garrett stood and stretched out his arms. She stepped into his embrace. There were no words, just a feeling of completeness such as he had never experienced before, even with Brittani. Pushing back reluctantly, Garrett turned Shari around by the shoulders and guided her to the sofa, where she sat.

He had orchestrated his moment. The only disappointment was the lack of a ring as Garrett knelt before her. Gathering her hands in his, he kissed them before looking up into her misty bedroom eyes.

"Sharmaine Carmen, no other woman can compare to your beauty, inside or out. I understand so clearly the Scripture in Jeremiah twenty-nine that says, *'For I know the thoughts that I think toward you...to give you an expected end.'* You are the end of my search for love. I'm finally complete."

A tear trickled down her cheek, and Garrett reached up and caught it with his fingertip. He rubbed the moisture against his thumb until it dried. Happy tears were the only kind he ever wanted to cause her in their marriage.

"God gave me the best of the best, and I will love you until my last breath. Will you marry me?" He paused, wishing again that he had a ring. "I looked in Boston for a ring that was perfect like you, but I found nothing that suited your perfection. I hope you don't mind shopping together."

The sparkle in Shari's eyes outshined the shimmery makeup she'd dusted on her face. "I love you so much, with or without the ring." She sniffed as she leaned forward and wrapped her arms around his neck. She gave him a short, sweet kiss, then pulled away. "But I still want my ring!"

Garrett laughed. He loved it when her spitfire personality popped out. "And I want you to have it."

Shari leaped to her feet. She could barely contain her excitement. She almost knocked Garrett flat on his back as she raced to the front door. After throwing it open, she screamed like a madwoman, "I'm engaged!"

Knowing her mother, she probably had a heads up that this was coming and had been waiting with the neighbor for Shari's answer. Her suspicions were confirmed when her mother's friend's porch light flickered off and on several times in rapid succession.

She knew her behavior was out of her character, but this was a once-in-a-lifetime moment. She was in love, she was loved, and she was officially a fiancée.

Laughing, Garrett walked up behind her and wrapped his arms around her. He chuckled as he began to sway back and forth. "I guess that means you're happy?"

"Maybe a little." Giggling, she twirled around and looped her arms around his neck. "Okay, deliriously happy." Was this the way Stacy had felt when Ted proposed?

After coaxing her to close the front door, Garrett guided her back to the living room. "I did come bearing a gift. Open it."

She sat again, and Garrett joined her, placing a box on her lap. After ripping off the gift wrap, she rummaged through the layers of tissue paper and discovered the figurine buried inside. It portrayed a man's hand slipping a ring on a woman's finger. The piece was all crystal except for the gold band. She had never seen anything like it. "Wow, it's beautiful. I love it."

Garrett kissed her cheek. "It doesn't replace an engagement ring, but I couldn't come here and propose without a gift." He reached for his phone and checked the time. "And a proposal wouldn't be complete without dinner for two. Come on. I made reservations at Fond, so we'd better go."

With all this eating out, it seemed her man was trying to fatten her up. As she got to her feet, Garrett twirled her under his arm like a ballerina. She grabbed her purse, and they walked out the front door moments later. She glanced across the street and spotted her mother and Mrs. Franks peeping out of another neighbor's window. Shari waved at them, and they fervently returned the gesture.

After Garrett pulled away from the curb, Shari took his hand in hers, closed her eyes, and smiled. Her bliss was indescribable, and she was thankful that Garrett allowed her the quietness to dwell in it.

Their candlelight dinner celebration was enchanting, from the exquisite meal to the unparalleled ambience. Plus, there were no interruptions. It was just the two of them in their own world, barely eating but gazing into each other's eyes with frequent whispers of "I love you." Shari hated to see the night come to an end.

By the next morning, she found out that her mother hadn't wasted any time spreading the news. Although Stacy already knew, she insisted on hearing the details from Shari. Then Shae called, and after Shari described the evening, her sister shared that she was now dating a professional baseball player who had won her heart. It wasn't until late the next morning, after two court appearances, that Shari was able to connect with Brecee.

"Girl, I'm so loving the life you're living. You've got drama with an ex-fiancée, babies, a low-down and dirty cousin, demons, and a marriage proposal. Did I leave anything out?"

Shari laughed as she scribbled on a pad at her desk: *Attorney Nash. Mrs. Garrett Nash. Sharmaine Carmen Nash.* She scratched out "Carmen." She wanted Garrett's name and his alone.

She stopped mid-sentence when her office door opened and Garrett stuck his head in. Her heart fluttered at the sight of her fiancé. "Brecee, I've got to go. A tall, handsome stranger just walked in. Maybe he needs representation."

"Right." Brecee giggled. "Tell my soon-to-be brother-in-law I said hi."

"I will." Shari disconnected, then stood, admiring Garrett's long strides to her desk.

Without speaking, he cupped her face with his hands. Anticipating his next move, Shari held her breath. Her eyelids fluttered as Garrett leaned closer, brushing his lips against hers before tickling her with his mustache.

"Your secretary said it was okay to come in, since you didn't have a client and weren't on the phone, but I see you were on your cell. Anyway, the representation I want from you is to wear my ring and be my wife. Ready to go diamond shopping?"

"I can't wait!"

Peeping over the desk, he scanned her attire. "Just checking to see you've got on comfortable shoes."

"Yes." She modeled the pumps she'd stashed in her desk drawer a few weeks earlier.

Soon they mingled with the crowds along the brick pavement of Sansom Street, where Jewelers' Row housed hundreds of upscale jewelry boutiques. Scanning the display windows, they stopped in front of Safian & Rudolph. Shari tugged Garrett inside.

"Congratulations on your engagement," the salesman said as he welcomed them, then gave them a general introduction to the collections. He steered Shari to a glass counter display where sparkling diamond clusters battled one another for her attention. "We have over a thousand rings in stock, so I'm sure you and your fiancée will find something," he advised Garrett.

Shari nodded and tightened her arm around his. The magnificence of her surroundings was breathtaking. "I've never seen anything so beautiful."

The New Jerusalem will be unmatched! God said, quickening

her spirit. *A city made of pure gold and walls of jasper. There you will find precious stones, sapphires, chalcedony, sardius...*

The Lord's voice faded as Garrett squeezed her tighter. "I have—when I first saw you," he whispered.

She blushed at his compliment. "Thank you. How about a simple band set?"

"Hmm." He wound one of her curls around his finger as he assessed her. "A simple band is for a simple woman from a simple man with simple intentions. We're neither of those things. I'm pledging my life to you, and, just like my grandfather has a Queen, I'm eagerly anticipating mine."

She had no rebuttal, so they glanced from one counter to the next before lingering at the last one. Garrett pointed out a platinum ring that had caught his eye, but Shari insisted they visit other stores before making a commitment. And they did, but they returned thirty minutes later to purchase the platinum ring. It was dazzling, with forty-seven round diamonds weighing more than three-and-a-half carats. She almost fainted when she saw the price tag.

"Make a scene, and, woman, I will kiss you right here like I already own you," Garrett said, silencing her protest with a threat.

Shari considered calling his bluff to receive his so-called punishment, but the smart thing was for her to back down and let the man shower her with gifts. "All right."

They left the jewelers completely satisfied with their purchase. "I guess this makes it official," Shari mused.

"No, it became official the day I set eyes on you."

Chapter Thirty-One

*E*very little girl wants a fairy-tale wedding when she grows up. What's your vision?" Garrett's mother, Phoebe, asked Shari. They were seated at her mother's kitchen table, planning the beginning stages of her wedding.

Shari already had her bridesmaids lined up—in addition to her sisters, Garrett's sister, Deborah, and Shari's best friend, Faith, would stand with her on her special day. It was a violation of the vow she'd made with her sisters, but they'd seemed okay with it.

Anchoring her elbow on the dining room table, Shari smiled. "Hmm. My dream wedding would include riding in a horse-drawn carriage, like they did in the movie *White Christmas*." She'd always found that idea romantic, albeit maybe not realistic in Philly, where she might freeze.

Her mother set aside the invitation samples she and Phoebe had been perusing. "Sharmaine Lynn Carmen, is that why you decided on a bitter cold January wedding?" She shivered. "We don't need to see a ninety-day forecast. There's almost a one hundred percent chance it will snow. But there could also be ice and subzero temperatures..."

"I know, it was a childish notion," Shari admitted, feeling silly as her mother pointed out the cons of her vision. She was about to concede when Garrett walked into the room.

The look he gave her was filled with love. Wrapping his arms around Shari's shoulders, he leaned down and kissed her head before rubbing his nose in her hair. She melted from his touch.

"We're getting married only once," he said. "If a horse-drawn carriage is what Shari wants, then I'll make it happen."

Shari turned around to face him. She reached up and rubbed his jaw as she whispered, "Thank you." Then he pressed his lips against hers.

"That man must love you if he's ready to freeze to death," her mother mumbled.

"He does," Phoebe declared.

Garrett pulled away, his nostrils flaring. "I do. Very much." Then to Shari, he mouthed, *"You're welcome."*

Shari's mother cleared her throat, as if to remind them that they had an audience. "Garrett, I love you like a son already, but you are a distraction to our powwow," she pretended to scold him.

"I think my future bride loves my distractions." Garrett gave her another kiss on the cheek and winked before he stood straight, but he kept his hand on her shoulder.

"Hush, Son," Phoebe said. "You two could enjoy a carriage ride in the spring or summer, and it'll be just as beautiful. Plus, six months to a year would give Annette and me more time to plan. We still need to choose a reception venue, make the menu selections, decide on the music, arrange the cake tasting..."

"We can help, Mom," Garrett said, picking up a pile of sample photos that Shari had set aside.

He pulled back her chair as if a silent command to follow him. She got to her feet, despite being clueless to what her fiancé might have planned.

"Shari and I can do the cake tasting on our own. We're the

ones who have to feed it to each other, after all. And I think we're both musically astute enough to choose our own band or DJ."

"I guess a once-in-a-lifetime love deserves a once-in-a-lifetime affair," Phoebe conceded, backing down.

Their mothers gave them a whimsical smile and said nothing more as Garrett grabbed their things and ushered Shari out of the house.

"Your mom and mine looked like they would be brainstorming all day, and I wanted to get you alone," Garrett said.

Shari elbowed him. "Part of the fun is the planning—the dress, hair-style, makeup, cake..." She rattled off the top ten items on her wish list as she got inside his SUV and clicked her seat belt.

"Babe, I don't care as long as you say 'I do,'" Garrett told her. "I can't marry you fast enough. A saved man can hold out only so long."

She laughed at his tortured expression and patted his hand. "I've held out for you, too. We've come this far, and the ninety days till the wedding will have passed before we know it." She tried to keep a straight face as she gazed at the defiant expression of her husband-to-be. Shari suspected she would see the same sulk frequently from their children. *Children.* She smiled. With Stacy pregnant, Shari didn't plan to wait too long to begin the journey of motherhood. "C'mon, let's go taste-test some cakes."

Garrett grunted as he started the ignition and drove off. "I should take you across the border and marry you today."

Poor baby. Shari giggled. He was probably serious.

Ninety days seemed to fly. The closer they got to the wedding, the more the realization set in that she was about to become Mrs. Garrett Nash. She couldn't keep the glow under wraps. The awe would manifest itself unannounced.

Shari couldn't resist touching Garrett whenever he was near, which explained why they were now holding hands in Bible class, forcing Garrett to scribble notes messily with his left hand instead of his right.

"I can't believe this is happening," Shari murmured close to his ear.

Although he was focused on the lesson, he paused and studied her with a worried expression, as if she was pregnant and her water had broken. "What's wrong, baby?"

"We're getting married," she said as tears filled her eyes. She couldn't help it. Blame the rock on her fourth finger. Every time she glanced at it, the effect was the same.

"Yes, we are." Garrett winked at Shari and exhaled.

Her love humbled him. He was the blessed one. Thank God he had submitted to the Lord's will, or he wouldn't have this jewel to call his own. He could have been stuck with Brittani, subject to the memory of her unfaithfulness for the rest of his life. But that was in the past. The woman beside him was his future.

"Stop doubting God that He will return," Pastor Underwood said, interrupting their private moment and drawing their attention to the front again. "Were closer now than we were yesterday. Keep your mind on Jesus..."

"You're too distracting, you know that?" Garrett whispered to Shari.

Someone seated in the pew behind them cleared her throat, and both of them looked over their shoulders.

The older woman frowned. "Brother Nash, Sister Carmen, I can't listen to Pastor's teaching while you two are carrying on like that."

"We're sorry, Mother Webster," Shari said, blushing.

Garrett didn't really know the woman, but he had seen her on Sundays, decked out with her matching hats, purses, shoes, and attire. Judging from the merriment dancing in her eyes, she wasn't all that annoyed with their behavior.

"Ah, it's nothing. Young love." The woman sighed, then squinted at them. "I plan to be at the church wedding, whether I receive an invitation or not, just so you know. I've known the Carmen family for years, and I was at Stacy's wed—"

This time, it was Garrett who cleared his throat. "Yes, ma'am. We'll be quiet." He squeezed Shari's hand as a cue, and they faced front again. He didn't say another word as he spied his fiancée fingering her engagement ring for the third time that night. Make that the fourth time. January 5th couldn't come fast enough.

With seventy-five days till the big day, the wedding chatter between Shari and Deborah was increasing in frequency and length. Instead of his grandfather interrupting the quality time Garrett spent with her, it was either his sister or one of Shari's calling to change some aspect of their nuptials. Shari seemed to enjoy the process, though, so Garrett didn't object.

One thing for which Garrett did have to pray for was patience when other brothers attempted to vie for Shari's attention, even though she was spoken for. They'd had their chance for years, and it was too late for them. At church several weeks later, a few men were holding court with her after the congregation had been dismissed. As Garrett stepped closer to the small group, he overhead one of them ask for legal advice.

Nine to five, he wanted to say, but he knew Shari wouldn't turn anybody away.

Seeming to sense his presence, she pivoted on one heel. "Hi."

He reined in his instinctual response—devouring her lips in an unforgettable kiss. What stopped him was the fact that they weren't married yet. Plus, once he started, he knew he wouldn't be able to stop.

"Excuse me, brothers." He lifted Shari's saxophone case from the floor. "I have to feed my fiancée. We'll see you next week at band practice."

Shari looped her arm through his and let him lead her away. "Stacy and Ted have invited us to dinner," She told him.

"Yeah?"

"Yes." Her dimples flashed. Garrett grunted as he nodded at a few saints they passed on their way out of the sanctuary. "The last time I was invited to dinner, at your mother's house, Ted growled at me when I reached for another roll."

"I know." Shari snickered. "But since she revealed her pregnancy during one of our sister video chats, she's been in entertaining mode. She's had Mom over, my uncle and aunt, and my cousins. Now it's our turn. I thought she would have less energy, but it's like she's on pregnancy steroids. I'm sure my sister will have Ted in check."

"What about you? Will my wife have me in check when we're having our baby?"

Closing her eyes, Shari grinned, then sighed. "I don't know, but I can't wait to find out."

"Are you saying you wouldn't mind starting our family sooner than later?"

"However the Lord wants to bless us, I won't complain." Her eyes sparkled with happiness.

"That's good to know." Garrett smiled, recalling what God had told him in prayer awhile back—that He would bless Shari's womb. "I can't wait to be a daddy."

The drive to Stacy and Ted's in North Philly took no time at all. Ted was in a jubilant mood as the proud papa-to-be as he catered to Stacy's every whim. It was actually comical. Things didn't turn serious until dinner, when Garrett asked him to pass the macaroni and cheese for a second helping. Only after Stacy elbowed him did Ted take a deep breath, grit his teeth, and reluctantly hand him the serving dish.

"Be nice," Stacy ordered him. "You know there's plenty more in the pan in the kitchen."

"That's for my late-night snack." He smacked his lips, and everyone else laughed.

The conversation soon turned to the wedding and then to baby stuff. Garrett couldn't wait for either event.

"I can't believe I'm going to be a daddy," Ted said. "If it's a boy, I hope he doesn't eat us out of house and home. Can you imagine our grocery bill?"

Rolling her eyes, Stacy shook her head. "I have a prelude to that already."

Ted's excitement was contagious. The way Shari squeezed his hand and stared into his eyes, Garrett wouldn't be surprised if they returned from their honeymoon with a baby being formed by God in her womb.

After dinner, they said their good-byes and stepped out into the chilly winter night. The sky was dark and clear, and the stars guided Garrett's drive to Shari's house.

"Forty-nine days before you're mine," he said at her door before gently capturing her face with his hands and kissing her good night.

"I'm surprised you don't know the time remaining down to the minute and second."

"I do."

After a long embrace, Shari pulled away and went inside.

The modesty that God required was killing him.

Chapter Thirty-Two

Shari bounced up the stairs of her house, humming an old Maurette Brown Clark selection "The One He Kept for Me." Those were the only words to describe the kind of happiness she felt. Before going to her room, Shari noticed that her mother's bedroom door was ajar, so she pushed it open and found her still awake. The doctor had ordered her to stay off her feet for a few days after she'd sprained her ankle while teaching dance lessons earlier that week.

"Hi, Mom." Walking farther into the room, Shari kicked off her shoes and climbed onto the bed.

"How was Bible class?" Her mother fingered Shari's curls.

She would definitely miss their bonding time together once she was married, but it was God's plan for her and Garrett to form the closest union possible and grow the next generation. "Pastor Underwood preached from First Thessalonians four and talked about the rapture."

Her mother nodded. "When Jesus comes back to gather the saints of God, the folks that are left behind will wish they had gone to church."

Switching her thoughts from Garrett to God, Shari agreed,

"That's going to be a great day... for some of us."

They chatted for a few more minutes, until Shari's smartphone played Handel's "Hallelujah Chorus." She got up and searched for her phone inside her purse. "It's Garrett," she told her mother.

"I know," she said with a smile. "I'm so glad that you decided to defend the love the Lord gave you rather than prosecute it. Tell him his future mother-in-law says hello."

Will do, Shari mouthed as she escaped to her bedroom for privacy. Although her conversation with Garrett was short, it was sweet and full of love. Soon she signed off so that she could call Shae and Brecee. Checking the time, she realized that Shae would still be working her shift at the television station, so she left a message on her home phone. Shari didn't want to chance interrupting her sister while she was on the air.

She called Brecee who answered on the first ring. "Hey, Sis. I can't get ahold of Shae—"

"Girl, where have you been? One date with that baseball player turned into two, and let's just say he may have struck a home run. Shae's still a little leery, though."

"I completely understand," Shari said. "I guess one bad relationship will do that to anyone. That's why I'm so thankful the Carmen sisterhood has my back. If the ballplayer is sent from God, maybe she'll be wearing a ring soon, too. What about you, surrounded by doctors and nurses?"

"I didn't get in this profession to find a husband." Brecee smacked her lips. "After hearing how you and Garrett met, and how Shae met Rahn, all I have to say is, the man who wants me better be just as unpredictable, exciting, and custom-made-fine by God."

Shari chuckled. Since Brecee was the baby, she had a fiercer, feistier, more rebellious spirit than the other sisters. She spoke her mind and had no problem backing up whatever came out of her mouth. Shari feared for the man who thought Brecee could be tamed. Her sister was a force to be reckoned with whenever she made up her mind about someone or something.

They chatted about their excitement of becoming aunts, which led to Brecee talking about some of the young patients under her care in her pediatrics residency and their prognoses. Shari decided to end the call before her sister managed to depress her. "Well, I'd better go. I have a brief to prepare for tomorrow. Love you."

True to her word, Shari reviewed the class-action suit set for trial the next morning. It was another case of identity theft, which was becoming increasingly commonplace thanks to information exchanged over social media and pin numbers associated with debit and credit cards.

Ten of her clients had filed suits against Cummins Computer Design for failing to dispose of their sensitive information, which had resulted in a compromise of their identities. When her eyes began to blur, Shari decided to call it a night.

The next day, Shari's heart fluttered in hopes that she would cross paths with her fiancé in the courtroom, but she was not privy to his schedule because of the nature of his work. But when she did see him, whether or not their eyes met, Shari knew he was multitasking, watching her and his charge.

Before the day was over, they had spoken twice and texted each other three times with their standard message: Thinking about you.

Later that night, after a long, hot bath, she read from her Bible. When she knelt beside her bed to pray, she couldn't explain it, but she felt unsettled in her soul. It wasn't the first time this had happened. The past two nights, God had awakened her in the middle of slumber and told her to pray.

The devil was busy somewhere, scheming to wreak havoc, roaming the earth to find whom he could devour. Someone was in dire need—or maybe it was Shari. She shook it off as a burden for intercessory prayer for someone else and climbed into the bed. Sleep came instantly.

Chapter Thirty-Three

appy New Year!" Garrett hugged Shari at the stroke of midnight during the annual Watch Meeting Night Service at church. "A new year, a new life. I'm days away from making you my wife."

On the day of the wedding, Shari and her sisters spent the morning at AnBrea Beauty's Salon in East Falls for the works. The hours of downtime until the ceremony were supposed to be relaxing, but all it did was make Shari antsy.

"Why did I suggest an evening ceremony?" she chided herself as she checked the time.

"Because you wanted an affair to remember," Stacy said in a calm voice as she rubbed her protruding baby bump. "It will be time before you know it."

And her big sister was right. Soon they were transported to the church, where Shari and the bridesmaids would finish getting ready. With her fashion sense, Faith applied Shari's makeup.

"This will give you a more dramatic look," her friend said as she applied various colors of eye shadow that Shari had ever thought would complement her dark skin.

"The gold shimmer will make your eyes seductive." Faith

stood back and admired her work, which received plenty of *oohs* and *aahs* from the other ladies in the room.

Phoebe glanced out the window. "It looks like the Lord will be sprinkling blessings on you and my son this evening. The forecast for snow has proven correct—they're predicting three inches or more." Her future mother-in-law seemed concerned. "I hope your guests can make it."

"It doesn't matter if they do or don't," Shari's mother told her daughter with a reassuring smile. Shari had never seen her mother so glamorous. "We're here to witness your marriage to a Christian man who I believe to be a man after God's own heart."

"What a difference a year makes," Deborah said, giving Shari's long fingers a loving squeeze. "My brother left Boston as a broken man, but you were able to put him back together again. You make his eyes light up that I doubt they'll ever go dim again."

"Thank you, Deborah." Shari's words choked in her throat. She glanced around the room and saw that everyone's eyes were glazed over with happiness for her.

When a knock sounded on the door, Shari took a deep breath to ward off the nervousness. "How is it possible to be ecstatic and scared at the same time?"

Her mother hugged her. "It's part of life, but you're marrying a Christian man who is also a Deputy U.S. Marshal. He will vow to protect you, and I believe he'll do an exemplary job."

"Thanks, Momma." She refused to cry, even tears of joy, as, one by one, the members of the bridal party slipped out of the dressing room. Once Shari was alone, she whispered a prayer. "Lord, I thank You for this man and for the opportunity to be his wife."

"It's time," Uncle Bradford whispered from the other side of the door.

"Coming." As Shari stepped out the room, she saw a latecomer hurry into the church, propelled by a gust of blustery wind. Because they had opted for a small, historic chapel for the cozy setting instead of the large sanctuary at Jesus Is the Way Church, they were at the mercy of the weather that assaulted the weakened hinges of the entry doors and swept powdery snow through the cracks.

Shari made her way down the short hall taking baby steps and soon made her appearance in the doorway to the chapel. The candlelight cast the perfect glow she had dreamed of. Garrett and his groomsmen stood at attention on one side of the altar, her bridesmaids on the other. She couldn't see Garrett's face, but she could feel his stare. Her heart fluttered. Instead of having the traditional wedding march music, her processional was "I Believe in You and Me," played by none other than her groom on his tenor saxophone.

When he blew the first note, Shari began to glide down the aisle. Wearing five inch heels, she focused on every step in order to avoid tripping and falling.

She was almost at her destination when the wind forced the unlocked door open and pushed her forward. Garrett shoved his sax into the empty hands of her cousin Victor and immediately steadied her.

"You look amazing, baby." Garrett's voice was low and husky.

Her hubby-to-be looked devastatingly handsome with a thin five o'clock shadow that had been trimmed. Shari reached out to touch his jaw, but he captured her hand and kissed her palm.

"Ready to be my wife?"

Swallowing, Shari could only nod as he guided her to the flower-draped brass archway where Pastor Underwood awaited them. He gave them an approving nod.

"Dearly beloved," the pastor began, "we are gathered here today in the sight of God and these witnesses to join together this man and this woman in holy matrimony." He paused, then looked over the rim of his reading glasses. "Who gives this bride away?"

In addition to Uncle Bradford's response, her mother, Aunt Camille, and even Victor and Dino's voices blended as a backup chorus.

Shari was amused by their antics, but Garrett grunted. "You've been in safekeeping."

"Marriage is more than hugs, kisses, and babies," Pastor Underwood continued. He admonished them to resist temptations laid by other men and women, warned then to be mindful of the devil's traps, and exhorted them not to take each other for granted. Finally, he led them in the exchange of the traditional marriage vows.

As the ceremony drew to a close, he said, "What God has joined together, let no man or woman separate, in the name of Jesus Christ, amen." He grinned at Garrett. "Brother Nash, you may now salute your bride."

Garrett's movements were deliberate as he slowly lifted her veil. "I love you," he whispered before gathering her in his arms and delivering the sweetest kiss that rendered her helpless.

She melted in his arms as he deepened the kiss, to the sounds of catcalls and applause.

Pastor Underwood beamed at the congregation. "Ladies and gentlemen, sisters and brothers, I present to you Mr. and Mrs. Garrett Nash."

All the guests were on their feet, clapping or taking photos, with camera flashes flickering across the room. Suddenly Shari was struck with the realization that she no longer was a Carmen. When Garrett had asked if she planned to retain her maiden name for professional purposes, her answer had seemed to both surprise and delight him.

"I've been a Carmen for thirty years, and I want to be a Nash even longer," she had informed him. "If I wear your ring, I'm wearing your name. I can't wait to change everything on my legal documents."

Garrett kissed her one more time, bringing her back to the present, before they took their stroll down the aisle. There was no other way to describe Garrett's leisurely pace. And it didn't appear as if Shari could rush him. Garrett grinned and slapped the hands of well-wishers as if they weren't going to have a receiving line. Or maybe he was stalling their carriage ride through the snow.

Once they reached the vestibule, the wind slammed the double doors open again, as if to salute them. Snow danced around their feet, and Shari caught a glimpse of their carriage. Instead of a white horse, she had requested a black stallion. She blinked at the amount of snow that had fallen since they'd entered the church. But it didn't matter. They were married, and no weather would derail the celebration.

The ushers hurried to shut the doors, and then Shari was separated from her husband for the first time as their attendants bundled them warmly for the elements. As if an imaginary line stood between them, they flirted with each other. Garrett winked; Shari blushed. She blew him kisses, and he pretended to catch them and place them over his heart.

Shari lifted an eyebrow, admiring the look of Garrett's tall, handsome, buff figure wearing a black top hat—definitely a black version of Fred Astaire. When he slipped on a full-length faux fur coat, she changed her opinion—*Super Fly*. Either way, her husband was fine and irresistible.

Maybe the same thoughts were going through Garrett's mind, for his nostrils flared when her sisters helped her into a white fur jacket. Tilting his head, he seemed amused when Brecee tried to delicately stuff her curls under a matching ball-shaped faux fur hat. Her mother handed her a fur muff for her hands.

Once Brecee gave him the nod, Garrett took two long strides to gather her in his arms again. "Princess, our chariot awaits us."

Inside the carriage, Garrett tucked a faux mink blanket around her and scooted her closer to him. Well-wishers stood outside to see them off, ringing tiny hand bells.

"Happy?" he asked her as the horse began to trot away, guided by the driver.

"Yes." She smiled and lifted her face toward the snow that seemed to shower her with wet kisses. Then she turned back to him. "I know it's love that you're willing to freeze just to make me happy."

"I'll let you in on a secret," he whispered in her ear. "I'm wearing thermal underwear."

They laughed between kisses and soft declarations of love until they realized their unhurried carriage driver had arrived at the reception site, two miles away. Garrett helped her down from the carriage, and she saw that the groomsmen had beaten them there and swept rather than shoveled a path through the snow. Garrett scooped her up in his arms and carried her inside.

"I don't know how tall your heels are, but you are not breaking your neck on our honeymoon night," he mumbled.

He didn't set her down until they were inside the banquet room. Large silver snowflakes hung throughout the space, but it was the floor-to-ceiling water fountain in the center that was the most breathtaking decoration. Shari blinked, then frowned when she realized that the hostesses and ushers, dressed in fairy costumes, were her mother's dance students.

"Welcome to your fairy tale, Mrs. Nash," Garrett said as the bridal party joined them to form a receiving line.

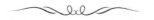

Garrett couldn't stop staring at his wife. She'd wanted a fairy tale. He got his happily-ever-after. The reception—from the company to the food to the musical entertainment—would always be a wonderful memory, but it was just a prelude.

When the snowfall surpassed four inches, Garrett's grandfather generously offered to put up any guests who hadn't made hotel reservations in a room for the night. Since the adjoining hotel had a four-star rating, none of the guests complained. Not to be outdone, Bradford Carmen offered to feed the guests breakfast with a lavish buffet the next day.

However, the inclement weather spoiled Garrett's plans to whisk his wife away to the Hershey Hotel. Thinking fast, his groomsmen scrambled to secure the honeymoon suite for them. After a few hours of pictures, dancing, and congratulations, they slipped out and took a private elevator to the top floor.

"I've loved you for so long," Garrett mumbled, nibbling on her lips as soon as the doors closed.

"I've waited for you so long."

When the elevator doors opened, Garrett lifted Shari in his arms once more. She giggled at his scowl when the swipe card didn't work after two tries. "I do not have time to return to the front desk for a new card."

Taking the card from his hand, Shari gently slid it in the slot, and the green light came on. "Voila."

From the moment he lowered her to the floor inside the suite, their eyes never left each other. He could tell she was a little nervous when he began to unzip her grown and she stopped him.

"I've never undressed in front of a man before, but I want to in front of my husband. Be patient with me."

Garrett nodded. He sat on the edge of the bed and loosened his bow tie. When the yards of lace and pearls crumbled at her feet, his jaw dropped. Slowly, his eyes perused his wife. She was wearing white fur shoes—he hadn't known they made such a thing. Her curls fell as she pulled pin after pin from her dark hair. When she finished, the package she presented to him was undeniable. The diamond on her finger shone as bright as the rhinestone in her navel—another surprise.

"You like?" she asked, looking doubtful, then moved toward him. "It was Brecee's idea. You like?"

Again, he nodded. When she was within reach, he wrapped his arms around her waist and gently kissed her belly. "I love all of you, and I'm glad we saved ourselves for each other. The Word of God is right. Fornication is a yoke because of the consequences. What we have is pure." He reached for the light switch, and the room went totally dark, except for the shaft of moonlight peeping through their window.

Chapter Thirty-Four

Marriage was far better than Shari had imagined it would be. She loved playing house with her husband, taking care of him, and discussing the details of their jobs. One of Garrett's favorite sayings, "My grandfather has his Queen, and now I have mine," always reminded her of his love when he didn't say those three words.

Shared prayer time was one of the benefits of the Nash marriage. Shari enjoyed snuggling under Garrett while he prayed. Even when she grew quiet, he kept going. Many nights, his whispered prayers lulled her to sleep.

One night, as they cuddled in bed with Garrett playing with her hair, Shari voiced a recent concern. "I'm wondering if I can have children." She couldn't help but frown. "I didn't get pregnant on our honeymoon, and I've been Mrs. Nash for four months and a day."

Garrett chuckled. "Baby, we can't rush God, but we can have fun until He sends us that blessing." He stroked her cheek in the dark. "We'll keep praying for God's will to be done in our lives. We can't go wrong with that."

"I know." She sighed. "I guess I'm just anxious about being a mommy."

You have made your requests unto Me, so don't be anxious, God whispered, reminding her of Philippians 4:6.

"Amen."

"I didn't say anything," Garrett pointed out.

"But God did."

"Well then, amen, my lovely wife." He brushed a kiss in her hair. "Let's get some sleep. I have an early-morning surveillance scheduled."

Shari awoke the next morning feeling refreshed in the empty bed. As she began her day, she smiled at the note Garrett had left her on the kitchen counter.

I love you more today than yesterday. I pray that the Lord will keep my wife safe, in Jesus' name. Amen.

"Two days until Saturday." Shari grinned. It was the norm for them to be inseparable on the weekends, whether they were at home doing laundry, cooking, and cleaning, or whether they were out and about, shopping or running errands. They took being "one flesh" seriously.

But on Saturday after breakfast, when it was time to head to the church for band practice, Shari sighed. "I wish we could play hooky today." She couldn't help her naughty thoughts regarding her husband.

"Say the word, woman, and I'll call John and have a ready excuse." Garrett grinned and mischievously wiggled his black silky brows before pulling her into a soothing embrace.

"Oh, I guess we shouldn't skip it. The Lord brought us together through the band, after all. We'd better go to practice, but the minute it's over, I want your undivided attention." Shari puckered her lips for a kiss, and Garrett delivered.

"I just remembered, the Odunde Festival is going on

downtown," Garrett reminded her. "Would you want to head over there after rehearsal?"

How could Shari have forgotten about the festival? For more than forty years, the weeklong event had drawn hundreds of thousands of people to experience the cultures of Africa showcased in one of Philly's oldest historically African-American neighborhoods. "Sounds like fun. It's a date."

The following Saturday, Garrett accompanied the men's ministry to an all-male prison while Shari attended band practice. Afterward, back at home, Shari wrapped herself in one of his shirts just to smell his scent. Lonely, she retrieved her "single life souvenir" book from a hatbox in her closet. Taking a seat on the floor amid her shoes, Shari crossed her legs and fingered the dried roses that she had strategically placed on the cover.

Opening the book, Shari smiled at the very first love note Garrett had sent her. It said, "You're mine, and I'm yours." The others weren't long letters on scented stationary, just notes on napkins, Post-it Notes, index cards—anything that had been within his reach at the time, it seemed—which made them all the more special to her. Shari liked knowing that she was in his thoughts at all times.

That hadn't stopped after they'd said "I do," and she hoped it never would. It seemed that her husband got a kick out of hiding notes in unexpected places, prompting her to be on a perpetual scavenger hunt for them, even if it meant emptying her purse.

One day, Garrett had forgotten to plant a love note in her bag, so he'd made a special delivery. Shari had been almost finished with her presentation in court when she felt someone's eyes on her in a way that made her shiver. It had seemed that the person was watching her every move—maybe because she was sharply dressed in her favorite powder-blue suit and matching heels.

While she had waited for the judge's response, she'd scanned the courtroom. In the back, on the last bench, she'd spotted her husband seated with his arms folded, appraising her attire. Garrett had smirked, then curved his lips into a naughty smile. Mischief danced blatantly in his eyes.

She had grinned as the judge called her name, ordering her and her client to the bench. Once the judge had advised her of the conditions of the young man's bond, he had moved on to the next case. For the next hour, she had argued two more cases, until finally the judge had dismissed the court for recess.

Garrett had stood as she walked toward him. He'd taken a different seat and pulled her down next to him as the court cleared out. "Hello, husband," she'd greeted him. "What are you doing here? I thought you were going to spend the day with Ted."

The brothers-in-law had planned to meet in order to go over some construction plans for the home she and Garrett were building and wanted Ted's advice since he was an architectural engineer.

"I forgot something." He'd leaned down and kissed her nose.

She'd closed her eyes, allowing the love vibes to run their course, until she shivered from his touch and the scent of his cologne. "What?"

"This."

She had frowned at the piece of paper until she realized it was a love note. She smiled before hugging him. "I definitely can't leave home without it. Thanks, babe."

"Now that my mission is accomplished, I'm heading out to meet with Ted. Just in case you couldn't get out, I gave your secretary a boxed lunch for you, so eat, Mrs. Nash." He'd stood, and so had Shari. "I'll see you at home." Garrett's swagger had caused her to shiver.

Thank God for memories. Grinning, Shari closed her souvenir book and put it away. As the hours dragged on, she decided to take a nap. When she stirred again, all she remembered were strong arms carrying her into the bedroom, then tucking her under the covers. In the background, his soft prayers were like a love song.

Later that week, Shari stood at the stove stirring a pot of spaghetti for dinner when the kitchen went black.

Turning around, she was surprised to see Garrett lighting two long taper candles. "What's this for?"

He grinned. "Happy five-months anniversary, Mrs. Nash."

"I thought only we women keep track of that." Touched by his gesture, Shari's eyes misted.

Once they finished their simple Italian meal, the night ended early when they retired to bed.

Chapter Thirty-Five

What happened? Shari silently asked sometime later when the marital bliss she'd been enjoying with her husband seemed to come to a shrieking halt. Suddenly, Shari wasn't as eager for Garrett's touches and kisses.

"Lord, should there be a cause for alarm?" she asked, scrutinizing her reflection in the mirror as she prepared to apply her makeup. Garrett had left for work hours earlier, and she had slept late since she didn't have any pressing court cases that morning.

Then it dawned on her. Could she be pregnant? She didn't look pregnant. Shari went through the motions of eating, dressing, and leaving for work, but en route, she decided to take a detour to her sister's house.

Stacy opened the door with her four-month-old son, TJ, in her arms. "What a surprise! C'mon in. I was just about to feed him. See Auntie came to visit?" She tried to coax the baby to grin. When TJ did, he revealed his first tooth.

Shari followed her into the kitchen. Toys were scattered all over the adjacent family room, as if her sister were operating a day care out of the home.

During breakfast, TJ put on a show. He spat, blew bubbles, and refused the pureed bananas Stacy tried to feed him. Occasionally, she managed to get him to swallow some baby food.

"What a workout." Stacy stood and worked her son out of his high chair. "Let me wash him up and lay him down for a nap. Oh, and you have to see the latest baby gadget Ted bought."

"Nothing will surprise me anymore." Since Shari's last visit, Ted had moved his son out of the nursery into a large bedroom filled with even more stuffed animals and toys. In addition to the crib, there was a playpen and a juvenile set of bedroom furniture.

"Okay, spill it," Stacy said. "You're too quiet. I know you, Mrs. Nash, and I should have heard Garrett's name mentioned at least three times by now." Folding her arms, Stacy tilted her head, waiting a second, before rambling on. "Did you two have your first fight? You know, Ted and I have spats all the time, but I always win." She grinned, then eyed Shari. "Well?"

"Well...I'm pregnant! At least, I think I am." Shari danced like a cheerleader, and her big sister joined her, but both of them quieted when they realized TJ had fallen asleep.

"Way to go, Garrett!" Stacy whispered excitedly. "Now TJ will have a playmate."

"I had something to do with it, too." Shari grinned, then followed Stacy downstairs and flopped on the sofa. Her smile faded as she confessed, "I'm happy and scared, and I've even gotten mad at him a couple of times." She gnawed on her bottom lip. "I've never been annoyed at my husband before—never. Am I supposed to become crazy like this?" Shari frowned. "Even the smell of his cologne makes me want to gag sometimes."

"It's just your hormones," Stacy assured her. "Ted got on my last nerve, too, especially when he would prepare a snack for me and then eat it before I could take my first bite. Sis, I put him on a hunger strike, cooking only for me. After two days, he knew I was serious. Ted made sure I'd eaten before he even added pepper to his food."

Shari wasn't amused. She checked her watch. She had to head to the office soon.

"Does Garrett know? Scratch that. You need to know for certain first."

"You've got a point. I'll stop at the store and get one of those home pregnancy kits." Shari grinned. "This is so exciting!"

That evening, Shari purchased a test, as planned. The next morning after Garrett left for work, she called Stacy to help calm her nerves as she followed the directions provided in the package. They both screamed with excitement as Shari read "pregnant" on the digital display.

"Welcome to the Mommy Club," Stacy cheered.

"I can't wait to tell Garrett, and don't you say anything to your big-mouthed husband," Shari fussed at Stacy. Ted had never been good at keeping secrets, especially when it was major news.

Two days later, when Stacy called to check up on her, Shari had to admit that she hadn't mentioned a word about her pregnancy to Garrett, even though she was more than ready to spill the beans.

Shari sighed. "I want to tell him with a romantic dinner or show him the positive pregnancy test and let him guess what we are having. But romance and creativity are overrated right now when I don't feel like myself. I hope this doesn't affect me in the courtroom, or my clients will have me thrown in jail," she joked.

"Don't start worrying. I'm sure you'll figure out how to tell him. In the meantime, Carmen sisters' pledge, I won't say a word to Ted until you give me the okay. Then I'll tell my 'big-mouthed husband.'" Stacy disconnected when her son began to cry.

A week later, Shari still hadn't told Garrett, and he seemed clueless about her perpetual sleepiness and her slight weight loss.

Humph. I'll tell him when I tell him, she thought, studying her complexion in the mirror. Her mood swings were starting to get on her own nerves. Forget the romance. She would just come right out and tell him tonight at dinner.

Garrett rubbed his hand over his face. He was tired, and he and his partner still had one fugitive to pick up before they could call it a day. Shari had been restless at night lately with the result that he hadn't been sleeping well, either. Yawning, all Garrett wanted was to do was go home and crawl in bed with his wife and sleep.

His wife. He smiled and lifted the framed picture of his favorite wedding moment—their first kiss as husband and wife—from his desk. "I love you," he whispered, as if the photo could answer him back. He leaned back in his chair and closed his eyes.

During their honeymoon, Garrett and Shari had been like junkies feasting on their love. Then, breakfast, lunch, dinner, and quick phone calls during the day were like snacks; waking up each morning wrapped in each other's arms was dessert.

Even in public, he sometimes struggled to restrain his affections. In the bandstand at church, when they were supposed to be watching the director, his eyes were on his wife. Whenever Shari looked his way, he would wink.

They often indulged in food-fight-style tussles in the shower, with soap and shower gel as their weapons. Then they would emerge, only to play tag with Shari's perfume spritzer. Thank God for ordaining marriage. Then, wrapped in their robes, they would collapse on the carpet, continuing their kisses before composing themselves for their morning ritual of prayer. *Sweet.*

Shari would snuggle at his feet while he knelt at their bedside. With her head bowed and eyes closed, she would wait for him to lead them in prayer. He loved when she did that.

The more Garrett prayed, the more he poured out his heart. "Lord, Your mercies are new every morning. You're magnificent. Jesus, it's because of Your blood that I'm washed. God, help us never to questions the trials You set before us, because we know You are faithful to bless us. Your will is perfect..."

Shari always ended their prayers by saying, "Thank You, Lord, and thank You for giving me a strong and loving husband, in Jesus' name." Together, they always said, "Amen."

But lately, something had been going on with her—with them—and he couldn't put his finger on it. Garrett didn't want to make a big deal out of it, in case it was a normal case of marital "growing pains." He definitely didn't want to call his parents or his grandfather for advice. They would panic and be on the next flight to Philly. "Jesus, what am I missing?" he asked during his private prayer time one morning.

I gave thee a wife to love, honor, cherish, and to be fruitful, the Lord whispered.

Hadn't he done all that? Garrett was sure he left no doubt in Shari's mind that he loved her. As a husband, he had never disrespected her or demanded she side with him in any disagreement. As for cherishing her? "Whew, Jesus, You know how much more I treasure Your gift than the one I previously chose." And be fruitful? Garrett froze. Could his wife be expecting? Excitement warmed the blood in his body. But before he jumped to conclusions, he would feel her out—tonight.

Chapter Thirty-Six

Shari walked through the front door of their condo after work feeling exceptionally hungry and tired. Stacy had told her to expect that. Her olfactory senses were on heightened alert when she sniffed jasmine in the air. For a moment, Shari was trying to register whether her body approved or disapproved of the odor. Where did it come from, anyway?

Her vision blurred, causing the lamps on the end tables to resemble flickering candles. The pregnancy went in for the kill when a tall bar of dark chocolate walked toward her. The hallucination was worth it.

"Hi, baby."

"Garrett? You're home early." She searched his face as he came nearer, closing the space that separated them.

"Shhh. No words right now." He relieved her of her briefcase and handbag, set them down, and then turned her around and slipped off her suit jacket.

Shari wanted to purr at his pampering. When Garrett scooped her up in his arms, she released a sound—was it a sigh or a moan? Regardless, she cuddled closer as he carried her into their bedroom.

Pillows of all shapes and colors were stacked on their queen-sized bed, which was covered with flower petals in abundance. She saw roses in colors she hadn't known existed. She sucked in her breath. She realized it was their scent she had smelled as Garrett laid her on top of the bed.

"Close your eyes," he whispered, tickling her ear.

A giggle escaped as she followed his instruction. The next thing Shari knew, Garrett had slipped off her four-inch heels. She couldn't help the "ooh" that slipped out when his large, coarse hands cupped her small feet. The massage was scandalous.

"Are you relaxed?"

"Mmm-hmm." Shari was so comfortable, she was about to roll over and take a catnap.

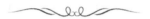

Oh no, she was not going to sleep on him—not when he had a romantic evening planned for them. But she looked so peaceful and beautiful that Garrett couldn't bring himself to disturb her. Backing out of their bedroom, he dimmed the lights and closed the door. He would give her thirty minutes—tops— then he was coming in.

In the kitchen, Garrett hummed an unknown tune as he loaded a plate with roast beef, pasta, a steamed vegetable medley, and rolls. Of course, his wife probably wouldn't eat it all, but that's what Hubby was there for—to be the cleanup man.

Glancing at the clock, Garrett smiled. He had given her twelve extra minutes of slumber. After arranging everything on the tray, he headed back to the bedroom. When he opened the French doors, Shari stretched, her eyelids fluttering. She scooted up against the pillows when she saw him.

"Hungry, Mrs. Nash?"

She nodded quickly.

His eyes never left hers as he slowly approached the bed. Her dark satin skin melted into the white sheets like creamy milk chocolate, and the vibrant rose petals added an explosion of color. Loose tendrils were the remnants of the tight curls that had greeted him at the door. And she was glowing.

Garrett set the tray on her lap. "I know I piled on the food. Don't worry—I'll eat most of it." He grinned sheepishly.

She arched an eyebrow, then lifted the fork. After a whispered grace, she dug in. "Don't count on it. Your baby and I need to eat." She stuffed her mouth and chewed.

Garrett dropped his own fork, spilling the vegetables he had just speared. He held his breath as his heart pounded. The innocent look on his wife's face was a tease.

Standing, Garrett moved the tray before Shari could reach for a roll. "We'll eat later." He set it on the bedside table and climbed in bed with her. He took her hands in his. "How far along?"

"Eight weeks." Her eyes watered. "Sorry I didn't tell you sooner. I was waiting for the right moment."

"You've got it. This is it, baby. I'm sorry I didn't notice anything before." He closed his eyes. His family would be thrilled. Jamal would have a first cousin, his sister would have a niece or nephew, and his grandparents would get another grandbaby to add to their tree.

Briefly, he thought about the other babies recently added to the Miller family. At Shari's suggestion, the Millers had sought counsel for visitation rights to see Brittani's twins. The case could very well be in litigation until the babies turned one. Plus, Brittani was not adjusting well to the single-parent lifestyle. Hopefully, Garrett's seed would restore some of his grandfather's happiness.

"Thank you for being my queen and for all the little princesses you'll give me."

She rubbed his jaw. "Princes, too, and you're welcome." Shari smacked a kiss on his lips.

Before the night was over, Garrett had to warm up their food three times, because the only thing they focused on was each other.

Chapter Thirty-Seven

Shari was still pouting after her latest obstetrician appointment. Dr. Johnson had placed her on a restricted diet.

"Your baby is doing well," she'd said. "Strong heartbeat, but watch your weight and your blood pressure."

After exchanging a worried look with Garrett, Shari had asked, "Should we be concerned?"

"Oh, no. Women who are pregnant sometimes develop conditions that they didn't suffer from prior to the pregnancy, such as diabetes, migraines, and high blood pressure. I'll monitor you, but you and your baby are very healthy."

Shari had given an audible sigh of relief. "What about my frequent headaches?" As she'd rubbed her stomach, Garrett had rested his hand on top of hers.

"More rest. Rest and diet are key to any pregnancy," the doctor had emphasized.

Garrett had interpreted that advice to mean bed rest, no cooking or cleaning, and cutting back on her cases. At first, Shari had been resistant to idea of losing her independence; but with every tender look from her husband, he'd managed to make her comply to his requests with little effort.

Six months later, Shari and Garrett moved into a new five-bedroom house in Salford Township. They threw a grand celebration that was a dual housewarming party/baby shower.

Stacy and Ted, as well as Shae and her baseball player husband, Rahn Maxwell—now the newlyweds in the Carmen family—flew to Philly for the occasion. Brecee, the solo single Carmen sister, was also in attendance, as were Shari's in-laws in large numbers.

Shari felt the baby kick, and she rubbed her stomach. According to the ultrasound, it was a boy. Garrett and the other men in the family couldn't have been happier.

"I can't believe Garrett hired a nutritionist to prepare my meals." Shari feigned annoyance, but she knew her sisters and mother saw right through her.

"You got that right, Mrs. Nash." Garrett strolled in the room and smacked a juicy kiss on her lips, generating a round of oohs and aahs from family members.

Garrett's mother gave her a wide grin. "You're my daughter-in-law, and I expect nothing less from the son we reared. He adores you, and we do, too. So, try to enjoy being pampered."

"Don't get mad at your hubby," her mother told her, wearing a whimsical expression. "It's that precious baby boy who is taking over your body."

"Sis, I feel ya." Stacy tightened her told on TJ, who had his eye set on the discarded gift wrap and bows. "Remember, I developed gestational diabetes, and no one in our family has a history of that disease."

Shari nodded. "My doctor said that stuff happens, but it should go away after the baby comes."

"Every pregnancy is different," Queen added. "I had seven of them, all girls, and I suffered migraines with five of them."

"I'm not liking those odds." Shari grimaced, feeling a little uneasy about what future pregnancies might bring.

Her mother must have sensed her deteriorating mood, for she put in, "But nothing takes away from, or can compare with, the joy of the new life that God gives you, growing and developing inside of you. Concentrate on your excitement over finding out who your son will look like, whose personality he will inherit, and so forth." Her smile made Shari grin. "At thirty weeks, your baby is packing on the ounces, and his eyelashes are filling in."

Curious about her mother's quick knowledge, Shari reached for the 3-D baby book she had received from Dr. Brecee Carmen, now the family's resident board-certified pediatrician, and searched the pages. Her jaw dropped when she read about the baby's latest developmental milestones. "Mom, you remember each week after all these years?"

Laughing, her mother swatted a hand in the air. "By the fourth pregnancy, I could recite the information back to my doctor. Of course, I had to brush up on my notes when Stacy had TJ."

Snickers filled the room. Her mother had everyone going for a minute. Shari rubbed her stomach, hoping to make the baby move again, or just to let him know she was there.

"All I know is, I want two boys...maybe three," she said.

"Three? You haven't delivered one yet." Queen lifted a brow and smiled.

"I know." She paused when Garrett brought her a glass of milk. She looked into his eyes and saw all the love she could ever ask for. "But I want handsome sons like their daddy." That comment earned her another kiss.

"Saul wanted two daughters," Shari's mother said. "He got his wish, plus two bonuses."

"Enough about baby talk," Moses said, halting the conversation. "Both our families are here, and so are our instruments. Seems to me we should have a friendly battle of the bands between families."

"Challenge accepted," Garrett said with a smirk.

"Whose side are you on, anyway?" Deborah teased her brother.

"My wife's, of course."

When building their home, they had included a designated music room, set up with a small stage for the purpose of family get-togethers. There were twelve seats set up like a home theater. Once everyone had assembled in the room, Shae settled behind the drum set, Brecee got out her guitar, and Stacy slid onto the piano bench. Even their mother warmed up on her flute. Garrett and his grandfather strapped on their saxophones. Jamal tapped expectantly on his congas. It seemed everyone was in place.

Unfortunately, Shari had to opt out, under the urging of her husband. The sound was like music to her ears. Even the most skilled drumline had nothing on the Carmen/Miller music duo. The baby kicked in response when Garrett played a solo on the sax. Shari smiled and caressed her stomach, wondering which instrument her son would be drawn to.

After they had covered a repertoire of classical, R&B, jazz, and gospel selections, Shari yawned. That was when Garrett stopped playing and politely informed their families that he was going to get her to bed. "You're welcome to stay," he told them, "but the party is officially over."

Chapter Thirty-Eight

The baby books and Lamaze classes were nothing like the real thing. Garrett sympathized with his wife as she pushed, paused, and panted, as instructed, until she was exhausted. If it were possible, he would bear their child himself.

Seated at her bedside in the hospital, Garrett massaged the damp hair away from her face. "I love you, Shari. It will be over soon, and Garrison will be in our arms."

"I know. I keep reminding myself of that with each contraction." A tear slid down her cheek. "I love you, too, G."

Her voice was so weak, her stomach swollen with the gift God had promised them. Shari had gained more weight than the doctor had wanted her to, and she and Garrett were preparing to welcome a big baby boy into the world.

The monitors interrupted his musings, alerting Garrett that another contraction was gaining momentum. But Shari didn't stir. That had to hurt. Concern filled his mind as the door to Shari's hospital room slammed open. A group of doctors and nurses raced inside. They took one look at Shari and adjusted the knobs on the machine.

Garrett shot up from his chair. "What's going on? What's

happening?" But his questions were ignored as the medical personnel worked quickly.

When he heard someone say, "Were losing her," he lost it and roared, "No!"

"Mr. Nash, we may have to take the baby," Dr. Johnson informed him calmly. "We can't control Mrs. Nash's blood pressure."

Garrett panicked. "But my wife is going to be okay, right?" He'd never known fear like this.

The doctor didn't answer right away, since she was busy tending to Shari. "For now," she finally said in an offhand manner.

"And the baby? Is my baby okay?"

"We'll do everything in our power to make sure of it. Please join your family outside."

"Join your family outside"? Was the doctor delirious? Garrett couldn't leave his wife when she needed him most. His feet wouldn't move as he tried to sneak another peek at Shari, but the doctors and nurses hid her from his view.

Garrett felt lightheaded and began to hyperventilate. Someone ushered him out of the room, down the hall, and into a waiting room where a group of family members were gathered. "Something's wrong," he mumbled over and over.

His grandfather's first word when he saw Garrett was "Jesus." Then Garrett heard whispered prayers rising up from several people.

Shari's mother reached out and hugged him. "What's going on?" she asked softly.

Shaking his head, Garrett struggled to get his words out. "I don't know. I don't know."

"I'm sure everything will be all right," Stacy told him. "Ted nearly fainted when I was in labor for nineteen hours. It'll be okay." Her smile gave him little comfort.

His vision blurred, but he couldn't blink—it was as if he was in a trance. He tried to keep himself composed, but in reality, he was losing it. *Lord, please bless my wife and my son. You promised, Lord. You promised! Please, God.*

"While we wait, let's pray," his grandfather spoke up.

Garrett linked hands with his grandfather and Annette. He couldn't control the tremors in his body. Was he about to have a seizure? As Shae began to sniff, her husband, Rahn, wrapped his arms around her. Ted cleared his throat before grabbing hold of Stacy's hand. Brecee, usually the most vocal of the Carmen sisters, was unusually quiet, her head bowed. As the medical doctor in the family, did she understand what was going on?

Before Garrett could ask her, his grandfather began the prayer. "Father God, in the mighty name of Jesus, we come boldly to Your throne of grace, where we give You thanks above all for this joyous occasion. We bless Your name for anointing the marriage of my grandson Garrett and his beautiful wife, Shari. Now, Lord, we stand before You in need of grace and mercy for Shari and little Garrison. They're in trouble, and the doctors can do only so much. Lord, You are a God of testimonies, and we need one right now. We know that in You alone are life and healing, so we ask You to speak healing, Jesus..."

As the petitions were lifted up, the presence of the Lord descended and encamped around them. Their prayers quieted at the same moment Garrett's soul trembled, not from fear, but from comfort and hope. He knew that God had heard them.

Know that I am God. I created the heavens, the earth, and all that dwell upon the earth... His voice seemed to shake the room.

Garrett listened in awe until he felt another presence among them. His body tensed. "Lord, something's not right. I feel it. What is it, God?"

God continued to speak, but Garrett was distracted. "God,

protect us," he prayed. "Whatever is in this room, I can't see it, but I know something undesirable is here. Protect us, God."

Be not afraid, for I am the Lord thy God.

Mixed emotions raced through Garrett. Suddenly his natural eyes were heavy to the point that he couldn't open them. Meanwhile, in the spiritual realm, he came face-to-face with something a Star Trek fan would have labeled as eerie. He saw a long black robe draped over a figure; a hood covered its face and the arms moved within the sleeves, but he saw no hands.

"God, what just came into this room?"

Death.

Their wailing crescendoed. Everyone was in the spiritual realm with Garrett.

"Why is he here?" he asked of the Lord. "What does he want?" Garrett continued to question the Lord.

He's waiting on Me. I'm waiting on you.

Me? "God, please don't take my son. Not my boy, not my firstborn." He began to sob. "You promised me that You would bless the womb of my wife..."

I came for your wife.

All the air was sucked out of Garrett's body. Had he heard right? "You said Shari was my season. Jesus, I can't bear her season coming to a close so soon. Not my wife, either!"

The hooded being didn't bulge. Garrett's mind raced through the Scriptures. Surely, he could recall one about God's goodness and mercy. Why was the Lord giving him this option? How could he make a decision over a life—the life of his wife? Garrett was not in the proper mind to utter anything at the moment.

Suddenly, he remembered a point from the sermon Bishop Jackson had preached during Garrett's last trip to Boston. *"Should a man tell God no? Saints shouldn't possess something they aren't willing to give to God if He asks."*

Garrett wished he could see the face of Jesus—the gateway to God clothed in flesh—look Him in the eye, and offer anything as a sacrifice... just not his wife or his son. He would be willing to die to save them both.

I've already shed My blood so that *all men might be saved*, God rebutted, whispering from Hebrews 9:12-14.

Every movement in the room, even the air, seemed to pause in time. Opening his eyes, Garrett wasn't surprised to see everyone looking at him. Another phrase from Bishop Jackson's sermon rang in his ears: *"The saints shouldn't covet anything that, if God wants it, they don't have a heart and mind to give it to Him."* Garrett's shoulders slumped. "Yes, Lord, You may have my precious wife. Please take care of her."

Death turned and disappeared from the room. Almost instantly, Dr. Johnson opened the door.

"Congratulations, Mr. Nash. You have a healthy baby boy." She paused, seeming to gather strength. "But I'm sorry to say that Mrs. Nash did not make it." After delivering the blow, the doctor didn't hang around to answer questions but quickly backed out of the room and closed the door.

Delirium struck the family at once, but only Brecee lashed out, lunging at Garrett and pounding his chest.

"How could you? How could you let my sister die?"

Through blurred vision and a collapsed mind, he didn't feel a thing. Annette wrapped her arms around her youngest daughter, and together they wept until everyone else had surrounded them in a group hug.

"It was God's will," Annette said, trying to comfort Brecee.

"But God gave Garrett a choice. They could have had another baby!" She was inconsolable. "She was my sister!"

"But God didn't give him that option," Annette reasoned with her.

Uncle Bradford walked into the room, carrying flowers. He stopped in his tracks. "What's going on?"

Garrett was too numb to speak.

"My baby didn't make it," Annette finally said.

Bradford seemed to process the news, then pulled out his handkerchief and wiped his eyes. "I'm so sorry, but Shari will have another one."

Annette shook her head. "She's gone."

A nurse entered the room carrying his baby boy, but Garrett waved her off. This was no longer a joyous occasion. He was mourning, and no one could give him comfort.

"Your wife gave you a precious gift, Mr. Nash," the nurse tried coaxing him—to no avail.

Garrett refused to embrace Garrison. He couldn't. He folded his arms in protest. "My wife was my precious gift."

Annette took her grandson while Garrett retreated to a corner to grieve alone. Once he composed himself, he demanded to see his wife.

Chapter Thirty-Nine

Standing tall, Garrett focused on the door of the waiting room and commanded his feet to take one step in front of the other. Without asking any questions of him, his kinfolk parted, making a path for him. He bypassed his son, having no desire to count fingers and toes or to see whose looks the child favored. He blinked back tears as he opened the door and crossed the hall.

Garrett bowed his head. He wasn't ready to say good-bye to his queen. "God, why did I trust You?"

Precious in My sight is the death of My saints, God spoke from Psalm 116:15. She was washed in My blood.

"She was very precious to me, Lord, because You gave her to me," Garrett whispered back. What he really wanted to do was to scream at Jesus. He quietly opened the door to Shari's room, as if she were sleeping and he didn't want to disturb her. He cast his eyes on the remains of his wife—the lifeless part that God had left him after carrying away her soul. It was so quiet, a stark contrast to the commotion in the room when he'd left it.

Even in death, Sharmaine Nash was exquisite with her long black hair spilling across the pillow. The white sheets tucked around her reminded him of their wedding day. Sleeping Beauty had nothing on his wife.

Before Garrett broke down, he approached the bed and kissed her forehead, then took the seat next to her. "Baby, I'm so sorry. I'm so sorry." He wept, then sniffed. "I love you so much, but we know God loves you better than me, right?" He smiled as his eyes roved over everything that made his wife beautiful: long, thick lashes; silky locks—he fingered a curl; full lips; dimples; and unblemished dark chocolate skin. Beautiful dark skin that was satiny to the touch.

It wasn't fair that Brittani had delivered two boys and lived, yet his wife's life hadn't been spared while giving birth to one. Garrett quickly repented for his wayward thoughts. "I know..." he choked. "I know that Second Corinthians five, verse eight, says that to be absent from this body means you're in the presence of the Lord, waiting for that trumpet sound, when the dead in Christ shall rise first."

More tears fell as he rattled off every Scripture he could recall about the benefits of death for those who were saved, concluding with First Thessalonians 4:17-18: *"We which are alive and remain shall be caught up together with them in the clouds, to meet the Lord in the air: and so shall we ever be with the Lord."*

Squeezing her soft hands, Garrett rested his head on her chest—no heartbeat, no movement, no life. He continued to sob. "God didn't give us much time together, but I appreciate what He gave us..."

Before long, his family and Shari's entered the room, singing praises and worshipping God for the life she had lived. All of them had tears streaming down their faces as they looked at the bed. How they had the energy and presence of mind to lift up their voices in praise, Garrett didn't know.

When his son cried, Garrett looked at him for the first time. Annette still held him, but she motioned for Garrett to take him. He hesitated, then reached for the baby. Cuddling Garrison in his arms, he studied his son's features. A smile tugged at Garrett's lips. Garrison Moses Nash looked like the mother he would never know.

Chapter Forty

Three months later

Garrett sat in the congregation of Souls Deliverance Church in Nashville, Tennessee, at the invitation of the pastor. It was the third invite he'd accepted within two months. He'd already turned down four.

"Psalm nineteen, verse seven, tells us that God's law is perfect," Pastor Jacobs told his congregation. "I am a witness. In sickness, God's grace is perfect. In trials, His grace is still perfect. In victories, we proclaim that God's grace is perfect. The Lord is consistent. He never changes. He is the same yesterday, today, and tomorrow." He continued to extort the congregation for another twenty minutes or so.

At the conclusion of his message, Pastor Jacobs closed his Bible and wiped the sweat off his forehead. He took a deep breath, then extended his hands. "Is there anybody here who wants to be saved? Playtime is over. Stop faking church. Repent for the sins you've committed, then walk down to the altar, where the ministers are waiting to pray for you to receive the real thing."

Several people, mostly teenagers, took the lead. Some even requested baptism in the name of Jesus.

"Before we dismiss today, we have some special visitors," he announced. "I'd like to ask Brother Garrett Nash to come to the podium and share his testimony."

With his saxophone in his hand, Garrett walked up to the pulpit and shook the pastor's hand. First he played "How Great Is Our God," worshipping Jesus with his instrument, until most of the congregants were on their feet. When he finished, they released an exhilarating ovation of applause.

"Praise the Lord, church," Garrett said, adjusting the microphone. "Truly, that song is my testimony. Even when I don't understand God, He's still great and perfect, as the pastor preached." He closed his eyes to gather his thoughts. "Three months and two days ago, I became a widower. I lost my soul mate—the woman I truly loved, the woman I had prayed for, the woman God gave me."

A hush swept through the sanctuary. "Hours before Shari died, she gave me my son, Garrison—seven pounds, five ounces, and nineteen inches long." Garrett paused, dropped his head, and swallowed. "It's still hard talking about the darkest day of my life." A tear slid down his check.

"Bless him, Lord," people shouted from their pews.

Garrett wiped his face with a handkerchief before continuing. "I stand here today with restored faith in God. His ways aren't our ways. You see, the Lord visited me in that hospital room and asked me if I would give up my wife. The angel of death was standing by, waiting to do the Lord's bidding. "If He had been a mere man, I would have asked him if he were crazy."

Frowning, Garrett gnawed on his lip as he gripped the podium. "Sometimes, I wonder what would have happened if I had told God no. Would He have taken my wife, anyway? What would have been His 'plan B'?"

He looked out over the congregation and found the face he was searching for. He smiled, and she responded with an even brighter grin. "I'm a witness that God never takes away from us without relinquishing to us." Stretching out his arm, he summoned the woman. "I would like to introduce my wife. Bring Garrison with you, baby."

A few people applauded, but most remained quiet with curiosity, seemingly uncertain as to how they should respond. It wasn't shameful for a man or a woman to remarry quickly after the death of a spouse. Garrett assisted his wife up the stairs and gathered his son in his arms. He stepped away from the microphone so that she could speak.

"Praise the Lord, saints." Her hat and clothes commanded attention. She was stunning in white.

"Praise the Lord," many people answered back.

"My name is Sharmaine Nash, and I am the miracle God restored—" Like the snap of a finger, the rejoicing was combustible. The sounds of cheers, speaking in other tongues, and hand-clapping were almost deafening. Many stood to their feet; some of them even danced. Others wiped tears from their eyes.

"The trial wasn't my husband's alone but also my family's and mine," Shari went on. "God called us to put our faith on the line, believing the words He had spoken to my husband before we were married. You see, if we don't pay attention when God speaks to us, our faith will fail us. In the Bible, the Lord told Abraham that he would become the father of many nations, yet God told him to offer his son of the promise, Isaac, as a sacrifice. Abraham's faith is evident in Genesis twenty-two, verse five, when he tells the two young men who accompanied him and Isaac to the mountain that both he and Isaac would return after worshipping God on the mountain."

She paused. "My dear husband was put in a situation like Abraham's. Garrett loved me unconditionally, beyond comprehension, and God knew it. And God wanted to show my husband the benefits of sacrifice, just as He showed Abraham."

When Garrison started to fuss because he wanted his mother, Garrett walked closer to Shari but kept holding his son so that she could finish. "Go on, babe," he whispered. It was important that they both give this testimony.

"I was told that the doctors pronounced me dead at twelve minutes past noon. I was told that our families prayed until God visited them. I was told that while my poor husband was mourning my death, our families entered the room rejoicing, worshipping, and praising God. They were essentially celebrating my life as if they were attending my home-going service.

"Not even an hour had passed when I stirred, according to my family. You see, in whatever place Jesus had me, I heard the voice of God saying, *Trust Me, Shari. Trust Me*. I sat up, not knowing that I had died. Looking around my hospital room, I didn't know why my husband was crying, while others were praising God. When I saw my son, I rejoiced with them."

Garrett lifted one hand in the air in praise, then stepped to the microphone to conclude their testimony. "When the nurses came to investigate the commotion, they were frightened. The doctor had already pronounced my wife officially dead—no heartbeat, pulse, or brain waves. She had expired. But when they saw her alive and holding the baby, they said that we were making so much noise, we woke the dead." He grunted. "Nothing wakes the dead but the power of Jesus. God didn't allow me to see my wife pass away, but I was privileged to see her come to life again."

Shouts of "Amen" popped up throughout the sanctuary.

To conclude their testimony, Shari and Garrett sang the BeBe & CeCe Winans rendition of "Midnight Hour."

The entire congregation was standing. There wasn't a dry eye in the place. When the service was over, the number of people who wanted to shake their hands and offer hugs was overwhelming.

Since that fateful day, Garrett had become clingy, always keeping his wife and son close. He realized that in a blink of an eye, his life could change forever, but he had also learned that God was faithful to turn things around.

Chapter Forty-One

One year later

"What do you mean, my sister's pregnant? Have you lost your mind? How could you let that happen?" Brecee was in a stare-down with Garrett.

Did his sister-in-law really expect him to answer her final question? Shari's second pregnancy had happened against his better judgment, but with a wife as fine as his, how was he supposed to resist her charm?

Secretly, Shari's news had scared him, too. There were too many what-ifs. As far as Garrett was concerned, after that close call with losing Shari, their family was complete with one son. He didn't need any more princes or any princesses.

Not only had Garrett babied his wife since her miraculous restoration, but so had everyone else in the family, especially Dr. Sabrece Carmen.

To nobody's business, Garrett had been beyond careful in protecting her and loving her gently, but God had ordained their marriage, so they had to trust Him. But, in the back of his mind, he remembered what Dr. Johnson had said once the Lord had brought Shari back from the dead: *"In my profession, these things do happen from time to time—although rare, and it's a phenomenon. Mrs. Nash was lucky."*

"No, my wife and our family were blessed by the Lord, whether you can admit it or not." Garrett hadn't been able to abide her belittling the God he served. He had set her straight right away.

Still, Dr. Johnson had seemed unfazed. "I see. Well, based on this condition, I would recommend a tubal ligation. She definitely shouldn't attempt to have any more children."

"That's something I might agree with," Garrett had said.

Now, their houseguest stormed away continuing her tongue-lashing with his wife. Garrett snickered. Shari's persuasive spirit wouldn't allow her to back down to Brecee. She might win the argument with her baby sister, but Shari hadn't won the argument that had ensued when she'd shared the news with him.

Garrett had lain awake all night after she'd delivered the bombshell. Meanwhile, his sweet little wife had had the nerve to roll over and peacefully fall to sleep. The next morning, he'd picked up where she'd left off. "Baby, do you have any idea how scared I am?"

"We can't be fearful and hope to make it to heaven."

"I know what it says in Revelation twenty-one, verse eight, but I'm a coward when it comes to my wife. We might not have the same testimony the next time, and that scares me. You're irreplaceable."

The sound of pots banging around drew their attention, and Garrett had hurried to the kitchen. Somehow, his son had managed to pick the baby lock on the cabinet—yet again. Garrett had finally realized that he needed to accept not only the pregnancy but also God's will—again.

In the months that followed, as he and Dr. Johnson monitored Shari's progress, Garrett was perpetually taunted by the devil. He lost track how many times the devil told him that he would lose both his wife and his baby this time. He was agitated and angry unless he watched the glow emanating from Shari. She didn't seem afraid at all as her delivery date drew near.

Prayer time was extended as never before in the Nash household. Surprisingly, their toddler son enjoyed praying, even though he was usually asleep in Shari's lap by the time they said "amen."

Three weeks before her due date, Shari's water broke, and she went into labor. In the delivery room, it was like déjà vu; but this time, there was a prayer cloth in Garrett's pocket and holy oil dabbed on Shari's forehead. She required an emergency C-section, by which she delivered another son, whom they named Saul Carmen Nash in honor of her father.

"Mr. Nash, once again, your wife was lucky," the doctor told him, to which he gritted his teeth to keep from correcting her choice of words. *Luck* was not in his vocabulary. "But every pregnancy increases her risk of developing eclampsia again. I need your permission to perform a tubal ligation."

Yes, that would make his life simpler, but what would his wife want? She trusted him. *God, please help me!* Garrett shook his head. Life was a walk of faith. But test after test had yielded victory after victory.

In her scrubs, the doctor tapped her shoe impatiently. "Well? I need an answer now, Mr. Nash."

After sending up a silent prayer, he answered, "No."

She stared blankly at him. "Excuse me? Do you have any idea—"

"She trusts me to make the right decision, and she trusts God, which means I will trust the Lord. I say no to the procedure."

When she turned and walked away, Garrett called after her, "My wife is a criminal attorney, and I'm a Deputy U.S. Marshal. If her ovaries, fallopian tubes, uterus, or any other body parts are damaged in any way, you won't practice again."

The doctor didn't flinch as she turned around and left.

Once Shari was in recovery, Garrett relayed his conversation with her doctor.

She smiled. "Thank you. We have to trust God no matter what. The first delivery was your trial, but this second pregnancy was my walk by faith. Consider us even."

"Even." Garrett nodded. "I will always defend our love—always."

"Amen."

Author's Note

It was my honor to bring you this story filled with testimonies that actually occurred. As I wrote this novel, I had to bind the devil so that the power of God could be proclaimed to the captives and set them free.

If your book club or church group would like to know the spiritual backdrop to this story, I am available for speaking engagements and would gladly make arrangements to address your group.

Remember Karyn Wallace, one the inmates Shari met during the prison ministry? She has her own story in *Crowning Glory*. You won't want to miss this heartfelt story of redemption, and speaking of redemption, God sends his wrath upon Landon. Yet, the Lord is merciful. Don't skip Landon's riches to rags story in *Redeeming Heart*.

About the Author...

Pat Simmons has penned more than thirty-five titles. She is a self-proclaimed genealogy sleuth who is passionate about researching her ancestors, then casting them in starring roles in her novels. She is a three-time recipient of the Romance Slam Jam Emma Rodgers Award for Best Inspirational Romance. Pat describes the evidence of the gift of the Holy Ghost as a life-altering experience. She has been a featured speaker and workshop presenter at various venues across the country. Pat has converted her sofa-strapped sports fanatical husband into an amateur travel agent, untrained bodyguard, GPS-guided chauffeur, and administrative assistant who is constantly on probation. They have a son and a daughter. Pat holds a B.S. in mass communications from Emerson College in Boston, Massachusetts. Visit her at www.patsimmons.net.

Book Club Discussion

1. Talk about a situation where God gave you a direction that at the time didn't make sense but God revealed it in the end.

2. Talk about Shari and Garrett's spiritual life.

3. Situations like Brittani unfortunately happen in the church. Should Landon, the father, marry her?

4. God made a promise to Garrett like He did to Abraham. Discuss whether Garrett forgot what God had told him before Shari's miracle.

5. Share a testimony when you felt God's presence in a situation.

Other Christian titles include:

The Jamieson Legacy series
Book I: *Guilty of Love*
Book II: *Not Guilty of Love*
Book III: *Still Guilty*
Book IV: *The Acquittal*
Book V: *Guilty by Association*
Book VI: *The Guilt Trip*
Book VII: *Free from Guilt*
Book VIII: *The Confession*
Book IX: *The Guilty Generation*

The Carmen Sisters
Book I: *No Easy Catch*
Book II: *In Defense of Love*
Book III: *Redeeming Heart*
Book IV: *Driven to Be Loved*

Love at the Crossroads
Book I: *Stopping Traffic*
Book II: *A Baby for Christmas*
Book III: *The Keepsake*
Book IV: *What God Has for Me*
Book V: *Every Woman Needs a Praying Man*

Making Love Work Anthology
Book I: *Love at Work*
Book II: *Words of Love*
Book III: *A Mother's Love*

Restore My Soul series

Crowning Glory

Jet: The Back Story

Love Led by the Spirit

God's Gifts:

Couple by Christmas

Prayers Answered by Christmas

Perfect Chance at Love series:

Love by Delivery

Late Summer Love

Single titles

Talk to Me

Her Dress (novella)

Christmas Greetings

Anderson Brothers

Book I: Love for the Holidays (Three novellas): *A Christian Christmas, A Christian Easter, and A Christian Father's Day*

Book II: *A Woman After David's Heart* (Valentine's Day)

Book III: *A Noelle for Nathan* (Book 3 of the Andersen Brothers)

In *Love by Delivery*, Senior Accounts Manager Dominique Hayes has it all money, a car and a condo. Well, almost. She's starting to believe love has passed her by. One thing for sure, she can't hurry God, so she continues to wait while losing hope that a special Godly man will ever make his appearance. Package Courier Ashton Taylor knows a man who finds a wife finds a good thing. The only thing standing in his way of finding the right woman is his long work hours. Or maybe not. A chance meeting changes everything. When love finally comes knocking, will Dominique open the door and accept Ashton's special delivery?

In *Late Summer Love*, it takes strategies to win a war, but prayer and spiritual intervention are needed to win a godly woman's heart. God has been calling out to Blake Cross ever since Blake was deployed in Iraq and he took his safety for granted. Now, back on American soil, Blake still won't surrender his soul--until he meets Paige Blake during a family reunion. When the Lord gives Blake an ultimatum, is Blake listening, and is he finally ready to learn what it takes to be a godly man fit for a godly woman?

In *Crowning Glory*, Book 1, Cinderella had a prince; Karyn Wallace has a King. While Karyn served four years in prison for an unthinkable crime, she embraced salvation through Crowns for Christ outreach ministry. After her release, Karyn stays strong and confident, despite the stigma society places on ex-offenders. Since Christ strengthens the underdog, Karyn refuses to sway away from the scripture, "He who the Son has set free is free indeed." Levi Tolliver, for the most part, is a practicing Christian. One contradiction is he doesn't believe in turning the other cheek. He's steadfast there is a price to pay for every sin committed, especially after the untimely death of his wife during a robbery. Then Karyn enters Levi's life. He is enthralled not only with her beauty, but her sweet spirit until he learns about her incarceration. If Levi can accept that Christ paid Karyn's debt in full, then a treasure awaits him. This is a powerful tale and reminds readers of the permanency of redemption.

Jet: The Back Story to Love Led By the Spirit, Book 2, to say Jesetta "Jet" Hutchens has issues is an understatement. In Crowning Glory, Book 1 of the Restoring My Soul series, she releases a firestorm of anger with an unforgiving heart. But every hurting soul has a history. In *Jet: The Back Story to Love Led by the Spirit*, Jet doesn't know how to cope with the loss of her younger sister, Diane.

But God sets her on the road to a spiritual recovery. To make sure she doesn't get lost, Jesus sends the handsome and single Minister Rossi Tolliver to be her guide.

Psalm 147:3 says Jesus can heal the brokenhearted and bind up their wounds. That sets the stage for *Love Led by the Spirit.*

In *Love Led By the Spirit*, Book 3, Minister Rossi Tolliver is ready to settle down. Besides the outwardly attraction, he desires a woman who is sweet, humble, and loves church folks. Sounds simple enough on paper, but when he gets off his knees, praying for that special someone to come into his life, God opens his eyes to the woman who has been there all along. There is only a slight problem. Love is the farthest thing from Jesetta "Jet" Hutchens' mind. But Rossi, the man and the minister, is hard to resist. Is Jet ready to allow the Holy Spirit to lead her to love?

LOVE AT THE CROSSROADS SERIES

In *Stopping Traffic*, Book 1, Candace Clark has a phobia about crossing the street, and for good reason. As fate would have it, her daughter's principal assigns her to crossing guard duties as part of the school's Parent Participation program. With no choice in the matter, Candace begrudgingly accepts her stop sign and safety vest, then reports to her designated crosswalk. Once Candace is determined to overcome her fears, God opens the door for a blessing, and Royce Kavanaugh enters into her life, a firefighter built to rescue any damsel in distress. When a spark of attraction ignites, Candace and Royce soon discover there's more than one way to stop traffic.

In *A Baby for Christmas*, Book 2, yes, diamonds are a girl's best friend, but in Solae Wyatt-Palmer's case, she desires something more valuable. Captain Hershel Kavanaugh is a divorcee and the father of two adorable little boys. Solae has never been married and longs to be a mother. Although Hershel showers her with expensive gifts, his hesitation about proposing causes Solae to walk and never look back. As the holidays approach, Hershel must convince Solae that she has everything he could ever want for Christmas.

In *The Keepsake*, Book 3, Until death us do part…or until Desiree walks away. Desiree "Desi" Bishop is devastated when she finds evidence of her husband's affair. God knew she didn't get married only to one day have to stand before a judge and file for a divorce. But Desi wants out no matter how much her heart says to forgive Michael. That isn't easier said than done. She sees God's one acceptable reason for a divorce as the only opt-out clause in her marriage. Michael Bishop is a repenting man who loves his wife of three years. If only...he had paid attention to the red flags God sent to keep him from falling into the devil's snares. But Michael didn't and he had fallen. Although God had forgiven him instantly when he repented, Desi's forgiveness is moving as a snail's pace. In the end, after all the tears have been shed and forgiveness granted and received, the couple learns that some marriages are worth keeping.

In *What God Has For Me*, Book 4, Halcyon Holland is leaving her live-in boyfriend, taking their daughter and the baby in her belly with her. She's tired of waiting for the ring, so she buys herself one. When her ex doesn't reconcile their relationship, Halcyon begins to second-guess whether or not she compromised her chance for a happily ever after. After all, what man in his right mind would want to deal with the community stigma of 'baby mama drama?' But Zachary Bishop has had his eye on Halcyon since the first time he saw her. Without a ring on her finger, Zachary prays that she will come to her senses and not only leave Scott, but come back to God. What one man doesn't cherish, Zach is ready to treasure. Not deterred by Halcyon's broken spirit, Zachary is on a mission to offer her a second chance at love that she can't refuse. And as far as her adorable children are concerned, Zachary's love is unconditional for a ready-made family. Halcyon will soon learn that her past circumstances won't hinder the Lord's blessings, because what God has for her, is for her...and him...and the children.

In *Every Woman Needs A Praying Man*, Book 5, first impressions can make or break a business deal and they definitely could be a relationship buster, but an ill-timed panic attack draws two strangers together. Unlike firefighters who run into danger, instincts tell businessman Tyson Graham to head the other way as fast as he can when he meets a certain damsel in distress. Days later, the same woman struts through his door for a job interview. Monica Wyatt might possess the outwardly beauty and the brains on paper, but Tyson doesn't trust her to work for his firm, or maybe he doesn't trust his heart around her.

In *A Christian Christmas*, Book 1, Christian's Christmas will never be the same for Joy Knight if Christian Andersen has his way. Not to be confused with a secret Santa, Christian and his family are busier than Santa's elves making sure the Lord's blessings are distributed to those less fortunate by Christmas day. Joy is playing the hand that life dealt her, rearing four children in a home that is on the brink of foreclosure. She's not looking for a handout, but when Christian rescues her in the checkout line; her niece thinks Christian is an angel. Joy thinks he's just another man who will eventually leave, disappointing her and the children. Although Christian is a servant of the Lord, he is a flesh and blood man and all he wants for Christmas is Joy Knight. Can time spent with Christian turn Joy's attention from her financial woes to the real meaning of Christmas—and true love?

In *A Christian Easter*, how to celebrate Easter becomes a balancing act for Christian and Joy Andersen and their four children. Chocolate bunnies, colorful stuffed baskets and flashy fashion shows are their competition. Despite the enticements, Christian refuses to succumb without a fight. And it becomes a tug of war when his recently adopted ten year-old daughter, Bethani, wants to participate in her friend's Easter tradition. Christian hopes he has instilled Proverbs 22:6, into the children's heart in the short time of being their dad.

In *A Christian Father's Day*, three fathers, one Father's Day and four children. Will the real dad, please stand up. It's never too late to be a father—or is it? Christian Andersen was looking forward to spending his first Father's day with his adopted children---all four of them. But Father's day becomes more complicated than Christian or Joy ever imagined. Christian finds himself faced with living up to his name when things don't go his way to enjoy an idyllic once a year celebration. But he depends on God to guide him through the journey.

(All three of Christian's individual stories are in the Love for the Holidays anthology (Book 1 of the Andersen Brothers series)

In *A Woman After David's Heart*, Book 2, David Andersen doesn't have a problem indulging in Valentine's Day, per se, but not on a first date. Considering it was the love fest of the year, he didn't want a woman to get any ideas that a wedding ring was forthcoming before he got a chance to know her. So he has no choice but to wait until the whole Valentine's Day hoopla was over, then he would make his move on a sister in his church he can't take his eyes off of. For the past two years and counting, Valerie Hart hasn't been the recipient of a romantic Valentine's Day dinner invitation. To fill the void, Valerie keeps herself busy with God's business, hoping the Lord will send her perfect mate soon. Unfortunately, with no prospects in sight, it looks like that won't happen again this year. A Woman After David's Heart is a Valentine romance novella that can be enjoyed with or without a box of chocolates.

In *A Noelle for Nathan*, Book 3, is a story of kindness, selflessness, and falling in love during the Christmas season. Andersen Investors & Consultants, LLC, CFO Nathan Andersen (A Christian Christmas) isn't looking for attention when he buys a homeless man a meal, but grade school teacher Noelle Foster is watching his every move with admiration. His generosity makes him a man after her own heart. While donors give more to children and families in need around the holiday season, Noelle Foster believes in giving year-round after seeing many of her students struggle with hunger and finding a warm bed at night. At a second-chance meeting, sparks fly when Noelle and Nathan share a kindred spirit with their passion to help those less fortunate. Whether they're doing charity work or attending Christmas parties, the couple becomes inseparable. Although Noelle and Nathan exchange gifts, the biggest present is the one from Christ.

MAKING LOVE WORK SERIES

This series can be read in any order.

In *A Mother's Love*, to Jillian Carter, it's bad when her own daughter beats her to the altar. She became a teenage mother when she confused love for lust one summer. Despite the sins of her past, Jesus forgave her and blessed her to be the best Christian example for Shana. Jillian is not looking forward to becoming an empty-nester at thirty-nine. The old adage, she's not losing a daughter, but gaining a son-in-law is not comforting as she braces for a lonely life ahead. What she doesn't expect is for two men to vie for her affections: Shana's biological father who breezes back into their lives as a redeemed man and practicing Christian. Not only is Alex still goof looking, but he's willing to right the wrong he's done in the past. Not if Dr. Dexter Harris has anything to say about it. The widower father of the groom has set his sights on Jillian and he's willing to pull out all the stops to woo her. Now the choice is hers. Who will be the next mother's love?

In *Love at Work*, how do two people go undercover to hide an office romance in a busy television newsroom? In plain sight, of course. Desiree King is an assignment editor at KDPX-TV in St. Louis, MO. She dispatches a team to wherever breaking news happens. Her focus is to stay ahead of the competition. Overall, she's easy-going, respectable, and compassionate. But when it comes to dating a fellow coworker, she refuses to cross that professional line. Award-winning investigative reporter Bryan Mitchell makes life challenging for Desiree with his thoughtful gestures, sweet notes, and support. He tries to convince Desiree that as Christians, they could show coworkers how to blend their personal and private lives without compromising their morals.

In *Words of Love*, call it old fashion, but Simone French was smitten with a love letter. Not a text, email, or Facebook post, but a love letter sent through snail mail. The prose wasn't the corny roses-are-red-and-violets-are-blue stuff. The first letter contained short accolades for a job well done. Soon after, the missives were filled with passionate words from a man who confessed the hidden secrets of his soul. He revealed his unspoken weaknesses, listed his uncompromising desires, and unapologetically noted his subtle strengths. Yes, Rice Taylor was ready to surrender to love. Whew. Closing her eyes, Simone inhaled the faint lingering smell of roses on the beige plain stationery. She had a testimony. If anyone would listen, she would proclaim that love was truly blind.

In *Guilty of Love*, when do you know the most important decision of your life is the right one?

Reaping the seeds from what she's sown; Cheney Reynolds moves into a historic neighborhood in Ferguson, Missouri, and becomes a reclusive. Her first neighbor, the incomparable Mrs. Beatrice Tilley Beacon aka Grandma BB, is an opinionated childless widow. Grandma BB is a self-proclaimed expert on topics Cheney isn't seeking advice—everything from landscaping to hip-hop dancing to romance. Then there is Parke Kokumuo Jamison VI, a direct descendant of a royal African tribe. He learned his family ancestry, African history, and lineage preservation before he could count. Unwittingly, they are drawn to each other, but it takes Christ to weave their lives into a spiritual bliss while He exonerates their past indiscretions.

In *Not Guilty*, one man, one woman, one God and one big problem. Malcolm Jamieson wasn't the man who got away, but the man God instructed Hallison Dinkins to set free. Instead of their explosive love affair leading them to the wedding altar, God diverted Hallison to the prayer altar during her first visit back to church in years.

Malcolm was convinced that his woman had loss her mind to break off their engagement. Didn't Hallison know that Malcolm, a tenth generation descendant of a royal African tribe, couldn't be replaced? Once Malcolm concedes that their relationship can't be savaged, he issues Hallison his own edict, "If we're meant to be with each other, we'll find our way back. If not, that means that there's a love stronger than what we had." His words begin to haunt Hallison until she begins to regret their break up, and that's where their story begins. Someone has to retreat, and God never loses a battle.

In *Still Guilty*, Cheney Reynolds Jamieson made a choice years ago that is now shaping her future and the future of the men she loves. A botched abortion left her unable to carry a baby to term, and her husband, Parke K. Jamison VI, is expected to produce heirs. With a wife who cannot give him a child, Parke vows to find and get custody of his illegitimate son by any means necessary. Meanwhile, Cheney's twin brother, Rainey, struggles with his anger over his ex-girlfriend's actions that haunt him, and their father, Dr. Roland Reynolds, fights to keep an old secret in the past.

In *The Acquittal*, two worlds apart, but their hearts dance to the same African drum beat. On a professional level, Dr. Rainey Reynolds is a competent, highly sought-after orthodontist. Inwardly, he needs to be set free from the chaos of revelations that make him question if happiness is obtainable. To get away from the drama, Rainey is willing to leave the country under the guise of a mission trip with Dentist Without Borders. Will changing his surroundings really change him? If one woman can heal his wounds, then he will believe that there is really peace after the storm.

Ghanaian beauty Josephine Abena Yaa Amoah returns to Africa after completing her studies as an exchange student in St. Louis, Missouri. Although her heart bleeds for his peace, she knows she must step back and pray for Rainey's surrender to

Christ in order for God to acquit him of his self-inflicted mental torture. In the Motherland of Ghana, Africa, Rainey not only visits the places of his ancestors, will he embrace the liberty that Christ's Blood really does set every man free.

In *Guilty By Association*, how important is a name? To the St. Louis Jamiesons who are tenth generation descendants of a royal African tribe—everything. To the Boston Jamiesons whose father never married their mother—there is no loyalty or legacy. Kidd Jamieson suffers from the "angry" male syndrome because his father was an absent in the home, but insisted his two sons carry his last name. It takes an old woman who mingles genealogy truths and Bible verses together for Kidd to realize his worth as a strong black man. He learns it's not his association with the name that identifies him, but the man he becomes that defines him.

In *The Guilt Trip*, Aaron "Ace" Jamieson is living a carefree life. He's good-looking, respectable when he's in the mood, but his weakness is women. If a woman tries to ambush him with a pregnancy, he takes off in the other direction. It's a lesson learned from his absentee father that responsibility is optional. Talise Rogers has a bright future ahead of her. She's pretty and has no problem catching a man's eye, which is exactly what she does with Ace. Trapping Ace Jamieson is the furthest thing from Taleigh's mind when she learns she pregnant and Ace rejects her. "I want nothing from you Ace, not even your name." And Talise meant it.

In *Free From Guilt*, it's salvation round-up time and Cameron Jamieson's name is on God's hit list. Although his brothers and cousins embraced God—thanks to the women in their lives—the two-degreed MIT graduate isn't going to let any woman take him down that path without a fight. He's satisfied with his career, social calendar, and good genes. But God uses a beautiful messenger, Gabrielle Dupree, to show him that he's in a spiritual deficit. Cameron learns the hard way that man's wisdom is like foolishness to God. For every philosophical argument he throws her way, Gabrielle exposes him to scriptures that makes him question his worldly knowledge.

In *The Confession*, Sandra Nicholson had made good and bad choices throughout the years, but the best one was to give her life to Christ when her sons were small and to rear them up in the best Christian way she knew how. That was thirty something years ago and Sandra has evolved from a young single mother of two rambunctious boys, Kidd and Ace Jamieson, to a godly woman seasoned with wisdom. Despite the challenges and trials of rearing two strong-willed personalities, Sandra maintained her sanity through the grace of God, which kept gray strands at bay. Now, Sandra Nicholson is on the threshold of happiness, but Kidd believes no man is good enough for his mother, especially if her love interest could be a man just like his absentee father.

THE CARMEN SISTERS SERIES

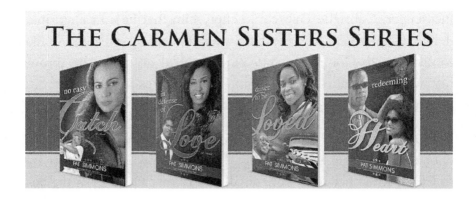

In *No Easy Catch*, Book 1, Shae Carmen hasn't lost her faith in God, only the men she's come across. Shae's recent heartbreak was discovering that her boyfriend was not only married, but on the verge of reconciling with his estranged wife. Humiliated, Shae begins to second guess herself as why she didn't see the signs that he was nothing more than a devil's decoy masquerading as a devout Christian man. St. Louis Outfielder Rahn Maxwell finds himself a victim of an attempted carjacking. The Lord guides him out of harms' way by opening the gunmen's eyes to Rahn's identity. The crook instead becomes infatuated fan and asks for Rahn's autograph, and as a good will gesture, directs Rahn out of the ambush! When the news media gets wind of what happened with the baseball player, Shae's television station lands an exclusive interview. Shae and Rahn's chance meeting sets in motion a relationship where Rahn not only surrenders to Christ, but pursues Shae with a purpose to prove that good men are still out there. After letting her guard down, Shae is faced with another scandal that rocks her world. This time the stakes are higher. Not only is her heart on the line, so is her professional credibility. She and Rahn are at odds as how to handle it and friction erupts between them. Will she strike out at love again? The Lord shows Rahn that nothing happens by chance, and everything is done for Him to get the glory.

In *Defense of Love*, Book 2, lately, nothing in Garrett Nash's life has made sense. When two people close to the U.S. Marshal wrong him deeply, Garrett expects God to remove them from his life. Instead, the Lord relocates Garrett to another city to start over, as if he were the offender instead of the victim.

Criminal attorney Shari Carmen is comfortable in her own skin—most of the time. Being a "dark and lovely" African-American sister has its challenges, especially when it comes to relationships. Although she's a fireball in the courtroom, she knows how to fade into the background and keep the proverbial spotlight off her personal life. But literal spotlights are a different matter altogether.

While playing tenor saxophone at an anniversary party, she grabs the attention of Garrett Nash. And as God draws them closer together, He makes another request of Garrett, one to which it will prove far more difficult to say "Yes, Lord."

In *Redeeming Heart*, Book 3, Landon Thomas (In Defense of Love) brings a new definition to the word "prodigal," as in prodigal son, brother or anything else imaginable. It's a good thing that God's love covers a multitude of sins, but He isn't letting Landon off easy. His journey from riches to rags proves to be humbling and a lesson well learned.

Real Estate Agent Octavia Winston is a woman on a mission, whether it's God's or hers professionally. One thing is for certain, she's not about to compromise when it comes to a Christian mate, so why did God send a homeless man to steal her heart?

Minister Rossi Tolliver (*Crowning Glory*) knows how to minister to God's lost sheep and through God's redemption, the game changes for Landon and Octavia.

In *Driven to Be Loved*, Book 4, on the surface, Brecee Carmen has nothing in common with Adrian Cole. She is a pediatrician certified in trauma care; he is a transportation problem solver for a luxury car dealership (a.k.a., a car salesman). Despite their slow but steady attraction to each other, neither one of them are sure that they're compatible. To complicate matters, Brecee is the sole unattached Carmen when it seems as though everyone else around her—family and friends—are finding love, except her.

Through a series of discoveries, Adrian and Brecee learn that things don't happen by coincidence. Generational forces are at work, keeping promises, protecting family members, and perhaps even drawing Adrian back to the church. For Brecee and Adrian, God has been hard at work, playing matchmaker all along the way for their paths cross at the right time and the right place.

In *Couple by Christmas*, five year old Tyler Washington wants his daddy to marry this mother. The problem is both his parents were once married, then divorced two years ago. But it's Christmas time and the holidays are not the same. This year, Derek has custody, and he knows the loneliness his ex-wife will face on Christmas Day without their son. He experienced it the previous year. His past regrets and Tyler's request have Derek thinking. Maybe, just maybe, Robyn would be willing to do things as a family again for Tyler s sake. At best, act as a couple for Christmas.

In *Prayers Answered by Christmas*, Christmas is coming. While other children are compiling their lists for a fictional Santa, eight-year-old Mikaela Washington is on her knees, making her requests known to the Lord: One mommy for Christmas please. Portia Hunter refuses to let her ex-husband cheat her out of the family she wants. Her prayer is for God to send the right man into her life. Marlon Washington will do anything for his two little girls, but can he find a mommy for them and a love for himself? Since Christmas is the time of year to remember the many gifts God has given men, maybe these three souls will get their heart s desire.

In *Christmas Greetings*, Saige Carter loves everything about Christmas: the shopping, the food, the lights, and of course, Christmas wouldn't be complete without family and friends to share in the traditions they've created together. Plus, Saige is extra excited about her line of Christmas greeting cards hitting store shelves, but when she gets devastating news around the holidays, she wonders if she'll ever look at Christmas the same again.

Daniel Washington is no Scrooge, but he'd rather skip the holidays altogether than spend them with his estranged family. After one too many arguments around the dinner table one year, Daniel had enough and walked away from the drama. As one year has turned into many, no one seems willing to take the first step toward reconciliation. When Daniel reads one of Saige's greeting cards, he's unsure if the words inside are enough to erase the pain and bring about forgiveness. Once God reveals to them His purpose for their lives, they will have a reason to rejoice.

In *My Rock*, three sisters living in three different cities (Baltimore, St. Louis, and Nashville) make a pact to share responsibilities for their aging relative after authorities find Aunt Tweet across state lines. Her destination had been a neighborhood grocery store. The siblings soon learn the definition of caregiver includes a cup full of patience, a slight sense of humor, and when to cry out for help. Women juggle between career and family all the time, but Tabitha Knicely (St. Louis) is struggling to find a balance. Romance is the last thing she's trying to add to her list. The Aunt Tweet she knew all her life is not the same one who is residing in her home when she accepts the role as a caregiver for six months. Overwhelmed can't begin to describe her emotions. Marcus Whittington is an opinionated, successful business owner, but he has a soft side when it comes to the elderly. They remind him of good memories of his grandparents. When Aunt Tweet is the mystery woman who stakes out his porch, he becomes concerned that she is not being taken care of properly. He sheds his misconceptions about what Tabitha isn't doing right when he discovers that every caregiver needs a caregiver. Marcus knows in order to win Tabitha's heart; he has to charm Aunt Tweet's too.

SINGLE TITLES

In *Talk To Me*, despite being deaf as a result of a fireworks explosion, CEO of a St. Louis non-profit company, Noel Richardson, expertly navigates the hearing world. What some view as a disability, Noel views as a challenge—his lack of hearing has never held him back. It also helps that he has great looks, numerous university degrees, and full bank accounts. But those assets don't define him as a man who longs for the right woman in his life. Deciding to visit a church service, Noel is blind-sided by the most beautiful and graceful Deaf interpreter he's ever seen. Mackenzie Norton challenges him on every level through words and signing, but as their love grows, their faith is tested. When their church holds a yearly revival, they witness the healing power of God in others. Mackenzie has faith to believe that Noel can also get in on the blessing. Since faith comes by hearing, whose voice does Noel hear in his heart, Mackenzie or God's?

TESTIMONY: *If I Should Die Before I Wake.*

It is of the LORD's mercies that we are not consumed, because His compassions fail not. They are new every morning, great is Thy faithfulness. Lamentations 3:22-23, God's mercies are sure; His promises are fulfilled; but a dawn of a new morning is God' grace. If you need a testimony about God's grace, then If I Should Die Before I Wake will encourage your soul. Nothing happens in our lives by chance. If you need a miracle, God's got that too. Trust Him. Has it been a while since you've had a testimony? Increase your prayer life, build your faith and walk in victory because without a test, there is no testimony. (eBook only)

In *Her Dress*, sometimes a woman just wants to splurge on something new, especially when she's about to attend an event with movers and shakers. Find out what happens when Pepper Trudeau is all dressed up and goes to the ball, but another woman is modeling the same attire. At first, Pepper is embarrassed, then the night gets interesting when she meets Drake Logan. *Her Dress* is a romantic novella about the all too common occurrence—two women shopping at the same place. Maybe having the same taste isn't all bad. Sometimes a good dress is all you need to meet the man of your dreams. (eBook only)

**Check out my fellow Christian fiction authors writing about faith, family, and love. You won't be disappointed! www.blackchristianreads.com

**Check out my friends at Sweet Romance Reads. www.sweetromancereads.com

**Don't forget, 1+1=2. Posting a review, telling one reader, equals two sales.

Made in the USA
Las Vegas, NV
25 January 2023

66256326R00157